THE KNIGHT, THE GNOME, AND THE FOX

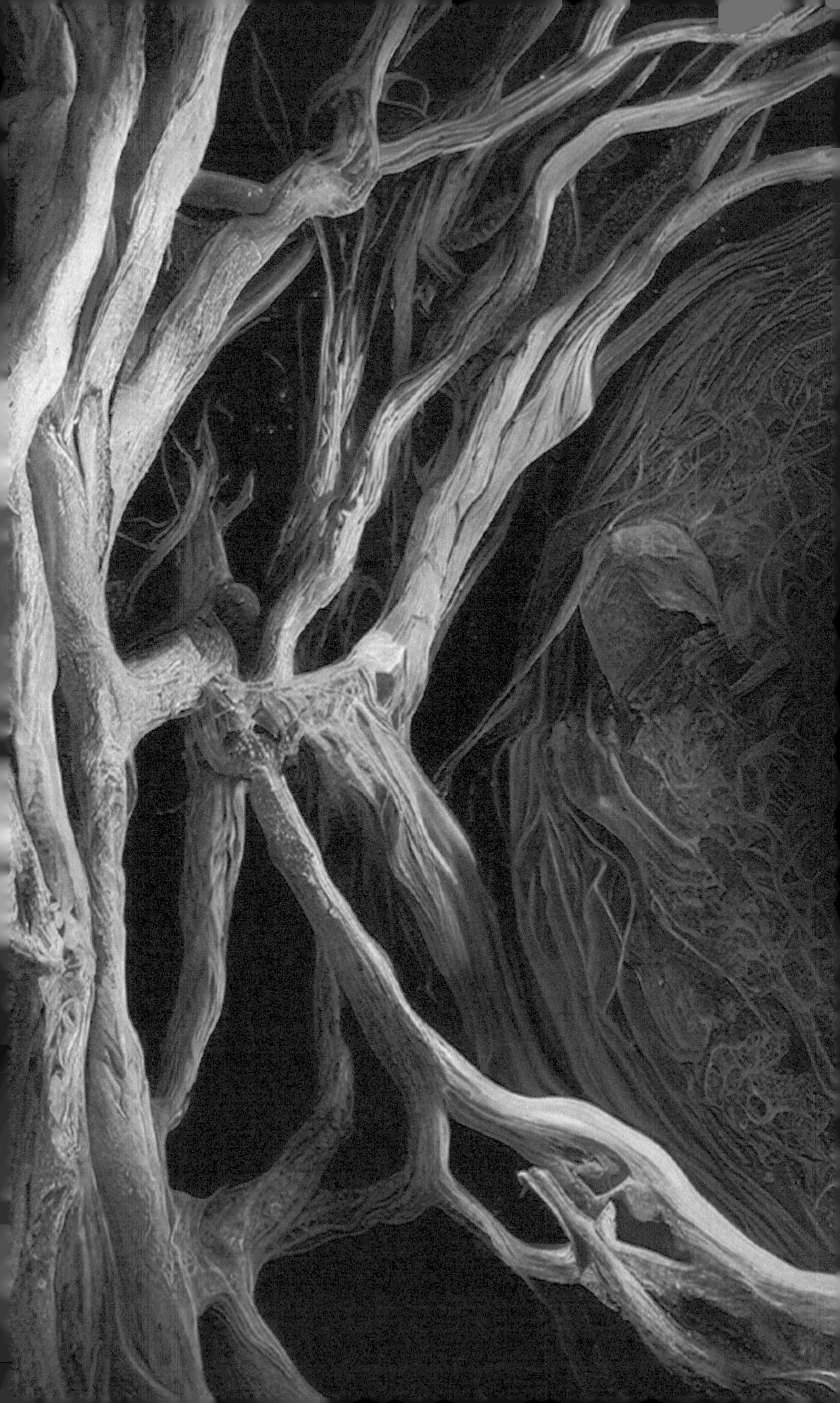

THE KNIGHT,

THE GNOME, AND THE FOX

D. A. SPRUZEN

Table of Contents

1

My three-year-old daughter Rose climbed onto a stool and lifted the cloth to peek at the Christmas cake on top of the piano every now and then. Her little nose twitched as her blonde hair fell around her cheeks like a curtain. She was beside herself with excitement, which started with a visit to a department store Santa Claus. Hunter—my lover and Rose's father—insisted on joining me. Hunter doted on our little girl, which had come as a great relief. After all, he was a Norse god who had lived through many lifetimes and sired countless children. His wife Lin had borne most of those children, of course. She was very fond of Rose, but not doting by nature. Not jealous either, or I wouldn't be here to tell the tale.

"What is Santa?"

"He brings Christmas presents to good boys and girls all over the world after they've gone to sleep on Christmas Eve."

"How does he get to all those places in just one night?"

"Magic reindeer pull him in his sled high into the sky."

"We went high in the sky, but we only got to three countries, and I know there are at least ten countries in the world."

"Well, that's the power of magic."

"And how does he have room in his sled for so many toys?"

"Magic."

The magic answer finally ended the discussion. Once we got to the mall and into the line, she looked through the flimsy archway at Santa, head tilted to one side, obviously thinking deep thoughts. "Is that person helping him his wife?"

"Yes, I believe that is Mrs. Claus."

"He's old and she's young. Poor Mrs. Claus."

I knew those around us were highly entertained, but I kept my eyes on Rose. She'd have been humiliated if she realized she was being laughed at.

Finally, her turn came. "Well, little girl, what is your name?"

"Rose. And I suppose you are Santa Claus."

"I am. And has Rose been a good girl this year?"

"I always try to be good. Have you been good?"

He laughed, his big belly pulsing up and down—so at least that was real. "Santa has to be good for the magic to work. What are you hoping to get for Christmas?"

"Another Flower Fairy book and a tricycle."

He glanced at me and I nodded. "I think I can manage that."

Hunter uttered a grunt of approval.

"But it's got to be a pink tricycle."

That wiped the smile off Hunter's face. He'd come home with a green tricycle a couple of weeks ago, so hearing that Rose wanted a pink one deflated him more than a little. "Ohh," he sighed.

"You shall have your tricycle, and maybe even the book. Make sure you go to sleep early on Christmas Eve."

"I will. And you'd better get an early start with all those children to visit. Have you finished making all the toys?"

"Indeed I have. And my elves are still in the workshop, putting the finishing touches on some of them."

On the way home, I asked Rose, "Why did you say 'poor Mrs. Claus'?"

"Because she is young and he is old. Too old for dancing and going to parties like big girls do on TV."

"But perhaps she loves him. Santa is a very good elf who makes children happy all over the world."

"Still. What about the rest of the year? She must get very bored."

The child could be insufferably precocious sometimes. I heard Hunter chuckling to himself, but it worried me a little. In any event, Rose was well pleased with her visit, but over the next few days, the excitement built to the point where she couldn't settle down for her naps. She got downright cranky.

"Long walks would help," said my Auntie Peggy. "Just before lunch."

She was right. I found that Auntie usually was.

I exhausted the poor child by not taking the stroller to the playground, so she had to keep going. Hunter played with her in the garden too, weather permitting. When Sven and Margareta—Hunter and Lin's kids—came home, they took her out to a big playground farther away.

Every time Rose went out, Hunter shut himself in the garage for a few hours painting the tricycle pink. He became quite exasperated. "Can you believe it took four coats?"

We prepared for days. The traditional Christmas puddings finally arrived from Harrod's, a famous department store in London. These puddings should be made at least several months before Christmas, if not a year, which Lin couldn't be bothered with.

"Boiling them is a pain. You have to keep watching them and replenishing the water," she said. "You remember I told you about the young nanny who worked for me in England in the early 1900's? She showed me how to do it, but I resolved not to bother. Harrod's makes them just as good."

Dora, Lin, Auntie Peggy, and I assembled all the ingredients for the traditional British Christmas cake, including sultanas, currants, brown sugar, ale, and brandy. A week ahead of the big day, we assembled everything into a fragrant batter that everyone in the house stirred while they made a secret wish. It was fun watching the expression on everyone's face as they closed their eyes and thought about their heart's desire. Margareta frowned deeply, which I noticed concerned Lin. Sven smirked, which seemed to bother his mother just as much. Lin and Hunter each glanced at their children and Rose before making their wish. I knew there was only one thing Lin and Hunter wished for. They already had eternal life and perfect health, but their children were not immortal, a cruel trick of the universe. Their powers had weakened after Ragnarok, the final battle, although they were still superhuman, particularly Lin. Terrible injuries had weakened Hunter more than Lin.

I wished for my daughter Rose's good health and Hunter's continued love.

The huge cake baked in a slow oven for six hours, permeating the house with its fruity aroma. After a couple of days, Lin decorated it with what she called royal icing, which dried fairly hard. First she sealed the cake in a sheet of marzipan so that crumbs wouldn't get into the white frosting. She fabricated a blue river across the surface, ruffled white icing into snow peaks, and placed little ornamental fir trees around the landscape. New this year, an elaborate sled, complete with Santa, reindeer and presents, completed the picture. It was magnificent and sat atop the piano covered by a cloth until the big day.

Margareta laid the table on Christmas Eve, taking great pains with the centerpiece, which she fashioned with holly, gold and red candles, and red roses.

"I bought special plates this year," Lin said, opening the dining room sideboard and bringing out white plates with gold rims laced with a holly design. "They'll look lovely with your flower arrangement, Margareta." She'd been gift shopping for weeks and apparently for other items too.

We'd decorated the tree in the family room with Rose's "help" the afternoon before. Lin, in particular, loved Christmas and all the trimmings. That had surprised me when I first came to them, considering that as Norse gods, she and her husband Hunter (formerly Hoenir) were once themselves the objects of worship. At least, Hunter was—Lin had been more of a handmaiden, albeit with godly qualities.

Sam, Auntie's Cavalier King Charles spaniel, decided that the new plush elf Lin wanted to put on the mantlepiece belonged to him and made off with it. I chased him, but that only made him run faster—whizzing around the kitchen island, through the family room, back to the kitchen, then out and down the corridor toward Hunter's study. Lin could have caught him in seconds, but she found the spectacle too entertaining. Finally, the wretched dog responded to Hunter's harsh command, stopped, and dropped. I slumped into the nearest armchair. The elf's pointed cap had come off, along with the hair. Auntie, thoroughly embarrassed by his bad behavior, said she could fix it and took it up to her room. Now it sat proudly looking down at us, the pine branch behind it concealing where the back of his jacket remained slightly tattered and saliva-smeared. The tree in the living room, decorated according to the gospel of chic, had been up for a week. Fortunately, nothing about it interested Sam.

Celebrating with our close friends and family was wonderful as usual—apart from the power cut in the early hours of Christmas Day that threatened to torpedo our traditional late lunch. It threw Dora, the maid, into a near meltdown and Auntie into her usual role of exerting a calming influence. The power was only out for an hour, but it set back the turkey, which had a domino effect on the rest of the menu. Lin called her guests, and we ate an early Christmas dinner instead.

Early on Christmas morning, we all gathered in front of a lively fire in the family room to open presents, still in our pajamas and robes. Dora brought in coffee and tea and joined us. Festive in her pajamas covered with cartoons of reindeer, Rose hopped from foot to foot until everyone was seated. Sven offered to play Santa. He donned a Santa hat, a comical sight, given his black tee shirt depicting a starkly white skull and crossbones.

"Rose, I think you need to come over here for this," he said, pointing to a large lumpy item covered in random sheets of wrapping paper taped together. She ripped into it, squealing with pleasure when she saw her pink tricycle with purple pom poms hanging from the handlebars. "Can I take it out now?"

"After we're all done here, and you are dressed," said Lin. "Everyone else would like to open their gifts."

Rose pouted a little, but soon got into the spirit of the thing, especially as she received plenty more gifts herself. Thank heavens only one was a plush animal, although it was a giraffe taller than her. Her room was already knee-deep in soft toys.

I'd done my usual agonizing over what to get people who could afford to buy anything they wanted. I finally jumped in and got everything in one fell swoop online: For Lin, a huge coffee table book about Scandinavia; for Hunter, an extra-large Irish sweater; for Auntie, a hip-length cashmere cardigan; for Margareta, a silk shirt; for Sven the mathematician, a biography of Niels Bohr; and for Dora, a pretty sweater. For my Rose, I went to the mall and found a red velvet dress that would swirl out when she spun around quickly. They were all happily received.

I got an elegant jade pendant from Hunter and Lin, a shirt from Auntie, and novels from the kids. Rose came to me proudly with a small package. "I got you a present, Mama. Papa helped me."

I opened the box to find a bracelet of intertwined gold chains. I gasped. "I've never seen anything so beautiful," I said. "Thank you so much, my love." I mouthed thank you to Hunter over her shoulder as I hugged her so tightly she squeaked in protest.

After breakfast, I took Rose downstairs to get dressed in old clothes so she could try out her new acquisition. Hunter joined us, carrying the trike to the playground, which had a large, smoothly paved surface. She went slowly at first, not quite sure of herself. Soon, Hunter ran beside her as she pedaled faster and faster until she tipped to one side, only saved by Hunter's dizzyingly quick reflexes. It was a long way down for such a huge man too. Gods sometimes move faster than the brain can catch up with one's eyes.

"You have to learn to only take your tricycle as fast as it can go. You could have had a nasty pain for Christmas," he told her.

"I wanted to see how fast I could go. I think I can go faster than the tricycle can. I still like it though. I like it very much. Santa brought just the right present, like he promised."

She couldn't have said anything nicer from Hunter's point of view. He puffed up with pleasure.

"We'd better go back," I said. "We have to get ready for the guests. Remember, you have your new dress to wear."

I wore the green wool dress I'd been wearing for holidays for a couple of years, but now I had a jade pendant that stood out beautifully on the darker background. Rose looked stunning in the red velvet with a matching bow in her blonde hair. Hunter and Sven complimented her profusely. Margareta appraised her for a moment, then said, "Very nice," which was high praise coming from her. The kids must have known that Rose was their half-sister, but they never asked about it and adored her anyway. They knew their parents were together forever—truly forever. They'd seen stranger things.

Joe, Helen, and Helen's daughter, Toni, were the first to arrive. Joe kissed Rose gently. "I don't want to mess up your gorgeous hair and make-up."

She simpered and said, "Mama doesn't let me wear makeup yet. Perhaps next year."

Helen and I looked at each other and shook our heads. Vanity, vanity. It starts early, given the right—or wrong—encouragement.

Lin, a private detective with her own agency, had worked with Joe on a few cases, and they had become friends. Before that, Joe served on the Salton Symphony board while investigating a serial killer—who turned out to be one of the board members. He liked the symphony so much, he decided to stay on, and Lin had joined the board shortly thereafter.

Lin had established a small theater in Salton a few years before, allowing local performing groups an affordable place to stage their shows. Her partner, Lettie, ran their detective agency now, only calling in Lin for difficult cases when she needed additional support. Lettie and her boyfriend, Bill, arrived soon after. Lettie, amusing and lively, sported black pants and one of those Christmas sweaters featuring Rudolph. Bill was the strong and silent type who wore an Irish sweater, had bushy facial hair, and was happy to sit back and observe. I don't know if Lettie realized Lin was "other." One could hardly ask.

Even Reem, a pediatric resident who worked day and night, was able to get away. She looked as calm and striking as ever with her dark chignon, perfect skin, and lithe figure. A Syrian refugee whom Lin had rescued from a sex-trafficking ring, she drove down from Philadelphia.

"Reem, Reem," Lin said. "It is so wonderful to see you again."

"Well, Lin, I have good news. I will be moving to a practice in Maryland at the end of my residency, so we'll be able to see each other more often."

Lin responded with hugs and tears, as she loved Reem like a daughter. In a previous lifetime in Egypt, Lin had had a daughter called Reema, whom she'd adored.

Dr. Ayre—formerly Eir, physician to the Norse gods—was the obstetrician who delivered Rose. She looked like a blonde Amazon in navy slacks and a royal blue cashmere turtle neck. She nearly always wore blue. At the beck and call of babies whose estimated time of arrival was rarely accurate and whose actual time of arrival is rarely convenient, she never knew when she'd be called away.

"I hope I can make it through Dora's magnificent dinner," she said before kissing each of us on both cheeks. "I actually had an evening to myself last night." She turned to Auntie. "Peggy, a word. I brought you a little something." She took Auntie aside and handed her a paper bag. Auntie told me later that the doctor had brought the wonderful gift of a special ointment for Auntie to rub into her arthritic joints. Dr. Ayre concocted a lot of those potions which had magical qualities. I'd benefitted greatly from one of them during childbirth and another the previous August after being bitten by a giant rat during an epic battle with Loki at the Thorens' house on the Chesapeake Bay.

Auntie Peggy had moved in during the COVID lockdown and never left. Lin and Hunter didn't think she should live alone anymore. I didn't either, but hadn't expected my employer to take her in. Margareta and Sven loved Auntie a lot. She was the grandmotherly type, and they had never known a grandparent, let alone any other older relative. She'd been the recipient of a bucket-load of secret teenage angst, although they were always respectful. It was as though Auntie completed the family.

Lin, as always the perfect hostess, looked radiant in a vivid scarlet silk gown—a color I could never hope to pull off. Christmas Day and its whirl of hilarity and happiness passed all too quickly. We spent New Year's Eve quietly. Margaret and Sven went to dinner at a Washington restaurant with friends. Lin and Hunter never celebrated in a big way. For them it was just another year with thousands more to follow. I didn't want to leave Rose because she was too unsettled after all her devoted admirers left, nor did I want to leave Auntie Peggy alone. Not that I would have had plans anyway. We watched a movie. They let me choose it this time. Lin had signed up for various streaming services, which gave me wide latitude. I chose a British thriller that had an intricate enough plot to keep Lin and me happy and enough action to keep Hunter happy. Auntie Peggy loved any British program, so she lapped it up.

Up until today, the weather hadn't been too bad, so I was able to take Rose out for walks. I usually took the stroller for when her little legs got tired, but now I didn't have to work off her Christmas frenzy. Sometimes I took Auntie Peggy out to lunch at the local shopping mall. Lin often joined us.

For the last three years, I had been recording Lin's memoirs with a view to shaping them into coherent books. At first we met nearly every morning. After Rose was born, it dwindled down to once a week. We hadn't done anything since before Thanksgiving, nearly as action-filled as Christmas, with most of the usual cast in attendance. I felt guilty about not earning my keep, although I knew she and Hunter thought of me as family. But being a "kept woman" just didn't feel right.

Now, here I was alone in the family room at the beginning of January, one minute missing the warmth and joy of the holidays, the next cherishing time to be alone with my thoughts and the TV remote. Auntie had gone to bed early, as she did so often these days. I'd put Rose down at seven. Hunter and Lin were visiting friends—I hadn't realized they had any apart from our usual gang—and the kids had gone back to their respective universities.

I'd closed the drapes a couple of hours before, but the gusty wind rattling the windows triggered a ripple of unease. A clap of thunder made me jump, unusual for January—one of the worst months in the year, second only to February. I hoped the noise hadn't woken Rose. I went out to the top of the stairs to listen, but all was quiet.

I had been enjoying the peace and quiet while I watched TV, but being all alone suddenly felt scary, distracting me from the denouement at the end of a murder investigation on a Caribbean island. When I got up to switch on another lamp, a flash of light bounced off the bookshelf by the fireplace. I walked over slowly to check, my nerves jangling.

A glittery Christmas tree ornament sat on three coffee table books stacked on their side—too big to fit upright. I remembered Rose being held up by her father, Hunter, to hang it on the tree front and center. It was a delicate thing, a golden fox made out of some sort of golden metal and sprinkled with silver snowflakes. Rose had been enchanted by it. She loved anything to do with animals, be it toys, stories, or shows that featured them. Someone must have put it there after taking it off the tree and forgotten to put it in the storage box with the other ornaments.

I picked it up and held it to the light, and it refracted off the "snow," which I realized consisted of tiny diamonds—fake?—that almost looked like dust in some places. It was so cold to the touch that I shivered. I placed it back on the books as gently as if it were made of glass. I sat back down and rewound my show, even though I was sure whodunnit. I was wrong, which I found both satisfying and annoying. I left it running to the next program. I'd choose something else after making myself a drink.

Restless, I wandered around the room to see if anything else had been overlooked. No, everything was in its place. You'd think the home of gods would look otherworldly in some way. Lin and Hunter's house leaned more toward modern Scandinavian—refined, but definitely of this world, especially when all dolled up for Christmas. Now it was back from tinsel and bauble to chic and sleek. Lin liked to take the Christmas decorations down on New Year's Day. I could see her point. Those sparkly things that feel so magical at Christmastime begin to look tacky in the days that follow.

It was all over until next year. Except, hopefully, for the cake. There should still be a few slices in the kitchen as no one could eat much of the rich confection at a time. First, a drink. I went behind the built-in bar to get some ice out of the mini-freezer and made myself a gin and tonic. I usually favored white wine but fancied something stronger. Back in my chair, I wasn't in the mood for the political show now running, so picked up the remote—and dropped it. Sitting next to it was the fox ornament, its snout facing the TV. I'm not sure if what I felt was fear or confusion. Probably a little of both. Sitting back, I ran through my choices. Ignore the thing and watch another show or two until Lin and Hunter came home (heaven knew when that would be). Put it back. Go to bed.

I got up and put the ornament back where I'd found it. It stung my palm like ice and seemed to vibrate slightly. Or was that me? Could this be an omen? Was something bad going to happen? *Hurry up, Hunter. Or Lin.* I didn't want to be alone anymore.

I searched the streaming services and found a thriller that looked promising—more of a Hunter choice than mine, but I was in the mood for something to hold my attention. It turned out to be a little too thrilling given the state of my nerves. I went to make another gin and tonic, sidling to the bar so I wouldn't have to take my eyes off the coffee table. Feeling around for the ice, my hand closed on something too large for a regular cube. The ornament felt colder than ever, and if foxes smiled, this one was doing it. I put it back in the freezer and completed mixing my drink.

I lost track of the show as I felt compelled to keep looking around to see if that damned fox had relocated again. I lay my head back and closed my eyes. *Think about positive things. Rose and her Christmas.*

I love all the trappings of Christmas nearly as much as Lin does. I think it's partly the scents—fir, turkey, the pudding and cake, eggnog—and the glow of decorations the color of jewels. The joy of celebrating with family and friends makes it a special time too.

I pictured the Christmas scene: the guests arriving, the tree lights winking, the colorfully wrapped gifts. Rose's squeals of excitement, everyone circulating and chatting. It was such a panorama of color, glitter, aromas, and chatter, I could hardly tell where I was standing and what I was eating, the room spun so fast.

Someone shook my shoulder. "Mary. Mary!"

I awoke with a start. "Lin, I'm so glad to see you. There's been a little problem." I turned off the TV and told her about the fox ornament. "I'm afraid I left it in the freezer."

"Serves it right. Silly creature."

"What do you mean?"

"It was an ornament Hunter gave me many, many years ago. He said he bought it at a little backstreet antique shop in Paris. He loves foxes, and he knows I love Christmas ornaments, so I was touched by such a thoughtful gift. But I knew at once there was something about it. It has a mind of its own. It likes some people and not others. It likes to tease. I was a little concerned when Hunter let Rose hang it on the tree, especially when she kissed it first. But all was well. It was teasing you, so it obviously likes you too."

"It certainly looked magnificent. What does it do if it doesn't like someone?"

"If someone it doesn't like touches it, it shatters. That's only happened twice. There are all kinds of apologies, embarrassment abounds, and it gets swept up and thrown away. Not ten minutes later, the person who broke it suddenly notices it back where it was before they touched it.

Talk about a freak-out. Great fun. I get around it by claiming I have two the same."

"Well, I was frightened."

"Sorry about that. The box it came in keeps it in check. I'll fetch it right now and put it away. Where did you say you found it?"

"On top of the coffee table books over there on the shelf."

She went over to the bookshelf and picked it up. "I knew it wouldn't stay in that freezer long. Naughty, naughty foxy." She marched out with it. Where was Hunter?

That was quite a story. I normally taped Lin's stories, but this had been unexpected.

Lin hired me to ghostwrite her memoirs—a fact we'd never revealed to Hunter, given his paranoia about anyone finding out who and what they were. He thought she just gave me a place to stay while writing my novel, as well as being a companion. Hunter and I had fallen in love and we'd had Rose. Lin didn't mind, as she enjoyed her own dalliances. Hunter still loved Lin, of course. They'd been together for thousands of years, so they both needed a change from time to time.

I went downstairs to my suite and got ready for bed. I had a hard time sleeping, so let my mind wander back to Christmas—it had put me to sleep earlier, after all.

Dora, a washed-up Greek wood nymph banished to Earth by Zeus, worked so hard to produce the Christmas feast every year—and so soon after Thanksgiving—but she didn't seem to mind. She had surpassed herself this time. She had made her usual golden, crispy-skinned turkey and many side dishes, including a mix of regular potatoes, sweet potatoes, butter and cheese, a dish soon scraped to the bottom. I thought all the oohs and aahs when she brought out the golden turkey, and then later when she paraded around the table with the flaming plum pudding, gave her enormous satisfaction. Our chorus seemed even louder this year. It's always nice to be appreciated. We all looked pretty silly in the paper hats that came inside the crackers Lin also ordered from Harrod's. A British tradition, it seemed. One person grasps a paper strip inside one fluted end, and someone else pulls the other. There is a minor bang, and the hat, a motto, and a little plastic toy fall out. Rose loved it, of course, but everyone else did too. It had become our tradition.

Lin and Hunter were generous with Dora, and she helped them with their rebirths. Lin and Hunter's immortality had become compromised over the millennia, so they had to undergo a physically challenging rebirth—Lin every 150 years when she was reborn a sixteen-year-old, and Hunter every 130 years when he was reborn as a baby. Lin always hired a nanny for him because she didn't fancy raising her own husband. Diapers and potty training are hardly romantic, and who could help remembering such things at awkward moments?

Dora wasn't wild about me. I knew very well that she and Hunter had enjoyed a few magic moments together, but she had learned to live with it, and she had a boyfriend now. She loved Rose though.

My eyes snapped open. The cake. I never looked for a leftover slice. They'd hear me with their godly ears if I started opening tins. And eating that kind of thing at bedtime was probably a very bad idea. I closed my eyes again.

I did accomplish one tremendous favor for Lin that winter. She had never been able to carry a cell phone or use any electronic device because her powers drained the battery almost immediately. That's why we still used an old-fashioned tape recorder in our sessions rather than a more modern contraption. Hunter didn't have that problem since his powers had weakened more than Lin's after he'd been so grievously wounded during Ragnarok. It was a situation that frustrated her a lot. We'd discussed it a few weeks before when I wondered aloud how she managed to drive her car—or ride in Hunter's—which has plenty of electronics. I wondered if the answer may lie with the floor mats or possibly the steering wheel cover. Silicone? Rubber?

One evening when Lin and Hunter came downstairs to kiss Rose goodnight, Lin said, "Mary, we've got to fix my device problem. I really want a cell phone, and an iPad would be nice too."

"She drains mine if she gets too close too," said Hunter. "Do you really think we can fix it?"

"I think it's possible because she doesn't drain the car's electronics when she drives. I think it's got something to do with silicone or rubber. I'll buy a cheap cell phone and charge it. First, we need to find out if it's all of her causing the problem or just part of her."

I spent hours doing online research about what might block what I thought must be some sort of magnetization coming off Lin. It was strange because metal objects didn't stick to her—only the batteries were affected. I bought a cheap cell phone and finally found some silicone gun cleaning cloths, and it took me a couple of days to sew them together into two sheets big enough to drape over Lin. I made one sheet smaller to cover her head to the shoulders and a bigger one like a ghost costume with a hole for her head and a couple of side slits. I asked Dora to keep Rose because Hunter wanted to watch the experiment.

It looked like a tatty ghost costume some teen had put together for Halloween.

"Let's start with your head," I said. I held the phone near her head and watched the battery signal. It stayed steady.

"I'm going to cover your head now. Stick out one hand." To my surprise, the battery still stayed charged. I thought it would definitely be her hands or her head. We did the other hand. Same result.

I let the sheets pool around her ankles. Maybe her heart. Nothing. Her feet? Surely not. I put the sheets back across her shoulders and had Hunter raise the sheet above one foot. Before I moved the phone all the way down, the battery signal dropped to the red zone. I wrapped it in the discarded head cloth.

"Well, that's a surprise. Lin, stand on the sheet, so we can see if that helps." The battery went dead. "I'm going to buy some silicone glue. We'll spread it all over the bottom of a pair of your shoes and see what happens."

I did more research. Silicone glue seemed to be used in many shoes, and the soles were often made of some kind of synthetic, although Lin usually wore expensive shoes that had leather soles. I stumbled on a few articles about a mineral called shungite. I ordered shungite dust on Amazon together with silicone glue. And that was the solution. Silicone glue alone didn't work. With plenty of shungite particles mixed in, it did. Lin had a working cell phone as long as her shoes had this glue mix spread over their soles, and they touched the ground. She was excited, like a kid with a new toy. She made sure to set it far away if she sat with her feet up or went barefoot. It entailed a tedious afternoon of applying glue to all her shoes, although I was glad to see her so happy. I was also relieved to have been able to relieve a problem so momentous to her.

Lin got on Facebook, Instagram, and spent hours on her iPad every morning while Hunter did whatever he did in his study. "It opens a new world," she declared.

"You've seen more of the world than anyone I know," I said, miffed that she wasn't focusing on our taping sessions anymore.

"Yes, but this is the world that other people see, that other people experience."

3

Lin, Dora, Auntie, and I were in the kitchen one afternoon having tea and the last pieces of Christmas cake when Joe called round and asked to speak to Lin in private. They talked in the dining room, and Dora served them coffee and mince pies. Both dining room doors were closed. I knew about the kitchen door, but I hadn't realized there was a pocket door in the opening to the living room. I was bursting with curiosity but took Rose and Sam out to the garden since it wasn't very cold. Rose loved to throw a ball for Sam, who rarely returned them, preferring her to run after him and grab it from between his paws. It was good exercise and fun to watch.

"Uncle Joe!"

I hadn't heard him come out. Rose flew into his arms.

"Hi, Joe, how's it going?" *Meaning, tell me what you and Lin were talking about.*

"Oh, I'm working a difficult case. I've asked Lin to lend a hand. Missing child." He looked sad. "It's been a week now."

"Oh, yes, I heard about it on the evening news yesterday. Poor parents. I can't imagine what they're going through." I shuddered, suddenly scared for Rose. I remembered the sonorous tone of the newscaster: *"Susan Wheeler, a young girl from the affluent suburb of Salton, has been reported missing. She attended the prestigious Woodacres school. Anyone with any information..."*

"Let's hope it's not too late," said Joe. "Rose, your hands are cold. I think it's time to go in. I have to go back to work too."

"You'll come to read to me soon?" Rose said, pouting a little.

"Of course." Joe picked her up and carried her back inside, Sam following close behind. He considered Rose to be his responsibility and kept a close eye on her.

I took Rose to the living room to watch Sesame Street. Lin soon joined us, sitting on the other side of Rose.

"I'm going to be busy for a while helping Joe with his missing child case," she whispered. "When I've finished, I'll fill you in."

"Okay," I said. "I just hope it has a happy ending."

"Me too." She held Rose's hand and lost herself in the program made for small children, full of innocent wonder and possibility.

We started again only a week later.

"**W**e got him," Lin said when she came down to breakfast at nine, late for her. She'd been in and out for the past week. I heard her come home before I fell asleep the night before. Hunter had already disappeared into his study. Rose was in the kitchen with Dora. "We saved the little girls too."

"Well done! I thought it was just one child missing." I was so relieved. Having a child of my own, I took these things personally. A girl disappeared, and my first thought was: could Rose be next? As a parent, I was learning true worry and fear.

"I watched him take another girl. Joe and his crew knocked down the door of the warehouse where he had taken them and caught him red-handed. He planned to sell them to the highest bidder."

"You mean…"

"Yes, for s-e-x."

"How awful. So, who was it?"

"I'll come downstairs when I've finished my breakfast. I'll tell you all about it. Man the tape recorder!"

"We could use the phone."

"I'll have my feet up. I always have my feet up. I tell better that way."

I finished the last of my coffee and went downstairs to my rooms to set up. I pulled a chair over to the small side table where I set up the recorder and plumped up the cushions on the chaise Lin liked to recline on when narrating her memoirs. This would be the first tape of the year and would seem out of step with the other volumes because this event happened so recently. Some of the stories I'd recorded went back hundreds or even thousands of years. It took some organizing to formulate a coherent volume—I'd have to consider reorganizing what went into which volume. I kept my own personal records that Lin didn't know about. They included my stories of family life with the Thorens, especially my relationship with Hunter.

Lin arrived just as I was heading to Rose's room to put away an armful of toys she'd left spread all over the floor. "Do you think she has enough toys?" she asked.

"No, she needs a few dozen more. Especially plush animals. I was actually wondering if we should give some away to poor children. We could involve her in the decision. Although I'm not sure where to find the right place."

"There's a shelter not that far away for women escaping from abusive relationships. They often have to get out of their houses in a hurry, so have to leave a lot behind. Their children would probably appreciate a few toys." *How do you know about such a place?*

"That sounds good. I'll talk to Rose later. She probably won't like it." I anticipated a tantrum or two. But I wanted to talk her around and get her to understand that not every child enjoyed her good fortune.

"Maybe do it with Hunter. He'll have a calming effect if she gets upset."

"Good idea. Shall I switch on the tape now?"

Lin reclined and assumed her rendition of a marble effigy.

Tape 1,
Volume 3

Joe told me the missing child had been abducted on her way home from Woodacres, her small private school on the other side of Salton. Susan Wheeler was ten years old and always walked to school and back, most of the way with friends who lived nearby. The day she disappeared, she'd told her friends that she'd left one of her books at school and had to go back to get it. They warned her the classrooms would be locked, but she insisted, telling them she'd see them in the morning. They said they were surprised because they didn't have a test the next day, and Susan always did well without studying much. She didn't seem to have trouble remembering things and didn't have to work as hard as they did.

Judging by what he'd been told, Joe considered that Susan's behavior was out of character, and he believed she'd arranged to meet someone. His face was well-known at the school after several visits, so he asked me to look around. The only other place Susan spent any time was at a ballet school, and her mother always went to walk her home in the evening.

I went to Woodacres school and asked to speak to the principal, claiming that my sister was moving to the area with her ten-year-old daughter, and I had promised to look at schools for her. My sister was a recent widow. The child was very bright but still grieving for her father.

The headmaster—as he pompously informed me was his title—was rather a frightening type, wrapped in business-like efficiency and tweedy outfits. After a stirring homily on school spirit, he flashed a smile at me, a startling expression that did nothing to improve his angular face. I didn't exactly dislike him but reckoned his excess of forced enthusiasm must wear on his charges.

His secretary was another matter—a cringing, middle-aged biddy who wanted nothing more than to fade into the background. I found her infuriating. Once the door to the headmaster's study door was firmly closed behind me, I asked about Susan.

"Miss Peabody, I heard that one of your girls recently went missing. It's concerning. Can you tell me anything about that?"

Miss Peabody reacted as if I'd slapped her, wincing and holding her cheeks with thin, veiny hands. "No, indeed, I don't know anything about that. The Head doesn't like us to talk about it. It's not allowed. Oh dear." She scurried behind her desk like a mouse running from a cat.

"I understand. I won't trouble you further. Good afternoon."

She mumbled something that might have been goodbye before flopping into her chair.

Well, that was a waste of time. Joe had given me the names and photos of the friends who usually walked to and from school with Susan. The next day I'd follow them and eavesdrop on their conversation. But for now, the ballet academy. It was Tuesday, the day when Susan usually took her class after school. On Thursdays too. Her friends told Joe she was pretty good. I'd taken ballet in London, then in Texas. Adult ballet classes were too basic for me. I hadn't the training to join a more advanced class but learned much faster than the others, so I didn't fit in anywhere. I loved it though. Maybe private classes would work better. Something to think about for later.

I heard the music through the open windows when I got halfway down the street—typical languid plié music, which meant class had just begun. When I entered, the young man at the front desk greeted me with a toothy smile. I gave him the same story I'd given the headmaster and asked if the class going on now was suitable for a ten-year-old girl with three years of ballet.

"It depends how competent she is," he said. "There are good teachers, and there are the other kind."

"She passed her Royal Academy of Dance grade four exam with honors," I said, wanting to wipe the smug smirk off his face. Royal Academy method is what we did in London. In Texas, the school claimed to teach "Vaganova style," but it was all rather sloppy and far from the way professional Russian dancers performed.

"We are not familiar with this academy." The young man sniffed.

"Which method does your school teach?" I asked.

"Monsieur Vronsky bases his teaching on his own illustrious background."

"May I watch the class?"

"Let me check." He sidled around the studio door when the music stopped between exercises. I peeped through a small glass panel in the door and saw that the students were still at the barre. "You may go in and sit at the back. There are a few chairs set out."

"Thank you."

This Vronsky—I searched his name on the Internet later and only came up with some fictional Russian character—was such a poseur. Flamboyant, and I suspected, even more so because of my presence. He flounced around, waving his arms dramatically as he half-heartedly demonstrated, his feet flopping around like dying haddocks. He taught no technique whatsoever, with "Turn out your feet more" being his most explicit command. It was one he should have followed himself. I looked around. The floor was scuffed, the varnish worn away in places. The walls needed a new coat of paint about five years ago. Vronsky's once-white shirt with peasant sleeves had turned gray with age and worn around the neck. The business was in trouble. Worth looking into.

I noticed that one girl's eyes were puffy as if she'd been crying. She was only going through the motions without a shred of enthusiasm. When the girls moved from the barre to the center, she gravitated to the back row. I would try to talk with her after class.

I suffered through the horrifying performance until the final curtsey. Vronsky strode toward me, his feet now turned out in an affected ballet walk. Hairy and obese, he looked like a pregnant performing bear.

"My assistant told me about your sister and her daughter. I hope you enjoyed our class," he said, in a "foreign" accent that encompassed snippets of inflection from just about anywhere.

"Indeed, I did," I said. "I will speak to my sister and highly recommend your school."

"Dear lady, thank you. I look forward to meeting the child."

"I noticed that one of your students looked very upset," I said. "Is she all right?"

"A sad tale. One of her friends is missing. The police fear the worst."

"Oh dear," I said. "How very distressing for her. Well, I have another appointment, so I must go. I hope to see you again soon."

His grip was surprisingly strong when we shook hands, so I returned the favor. He winced but was too proud to say anything until I let him go. I turned at the door to offer him a wiggly finger goodbye just as he started massaging his fingers. He pretended not to see me. When I went out to the lobby, the sad girl was just putting on her regular shoes.

"Hello," I said. "I was just watching the class because my niece might join it. Do you enjoy it?"

She glanced nervously at the assistant, who stared at us both. "Very much," she said.

"See you outside," I whispered.

We walked together down the street. "What's your name? Are you scared of the men at the ballet school?" I asked.

"I'm Jane. I don't like that ballet teacher much. And Mark, his assistant, can be really mean. He was especially mean to Susan." She stifled a sob.

"Susan?"

"She's my friend, and she was in my class at school as well as ballet. She went missing a week ago. I may never see her again." She started to cry. I put my arm around her.

"You know, Jane, the police are very good at this sort of thing. And I expect they have brought in all kinds of help. Try not to worry."

"This is my house," she said, as we stopped outside the wrought iron gate of a brick colonial. "Mom and Dad are still at work." She fished a key out of her ballet bag. "Thank you for being so nice."

"You're welcome," I said. "Did Susan tell you about any new friend or anything troubling her?" Jane bit her lip. "You know any little thing could be important."

"She said it was a secret. She said she was going to be famous and make a lot of money."

"How?"

"In Hollywood. She said she was going to be in a film."

"Who fixed this for her?"

"She wouldn't say. She swore me to secrecy."

"You run along, Jane, and take care of yourself."

The sad little girl turned to wave goodbye before entering her house. It occurred to me that someone might wonder if Susan had told any of her friends anything.

I pulled out my phone to call Joe as I walked toward home but shoved it back in my purse when I saw Mark up ahead. I flattened myself against a brick wall, over which grew a thick vine. Worried that he was going to Jane's house, I kept watching until he took another side road. I followed, wishing I'd had time to shape-shift. It takes me a while these days. As you know, our powers are not so strong anymore. A car drew up beside him. Vronsky. They argued for a while. Finally, Mark got in. I gave them a head start before I ran after them. As I've mentioned before, I run so fast that humans can't see me, but I need plenty of leeway, which is a problem if my target is moving slowly. They stopped outside a small house dating back to the fifties. The façade was unkempt, including the yard. There was definitely a money problem with these guys.

I ran all the way home before calling Joe. I told him what I'd found out and that I planned to follow Susan's friends the next day. He sounded hopeful and said he would run a check on the ballet school people. Someone had obviously lured Susan to a meeting about the supposed movie deal.

Next day I arrived at the school gates at what I thought was dismissal time—3 p.m. There was one cluster of girls chatting halfway down the street, and that was all. I ran after them.

"Excuse me, I was waiting for a couple of girls. Did school let out early?"

"We get out at two-thirty on Wednesdays."

"Do you know Ginny Parker and Tilly Pines? I need to ask them a few questions about Susan. You know, the missing girl?"

"Are you a detective or something?" asked one of them, her eyes shining and mouth pursed as if to say, "Ooh!"

"I'm a private detective helping the police with their inquiries."

"Ooh!" She couldn't resist it this time. "I'm Tilly." She pointed at a chubby girl next to her. "She's Ginny."

"I understand you were friends with Susan. I'm wondering if she told you if anything important was going on in her life. Nice or not. It's very important we know everything if we are to find her, even if she swore you to secrecy."

The girls looked at each other, consternation and indecision clear in their expressions as they looked at one friend and then another.

Tilly was the first to speak. "We were all friends, not just Ginny and me. We were ever so excited because Susan had this big secret. She was going to be a big star in a film. And she said maybe she could get us parts. But we promised not to tell because she'd promised him not to tell."

"Who did she promise not to tell?"

"She wouldn't say. But she seemed a bit scared of him. 'He'd kill me if he knew I'd said anything,' she said. "I don't think she meant to tell but just couldn't help herself.

Then she got scared because she'd told. She made us swear and cross our hearts." Tilly looked scared. "If he found out she'd told people, maybe he..."

"No, I'm sure that's not the case," I broke in hurriedly. "Try not to worry. Now, the day she disappeared, she went back to school because she'd forgotten something, I was told."

"Yes, it was really odd," Ginny said. "I think it was just an excuse. She was going to meet him."

"Did you actually see her go into the school?" I asked.

"I did," piped up a thin girl with big glasses. "I dropped my backpack and a bunch of stuff fell out, so I had to pick it up and stuff it back in. One of my books had lots of its pages messed up, so I tried to make them flat again. That's why I was behind the others. I saw her come in and go around the back where the teachers park their cars."

"Did you tell the police?" I asked.

"No. They never talked to me."

"Your parents didn't tell the police?

"I never told them. I never told anyone. Susan has a right to her secrets."

"What's your name?"

"Penny Martin. Am I in trouble?"

"No, but the police might want to hear your story. You know, when someone has disappeared and might be in big trouble, every little bit of information helps. Secrets are not important anymore."

"Yes, miss," she said, eyes downcast.

I called Joe again to relay what Penny told me. "Damn little girls and their secrets," he said.

I decided to keep watch on Vronsky and Mark for a few nights to see what they got up to in their spare time, starting that evening.

I went home to relax for a while. Rose woke up from her nap just as I got through the front door. She must have heard me because I heard her little voice calling, "Linny, Linny."

I went down and found her clambering out of bed, demanding a story.

"Potty first. Then story."

I waited for her in the living room. Rose trotted over to me, her latest Flower Fairy book under her arm. We snuggled in for a cozy few minutes.

Afterward, we went upstairs to the kitchen, and Dora poured Rose some apple juice, together with a plate of cookies and made coffee. You soon joined us, Mary. Auntie Peggy was still napping. I said I had to go back to work at dusk, so Dora sat down too, and we passed a pleasant hour chatting, sipping, and nibbling. Such moments are precious, you know. The small, simple moments.

Anyway, I changed into dark clothing and ran to Vronsky's house as night fell. They only had one decent-sized hedge I could hide behind. A visitor, arrived—a young man. He looked unkempt and hungry, which set off alarm bells. A light went off in an upstairs room, obviously a bedroom, judging by the various unsavory sounds I detected, thanks to my godly hearing abilities. Two people enjoying and one suffering.

This was a good time to look around the exterior. There was a small unlocked shed containing a few gardening implements but no little girl. I needed to get inside the house. The backdoor was unlocked, so I crept in. A door just outside the kitchen led to an unfinished basement filled with boxes overflowing with costumes and other things I assumed were props. There were no side rooms, and no big spaces behind the furnace or the water heater.

How many bedrooms were there upstairs? The guys were still hectically busy, so I deemed it safe to go up. There were two rooms currently unoccupied. The smallest was furnished with a twin bed and dresser and the other with a queen-sized bed and two dressers. No little girl. I ran back out of the house and waited again behind my friendly hedge. The boy left an hour later, tears pouring down his face. I'd track him down when this case was over and set him straight. Money and a pep talk.

That was on Wednesday, and I felt if anything big were to happen, it would be on Friday or Saturday. I was beginning to think these two guys were not involved in Susan's disappearance. Unless they'd sold her, what could be their motive? Maybe she'd seen something she shouldn't have. I would reserve judgement. I planned to return on Saturday night to see what they were up to but didn't hold out much hope. And the child had been missing for over a week. Time was running short, given the sad result of many such cases.

I decided I should hang around the school more because that's where Susan was last seen. The faculty parking lot might yield something.

On Friday, I waited until school was out and ran through a wrought iron arch to the parking lot. There were plenty of hiding places, fortunately. I chose a space where the dumpster almost but not quite covered a corner of the fence. It was the sort of place no one would look.

After about a half hour, a girl came through, looking around her nervously before waiting under the lamp over a back entrance door, hugging herself against the cold. It was not one of the girls I'd talked to. This one was a redhead, a petite pretty girl with a cute smattering of freckles across her nose and cheeks. Her short curls seemed to point in all directions. I should remind you at this point that my eyesight also has godly properties—ten times better than a cat's.

The back door opened. The headmaster spoke to the girl in a gentle tone that seemed out of character.

I risked sidling closer as it was nearly dark. "Don't be alarmed," he said. "I'll call your parents later and explain everything. It's your big chance. Remember what I told you. You're going to be a star. I know all the right people. And you look just the part."

"Yes, Mr. Carter," she said, her voice shaky.

Carter took her elbow and led her to a dark green Toyota. He started the engine and I called Joe.

"I'm at the school. The headmaster has just met with another girl, and he told her he's going to make her a star. They've gone off in his car. I will follow. They're going down Devon Street toward the industrial estate and that new mall development. Try to get there soon. No sirens." I didn't give him a chance to respond.

I set off running, pacing myself so that I still stayed invisible while not losing the car. I'm not sure I was invisible at all times as cars don't go that fast in town. I noticed Carter looking in his rear view mirror a couple of times and turning around to look. I spun in a tight circle to remain invisible until he gave up. A couple of drivers coming in the opposite direction did a double-take too.

The car turned into the industrial estate and parked outside a small stand-alone, one-story building. I texted the location to Joe. The place looked deserted with its boarded up ground-floor windows and weather-beaten, splintery door. I hid behind his car while they got out.

"Come on, Julie," he said.

"Is there anyone here?" she asked. "It doesn't look very nice, like a film place should."

"Oh, it's the right place all right," he said. "Come along."

He again grabbed her elbow and steered her to the entrance, which he unlocked with a deadbolt key. After they entered, I heard the door being locked from the inside.

About five minutes later, four police cars arrived, accompanied by Joe in his Camry.

"It's the headmaster," I said. "He just took another girl in there telling her he was going to make her a star. I hope Susan is in there. He's definitely the kidnapper. The door is locked."

Joe nodded to the four cops. "Break it down," he said. He pointed to the beefiest guy. "You go around the back and check for other exits."

They got a battering ram out of one of the car trunks and broke down the door in a minute. I hoped Carter wouldn't have time to hurt the girl—or girls. I ran in behind them into a cavernous unheated space. I made for a corner of the building where I heard some faint whimpering. Cold dampness rose from the concrete floor. I found a small cage where a young girl—Susan, judging by her photo—sat shivering and crying softly. A large padlock fastened the bolt. I took it both hands and twisted it this way and that until it snapped. Susan watched, shrinking away from me, her eyes wide with terror.

I said, "Don't worry. We are here to rescue you and take you back to your parents. You are safe now."

She crawled out of the cage and pulled herself up. "I'm so hungry." She could hardly walk. I supported her as we crossed the floor to where I heard shouting and screaming. I didn't want to subject Susan to more trauma but didn't dare leave her alone either.

Carter had Julie in a choke hold.

"It's over," said Joe.

"You leave me alone or she dies," Carter screamed, desperate as he faced all he had to lose.

"If she dies, you have a nasty accident," Joe said, his voice rasping with menace. "You have several choices here, some less unpleasant than others. Let her go and you'll get a fair trial."

"Fair trial? You must be joking."

"What were you going to do with them, anyway?"

"There are people. Very rich people. They like pretty little girls."

I pushed my way forward. "Headmaster, listen."

"You!" He spat. "A snake in the grass."

"Oh, so now you're the victim, are you?" I moved so fast, he didn't see me coming. I laid him flat. Even I winced when I heard his head hit the concrete. Julie ran over to Susan and they held on to each other, shivering and crying until Joe told one of the cops to take them to his car. He called for an ambulance.

"I'm a black belt martial arts expert," I told the other cops by way of explanation. They looked at me as if I had two heads. I could see their point pf view.

So, the case has been wrapped up, bar the trial. The girls are traumatized, but physically unharmed, the headmaster is ruined as, perhaps, is the school. The unsavory pastimes of Vronsky and Mark were all that was left.

I went back on the Saturday night when I found drunken revelry going on downstairs and shouts of pain upstairs. I barged in. "What is going on?" I yelled, going around the room unplugging everything I could see until the music stopped.

"Nothing to interest you," said one big bruiser as he strode toward me. I slapped him against the wall. He looked comically surprised before his staring eyes rolled back in his head as he slid down the wall in a heap.

"Who's next?"

No one. I ran upstairs, where I found the young boy I'd seen a few days earlier being tortured by two men with whips and prods. I laid them out too.

"Come with me," I told the boy. He pulled on his clothes as fast as he could, given his shaky state. We stood at the top of the stairs facing five or six men at the bottom wielding knives and sticks. I pushed him back around the corner. "Wait up here."

I ran down so fast, they didn't see me coming. I turned one knife on its owner, the other on his neighbor, the sticks got broken over several heads, and it was over in a moment. Except for Vronsky, who now came sauntering over holding a gun.

"Who shall I kill first?" he said. "You or him?" He waved his weapon toward the top of the stairs. I glanced up at the boy who'd been peeping around the landing but now dodged out of sight.

I ran, zig-zagging so fast that the shots he fired came nowhere close. I grabbed Vronsky's gun and pistol-whipped him.

"Come down now," I called. "They are all out for the count."

The boy's head peeked around the corner of the bannisters, taking in all the unconscious men on the floor. He tip-toed downstairs and gingerly stepped over the bodies.

"You bitch." The first guy I'd attacked held me with one massive arm and trained his gun on the boy. "Don't move, little boy. I've got a little time owing from you."

The boy whimpered. I had to more fast but carefully. Bullets ricochet. The man's hold tightened, starting to impact my breathing. I flung up my arms, knocking the gun across the room and tipping my attacker backward. I turned to finish him off, but the boy got there first, smashing some sort of trophy over the man's head. Twice. He pulled back his arm for a third strike when I caught it and forced him to drop the trophy, whose gold tones seemed to be peeling off. I was surprised it was heavy enough to do that kind of damage. I wiped it down with a drape I pulled off its moorings.

"Go outside, down the road to the left, and wait for me. I have to try to get rid of your prints."

I couldn't be sure of every surface the boy had touched, but I wiped down the stair railing, the bedroom and the front door handle.

I hurried outside and found the boy skulking by a tree around the first bend in the road. "That's the way to look suspicious," I told him.

We walked fast and far. After we'd covered a fair distance, he asked, "How'd you do that?"

"I'm a martial arts expert. How did you get here?"

"Cab."

"I'll call you one"

"No money. I never got paid."

"Why do you do this?"

"I'm no good at anything."

"Well, get good at something. Get a job. Any job. Start small. Work hard. Maybe take some classes. Did you finish high school?"

"No."

"Start there. Get your GED. Where do you live?"

"Here and there. Mom married a guy who hates me. I hate him too. I had to leave. He did things to me."

"So here you are, letting other men do things to you."

He shrugged. I handed him my card.

"There's a rooming house I know where you'll be safe. I'm going to take you there and pay them for three months. I want you to enroll for classes so you can get your GED. You could get into the community college to get job training of some kind after that. I'll pay. Don't blow it. Act wisely because I'll be visiting you and keeping tabs."

He cried a little. I squeezed his arm before calling a cab. He looked a whole lot brighter when I left him in a tiny bedroom with a door that locked. I hope he makes something of himself. I wonder if I'll hear about the mess in the Vronksy house from Joe. I'm not sure they'll all survive. Good riddance. Life and health are gifts they don't deserve.

Joe will get a lot of credit for saving the girls. The papers will be full of it. He deserves a break.

Lin sat up. "Very satisfactory."

"You deserve a little credit too, Lin."

"The girls are safe. That's all that matters. That's what I was bred to do. Go down to Midgard to rescue humans in peril. Only my lady Frigg isn't sending me anymore, and I'm already down here. But it's still the sort of thing I need to do—should and must do."

I admired her resolve. While she was away so much over that week, Hunter and I enjoyed several delightful trysts. Lin didn't object to our relationship, but by tacit agreement, we didn't get together when she was around. She kept her little transgressions offstage too. It was our version of civilized behavior.

St dinner one Friday night just before Valentine's Day—Lin and Hunter thought it silly and never celebrated—Lin announced she was going to stay with friends in Charlotte, North Carolina for a week.

"I haven't seen Beth for a year," she said.

"Who is Beth? I do not remember you ever mentioning her," said Hunter.

"Oh, you know, one of those neighborhood watch women. She was nice to me though, not like some of the other self-righteous cows."

"Moo, moo, moo." Rose always had to have her say.

"Quite," said Lin.

"I don't think…"

I broke in before we got into explanations that could tie us in knots. "Auntie Peggy, it's all right. Rose is just showing us she knows the sound a cow makes,"

"Clever girl," said Hunter, tousling Rose's hair. "It is time she saw one for herself."

"Yes, want to see a cow, and a sheep, and a horse, and a chicken." Rose nodded her head emphatically.

"There must be some farms near the Bay," I said. "I'll look into it. We should take her to the zoo for a start. I don't know why we haven't done it sooner."

"Let's do it next week," said Hunter. "Would you like to come, Auntie?"

"No, too much walking for me, I'm afraid. The ointment Dr. Ayre gave me helps a lot, but walking long distances is not very comfortable and tires me out these days."

I looked at her, suddenly realizing how much she'd slowed down. "I think it's time for a check-up, Auntie," I said.

"Oh, no dear, I'm all right. Just age creeping up on me. Like it does."

"Auntie," Lin said, "Mary is right. Better check that everything is in order."

"I'll call your doctor and make an appointment," I said. "I'll drive you there."

"No, I will," said Hunter. "Next week then."

Auntie sat back. "Very well, if you insist." She looked uncomfortable.

"I'll call him on Monday, I said." Auntie nodded, having resigned under pressure.

"And by the way, Dora will be away from Monday through Thursday. She will leave meals in the freezer," Lin said.

Hunter swallowed suddenly and looked up. "Wherever is she going? She has never gone away before."

"Well, now she has a boyfriend. They have a little vacation planned in Williamsburg."

"Well!" Hunter was too flabbergasted to say more. He finally closed his mouth, grunted, and focused on his plate again, shoving another bloody wedge of beef into his mouth.

We watched a couple of British shows on TV and went to bed early. Next day, Lin drove off just after breakfast,

Rose waving goodbye vigorously after presenting her with a bunch of dandelions.

"I will cook lunch for you one day," Hunter said before retreating to his study.

Auntie Peggy came down to my sitting room to read and do a little knitting. I read, and Rose played with her Christmas loot. We were having typical February weather, so it was very cold out. Snow was forecast for tomorrow. It was a good thing Lin would miss it. Funny time to go visiting. From Salton to Charlotte must be at least a five-hour drive.

Beth? *Yeah, right.*

Breakfast was fine for Auntie and me because she made eggs and toast. Hunter ate the eggs, but I'm sure he hankered for his steak. He put a good face on it though.

Hunter came down to me each night after Auntie had gone up to bed. It was so delicious waking up next to him. The morning cuddles were addictive, although Hunter always left before Rose awoke. I explained that questions might be asked when she started school and chatted about her home with her friends. Children don't understand discretion.

On Monday, I called Auntie's doctor and got an appointment for the next morning. Hunter and I took her, and Rose came too since we had no one to leave her with. Hunter would stay with her in the waiting room. We'd all go out to the local Turkish restaurant for lunch afterward, he said.

Dr. Barrett was the kind of GP seen on TV ads for minor remedies: gray-haired, portly, half-moon glasses, a pleasant smile, and a reassuring manner. I had explained my concerns when I called—out of Auntie's earshot.

"Lovely to see you again, Peggy. You look younger every time I see you."

Auntie giggled. "I bet you say that to all the ladies."

"Only the special ones," he said. "Well, Peggy, let's look you over, shall we? My nurse will show you to the examination room." He rose to open his office door. "Jane. Show this lady to a room, would you? Peggy, I'll be with you in five minutes."

He returned to his desk. "Mary, tell me about what you've observed."

"Auntie has been living with the people I work for since the lockdown. We're really part of the family now. She's slowed down over the past few months. I know her arthritis bothers her, but she seems to tire much more easily, even though she's in bed by ten and gets up at around eight. She takes a good nap every afternoon too. She says it's just old age, but I'm not so sure. She's only 74."

"Yes, I see your concern. We'll discuss it when I've examined her. You wait here."

I waited for almost an hour. What was taking so long? I didn't hear any loud noises from the waiting room, so maybe Hunter had taken Rose outside. When they returned, Auntie looked flustered. She sat in the chair next to me while Dr. Barrett seated himself at his desk.

"Well now," he said, looking at us over his glasses. "I will get the results of blood and urine tests tomorrow. Your blood pressure is a little higher than I'd like, so we'll start with diet. Here's a booklet about ideal diet and exercise. I did an EKG and found an anomaly. Peggy, I'm going to refer you to a cardiologist. My nurse is calling now to make an appointment for you. Don't worry too much. It doesn't seem to be anything major, but we must take this a step farther."

The nurse entered. "Dr. Leonard has an opening on Thursday at eleven," she said. "I took the liberty of making an appointment for you," she told Auntie.

"Thank you," Auntie said, her lips pursing above a clenched jaw.

"Any questions?" asked Dr. Barrett. "I'll call you when the test results come in."

"No, thank you. It's all quite clear for now."

We shook hands and left. The nurse handed us the referral to a practice in Fairfax, and we went outside to look for Hunter. We spotted them by the flower bed that flanked the parking lot. Rose was counting naked rose bushes. Hunter spotted us and hurried over.

"Well?"

"Auntie has to see a cardiologist on Thursday."

"Oh. It is a good thing we brought you to the doctor then."

"I suppose so," Auntie said, not sounding convinced.

"There are eight bushes, Mama," Rose announced.

"Clever girl."

Hunter strode toward the car. "Off to lunch now."

We drove the short distance to the restaurant. Hunter chose donner kebab, I ordered scallops, and Auntie, after exhaustively reading the expansive menu a couple of times, settled on the same chicken dish she always had. I ordered appetizers for all of us, including pastry rolls stuffed with cheese, Rose's favorite. She'd nibble on bits from all our plates.

The owner knew Auntie as she'd been going there for years and Hunter because he and Lin went from time to time and tipped well. He made sure our waiter was very attentive. I drank a glass of white wine, and Hunter drank red, as did Auntie, although she usually preferred white. "Red wine is good for the heart," she pronounced.

Spirits rose as we worked through our food. Hunter wasn't that interested in dessert, but Auntie and I had their terrific rice pudding made from ground rice.

After we got home, Auntie went upstairs for her nap, and Rose, Hunter, and I went downstairs for ours. Rose was soon asleep, so Hunter climbed in for a cuddle.

"Tomorrow, I will cook lunch," he murmured.

"What will you make?"

"I'll have to think about it."

"I don't mind cooking. I'm not very good at it, but I can try. Anyway, didn't Dora leave meals in the freezer?"

"Yes, but I want to do this."

"Okay." I had never even seen Hunter barbecuing, let alone setting foot in the kitchen.

We fell asleep, only waking when Rose wriggled her way between us. Now the proverbial cat was out of the bag. Oh well. The coziness enraptured me though.

Hunter left fairly early the following morning. "I have shopping to do," he said. He returned a couple of hours later with a huge steak, a whole salmon, a sack of potatoes, and salad stuff.

Auntie followed me into the kitchen. "I can cook for you," she said.

"Oh, no. I am going to cook this lunch," he said proudly.

Auntie said, "Well, I'll take Rose to the swings then."

"Will you be all right?" I asked. "It's quite a walk."

"I'll manage. It's important I get my exercise."

"Did the doctor tell you that?"

"It's in the book he gave me. It says that walking is often the best medicine."

Rose jumped up and down. She loved that playground. She just about dragged Auntie to the coat closet. Although it was very cold, at least there was no snow or ice. The light fall a couple of days ago had already melted away. They came back through the kitchen, bundled up to twice their usual width, and waddled out the side door.

"Lunch is at one," Hunter called after them.

"What are you going to do with the potatoes?" I asked Hunter.

"Roast them whole."

"I'll scrub them. How many can you eat?"

"At least two."

"I'll scrub six then. I'll do the salad too."

"Thank you. I will take care of the fish and meat. The fellow at that fancy store took away the fish head and insides, so I can just put a few things inside and roast it with the potatoes."

"It won't take as long as the potatoes," I said.

"How long?"

"I'll look it up."

There weren't any cookbooks in the house, so I went downstairs to consult my iPad. At least an hour for the potatoes and about thirty minutes for the salmon. And no time at all for the steak, knowing him.

I reported back to the head chef, who had stuffed the fish with butter, fresh dill, and seasonings. He poured some broth into a long pan before placing the fish in it, smeared butter over the skin, and carefully placed thin slices of lemon over the butter. I was impressed.

"You've done this before," I said.

"No, I went to Google."

"Me too. The potatoes need at least an hour, and the salmon thirty-five minutes."

"Thirty-five minutes sounds right."

I preheated the oven and scrubbed the potatoes. "Hunter, we must turn the oven down before putting the fish in. Remind me, so I don't forget."

"I will," he said.

I stabbed the potatoes several times, placed them on a baking tray and slid it onto the top shelf in the oven.

I made coffee and we sat at the kitchen table for a bit. He told me a story about an adventure he and Odin got up to when they were young. I resolved to type it up later before I forgot the details.

"Has it been thirty minutes yet?" Hunter asked.

I consulted my watch. "Yes, let me prod them to see how far along they are."

They felt too hard. "Let's leave them another fifteen minutes before putting in the salmon. I'll make a start on the salad."

I washed and chopped lettuce, tomatoes, green onions, a yellow bell pepper, and tossed them in the garlic dressing Hunter had bought. A large ceramic salad bowl sat on top of the fridge, so I opted to use that.

"Time to add the salmon," he said. "Should we cover it?"

"Yes, I forgot. Twenty minutes covered and fifteen minutes open."

I found the aluminum foil and squeezed the edges around the pan. Hunter put it in on the middle shelf.

I looked at my watch to check the time. That should be done right at one o'clock. I started to set the table in the kitchen, feeling there was no need to be formal.

"Will we not eat in the dining room?" asked Hunter. "This is a very special lunch."

Clearly, his male pride was at stake, so I transferred everything to the dining room, adding placemats, glasses, and cloth napkins, which I remembered Dora kept in a large drawer in one of the buffet drawers. I set the beautiful salad bowl in the middle. *Trivets.* If we ruined the table surface, there'd be trouble. I found the trivets in another drawer. Serving spoons. Platters. It was exhausting, searching for all these things, and then remembering more items I'd forgotten.

I looked at my watch. Time to uncover the salmon. Hunter was still at the kitchen island, sipping coffee and reading the paper. I found his obliviousness to my hectic adornment of the dining room irritating. There was more to lunch than just the cooking, and I'd done a lot of it.

"What about your steak?"

"Ah, yes. I see you have taken off the salmon cover. I will start cooking the oil."

He got out a large frying pan and put it on the burner. He found the oil and poured about half-an-inch into the pan.

"I don't think you need quite that much," I said.

"But I like my steak to be cooked very fast, so that means a lot of very hot oil."

"Okay, I'll be back in a few minutes. I need to freshen up. The platters are out."

"Take your time. Lunch will be ready by the time you get back up."

I went downstairs to use the bathroom and put on some lipstick. I noticed I'd splashed my shirt with salad dressing, so shoved it in the hamper and put on a fresh one. I'd better do a wash soon. Halfway up the stairs, an ear-rupturing roar startled me. I ran up to the kitchen in time to see Hunter, his face scarlet, pouring a bowl of water onto a flaming frying pan. After a dramatic flash, oil and water rolled all over the place, each following its separate paths. Hunter backed away, shouting what must have been every curse available in his old language and maybe a few more. His eyebrows had acquired random patches of singed stubs. He ran to the sink, running one of his hands under cold water. Aware of a sudden draft of freezing air, I turned to see Auntie Peggy and Rose in the doorway, rooted to the spot.

"Oh dear," said Auntie.

"Does Papa have an owie?" asked Rose.

To my shame, I hadn't asked. "Are you hurt, Hunter?"

"I burned my hand. Fucking oil. Fucking steak!"

Auntie hustled Rose out of the kitchen to divest her of her layers of clothes. I knew what was coming.

"Fucking steak hurt Papa," soon emanated from the hallway, followed by a stern lecture from Auntie.

The stove looked dismal. The microwave above the oven had blackened as had the stove top. Pools of water with oil slicks flecked with ash spread on and around the sad spectacle. I couldn't be sure about the state of the counters on either side. Granite should be tough enough to survive a little fire. I hoped.

"How did it happen?"

"I was reading a stock report on my iPad and forgot the oil. It fired up. So I poured cold water on it. Logical thing to do. But it almost exploded. I am lucky my face is not burned."

"I'm afraid you have lost some of your eyebrows," I said. "Most of your eyelashes look fairly normal though. Let me get you something for that hand. You may as well throw away that shirt though." Luckily, he'd removed his thick Irish sweater when he came in from shopping, so only the shirt took the brunt of hot oil and burnt bits of meat.

I turned off the oven and pulled out the salmon—probably overdone by now—and the potatoes. The first aid kit was in the hallway powder room. I found a packet of pads to soothe burns. I took them to Hunter and bound one to his burned hand with a length of bandage.

"I'm sorry. You'll have to make do with salmon for lunch," I said. "You did a beautiful job with that." That compliment soothed him somewhat.

I set the platters of potatoes and salmon on the trivets and called Rose and Auntie to the table. I'd worry about the state of the kitchen later. They sat and I served everyone. The salmon wasn't too bad. It was a big one, so probably needed the extra time. I fetched butter, salt, and pepper from the kitchen to put on the potatoes. We tucked into a pretty good meal, in spite of the war-torn kitchen.

"I hope your hand doesn't hurt too badly," said Auntie, breaking a heavy silence. Even Rose seemed to understand the situation was not to be taken lightly.

"It is feeling better with that pad Mary put on it."

Rose said, "I am sorry you have an owie, Papa."

He leaned over and kissed the top of her head. "Papa is fine now," he said.

After that, we chatted of inconsequential things. I was keenly aware of the next day's appointment, and I'm sure Auntie was too.

"I am going to clean the kitchen," Hunter announced after he'd eaten half the salmon and three potatoes.

"What about your hand? I'll help you," I said.

"No, my hand is feeling better. I will do it myself. You all go and take a nap."

I felt guilty leaving him, but he was adamant. I wondered if he'd have to replace the oven. Hunter and Lin healed miraculously fast, so maybe he wasn't feeling much discomfort.

Next morning, Auntie found one burner working, so she made the eggs as usual. The whole area still looked like a bombsite.

"We'd better call someone," I said.

"I do not know who," said Hunter. "I would rather get it all sorted out before Lin gets back."

"Dora returns tomorrow," Auntie reminded him. "I'd be more concerned about what she has to say. Lin tends to be more philosophical about things."

"Ah." Hunter looked more agitated than ever. "Maybe that kitchen place in town. They should know what to do. I will to call them now."

We went out for lunch to the local family restaurant that was very popular. Its parking lot boasted fancy cars and older, smaller models in equal measure. Something for everyone. The kitchen man was due at two, so we didn't linger.

The rep from the kitchen remodeling center was a slick character, wearing a maroon bowtie and navy blazer. Upon viewing the carnage, his first reaction was, "Tsk, tsk, tsk." He whipped out a measuring tape and laid it all around the countertops.

"We only want to replace the damaged counter," I said.

"Oh, dear, that will never do. It won't match, you see. It all has to go."

Hunter looked stricken. "I must consult my wife. She will have her own ideas."

"Well, I wouldn't take too long about it. We have a little sale going on right now. Only for a couple of days."

"I bet you say that to all the ladies," Auntie said, her tone far from the jovial one she'd taken with Dr. Barrett.

Kitchen Man ignored her. "New oven and microwave. The floor's a bit iffy too."

"Nothing wrong with that floor that a bit of elbow grease can't solve." Auntie replied in her iciest tone. She didn't like being disregarded.

"As you wish."

"I will send you an estimate by the end of the day," Kitchen Man said as he slid his notebook, pen and measuring tape into a briefcase that looked far too large to warrant such a minor toolkit.

After he left, Auntie said, "I don't like him. Too much the slick salesman."

"Well, I guess that's his job," I said.

Hunter sighed deeply. "If we have to replace all that stuff, we will wait for Lin. She must choose the color of the counters and the appliance brands. It is not as though they can finish before she comes, anyway. I hope she will forgive me. I hope she has had a nice time and will be in a happy mood. We will just have to eat out."

"If we go to the bakery early and get good bread, maybe croissants, it won't be too bad," I said. "Cheese, cold cuts, and French bread will be fine. At least we have the coffee maker and the electric kettle."

"I suppose you are right. I think I will go to my study."

Hunter was not a happy man. He didn't come downstairs that night.

Next morning, Hunter drove us all to Fairfax to see Dr. Leonard. Probably in his forties, he looked pleasant enough as he greeted us. Hunter said he'd take Rose to a coffee shop.

I stayed in the waiting room while Auntie went in for her tests. It was just over an hour before the nurse called me into the doctor's office where Auntie sat with her tense shoulders up around her ears as she waited for the diagnosis.

"Miss Lambert, I'm afraid you are suffering from arrhythmia. That means your heart is beating erratically, which is why you feel fatigued. You need a pacemaker. It's not a serious procedure, done under mild sedation and local anesthetic. It's a very small device that we insert in your chest, just under the skin. You will be a little sore for a week or so, must take it easy for a few weeks, then you can get back to normal—only better."

"An operation!" Auntie said. "I never thought…"

I hastened to reassure her. "I'm sure it's for the best, Auntie. You have been slowing down. You will feel much better after. That's worth it, isn't it?"

"I suppose you are right." She thought for a minute. "Doctor, is there no alternative treatment? I'm concerned about having anesthetic at my age."

"Oh, we don't give you a general anesthesia. Remember, I said local anesthesia. We only numb the necessary parts. It won't take long, and the sedation will make you very sleepy."

We went out to lunch again, a Vietnamese restaurant this time. It was a twenty-minute drive from Salton. I guessed Hunter was avoiding Dora, who would probably be home by now.

We drove home slowly. Hunter didn't say a word. As we turned into the driveway, we saw Dora unlocking the side door. Her boyfriend followed with a suitcase. Hunter pulled up in front of the garage. Upon hearing Dora's cry of outrage, we went to the front door by tacit agreement. Hunter unlocked it quietly but found himself confronted by a ball of fury, cursing in some language I didn't understand.

"I am very sorry," Hunter said, drawing himself straight as a ramrod. "I am going to my study."

"I will come with you, Papa," said Rose. They walked slowly along the passage, hand in hand. We stood in silence until we heard the door slam.

"Let's go to the kitchen and see what is to be done." Auntie steered Dora back to her domain, where I hoped she'd be able to calm her down.

There didn't seem much for me to do, so I went downstairs to read.

We ordered pizza for dinner. Dora ate hers in the kitchen, sulking and muttering. Tomorrow would bring Lin's wrath down on Hunter's head—maybe, depending on her mood.

Auntie went to bed early that night, fretting about her upcoming procedure, no doubt. The doctor hadn't wasted any time. It was set for the following Friday.

We were all on tenterhooks waiting for Lin to get back. She'd called to let Hunter know when she left, so we expected her that afternoon around four. She laughed when she saw the state of the kitchen.

You had a great time, Lin!

"We'll visit the kitchen shop tomorrow," she said. "I never liked that countertop, anyway."

The tension dropped from Hunter's shoulders. "Let us have a nice dinner out."

This time the meal was Italian and Dora joined us. The restaurant prepared a large round table for us in a corner. Auntie chose a salmon salad. "Salmon is good for the heart," she declared. Rose chose spinach ravioli in a cream sauce, like me. She couldn't finish such a large portion—and neither could I. We had great doggy bags for tomorrow's lunch though. Lin ordered more food to take away, so tomorrow's meals were taken care of.

After we returned home, I told Lin about Auntie's medical issue. I hadn't expected her to be quite so concerned.

"Is it dangerous, this surgery?"

"The doctor said it is a very common procedure and will make her feel much better."

"By the gods, I hope so. And that all will be well."

We went to bed soon after.

Lin and Hunter went to a kitchen store in Fairfax, not the one the sleazy salesman had come from. Lin seemed happy with her decisions. "So expensive," Hunter groused. Lin refrained from the obvious retort.

"Auntie, would you like to have a few days at the bay?" Lin asked at lunch.

"That would be lovely." Auntie looked happy. She was beginning to love the place too.

So off we went after Dora packed half the contents of the freezer and larder into chests. "We will leave some meals in the freezer," she said.

We returned on Tuesday as Sven and Margareta would both arrive on Wednesday.

"Was that planned?" I asked Lin.

"No, they are upset about Auntie. They will stay until Sunday."

Auntie had just gone to bed when they got in. They both tore upstairs and knocked on her door. They stayed up there for an hour. Laughter and cheerful voices filtered downstairs, so I was glad they were able to cheer her up. She'd been depressed since she got the diagnosis, although she'd perked up when we were at the bay as she sat by the big living room window, alternating her gaze between her book and the water.

Helen had very kindly offered to take care of Rose that morning as Dora insisted on coming, as did the kids. They looked as apprehensive as Auntie by this time. Only I was allowed to go through to pre-op with her. After the IV was inserted, Auntie's eyes soon started to droop.

"Time to go," announced a nurse as he wheeled her away. She barely registered him. I didn't even have time to kiss her goodbye. I went to find the others. They had created a family corner in the lobby. The kids consulted their phones while exchanging worried whispers, Lin read a magazine without turning the pages, and Dora gazed into space, her expression one of impending doom. Hunter drummed his fingers on a side table as he studied his shoes.

"You should have brought something to read," I told him.

"I do not feel like reading. I will go outside and walk around."

It was my aunt who was going under the knife, but I seemed the most composed of any of them. Then it struck me. This was alien. Hunter, Lin, and Dora had never needed a doctor or any sort of surgery. Perhaps the kids hadn't either. This was a catastrophic event in their eyes. And she was their auntie now too, very significant to young people who had never known any relatives. Dora had probably never had a real friend before either.

"This procedure has been done hundreds of time, just by this doctor," I said. "She'll be all right."

They looked at me as if I'd just told them the moon was shining.

A couple of hours passed with me trying to concentrate on a National Geographic article. Lin, trying to look her usual cool self, picked up one magazine after another while the kids did whatever kids do on their phones. Hunter alternated between pacing in the lobby and pacing outside. Dora hadn't moved an inch. Finally, the doctor appeared. I walked to meet him.

"Miss Lambert, your aunt is awake now. She came through it very well. She can go home tomorrow morning. The nurse will give her discharge instructions."

I turned to find the others practically standing on my heels.

"Very good news," said Hunter.

"You have a big family," said the doctor.

"Indeed, I do." Hunter patted my backside.

I suggested everyone could leave as I was going to visit Auntie. "I will wait for you," said Hunter.

I was surprised to see Auntie sitting up in bed with her arm in a sling. "The nurse told me that the sling could come off tomorrow, but it would be a good idea to wear it at night for a few days."

"You seem very alert. I thought you'd be drowsy."

"They have different stuff to wake you up these days. The doctor came to check on me and told me what to do after I go home. They'll give it to me in writing too. I must keep my arm close to my chest so as not to disturb the incision and pacemaker placement. I must not raise my elbow above my shoulder for several weeks. The doctor promised I'll feel much better in a week or two and completely recovered in six weeks. I've got to see him again next week." Her head fell back on the pillows.

"You are tired now. Sleep well, Auntie. I'm so glad it went well. You'll be full of energy again in no time."

"I certainly hope so after all this to-do."

The kids and I collected Auntie next morning and got her upstairs to bed. Dora had made chicken soup and the kids took it up to her, accompanied by Rose.

We ate a meal Dora extracted from the freezer, and we all felt much better. I hoped Auntie would feel better soon too.

The kids made a great fuss of Auntie until they left. They took Rose to see her too, telling her that she must be quiet as Auntie was tired after her operation. They took her cups of tea, her breakfast, then helped her downstairs on Sunday morning. I helped her dress, gingerly removing the sling—which she'd chosen to wear most of the time—before placing her arm through a sleeve.

After the kids left that evening, Rose said Auntie might feel lonely, so she would read her a story. She snuggled on

Auntie's good side in the living room and read the story of the brown chrysanthemum fairy. I hadn't realized she'd made such good strides with her reading.

"Have you been practicing?" I asked. "I didn't know you read so well."

"Auntie has been helping me," Rose replied. "She's quite good at it."

Auntie laughed, a welcome change after the tired, grateful smiles we'd seen the last few weeks.

I'd left Rose with Dora for the morning while I went shopping with Lin. She wanted some new clothes now that spring was finally putting out feelers. I wasn't that keen on going to shopping malls as Covid still lurked, but I'd had my vaccinations and wore a mask. Rose still wasn't eligible. She was only three and the new vaccinations for children, due out later next month, were not yet recommended for the under-fives. Not many children seemed to come down with it, but some did, and some died. It haunted me.

My worries dimmed in the excitement of a lovely pair of dark gray wool pants and a matching twin set—not the old fashioned kind, but a cashmere sleeveless top with a long jacket in pearl gray. I got some slick gray pumps, too. Lin wanted to buy me a purse, but I already had a beautiful black one she'd bought me a few months before. We finished the outing with a tasty, tangy lunch at a Vietnamese restaurant.

When we got home, we found Rose in her high chair, which she had almost grown out of, playing with what looked like a little plastic doll. She bumped it across the tray, saying, "Clip clop, clip clop." When Lin spotted it, she snatched it away, prompting an epic tantrum.

"Dora," Lin said in a tone resembling a growl, "where did this come from?"

Dora plucked Rose from the chair and soothed the outraged toddler, whose protests still reached for crescendo. "Hush, hush, my love. I'll find you a better one."

"I said, where did you get this?"

"I found it while I was putting away your underwear. It rolled out from the back of the drawer. It's only a little thing, and I knew Rose would like it."

"Well, it's something that is very precious and very private. How dare you take something of mine like that?" She didn't shout, but her voice carried menace and ice.

Her fury surprised me and Dora looked scared. It shocked Rose into thumb-sucking silence.

"I'm going to my room to take a nap. I will see you both at dinner."

After she stalked out, clutching the little horse, I patted Dora's arm. She looked ready for her own meltdown. "You weren't to know, Dora. You meant well." *You meant well* is a damning phrase at best, but it was all I could come up in the effort to be supportive. "She'll get over it." Rose reached out for me and yawned. "I'd better get Rose down for her nap. Thank you for looking after her. She really loves you, you know." I patted Dora's arm again. She almost smiled.

Dinner was uneventful. Lin seemed to have gotten over her snit, Hunter was jovial, Rose ate well, and Auntie Peggy remained blissfully unaware of the earlier drama. We watched television after Rose had gone to bed. *Midsummer Murders* was a British detective series we'd been following that took place in a fictional county in the southwest of England where murder seemed to be a weekly occurrence. The plots were good, though, and the characters believable. The show made a nice change from gun fights between impeccably coifed bimbos and hunks, closely followed by at least one car chase and a devasting explosion.

We went to bed early. Both Lin and I liked to read in bed, and I'd recently bought myself a Kindle. Kindles are wonderful and dangerous. I can carry hundreds of books in my purse, and it's easy to read in bed, but they are dangerous because a new book is only a click away. I already had twenty, and I'd only owned it for two months.

Next morning, Hunter took Rose to his study after breakfast, as usual. Lin said she'd see me downstairs in half an hour.

She came down and sat rather than reclined on the sofa.

"I want to explain my reaction to the thing Rose was playing with yesterday. I didn't mean to frighten her—I was just so upset."

"I realized that little figurine was special to you. I didn't get a good look at it, but it looked like a man on a horse."

"It was. It's very, very old and very, very valuable."

"What's it made of?" I asked.

"Let me tell you the story."

Tape 2,
Volume 3

A long time ago in the last half of the twelfth century, we were living in Lisbon, a place we seem to return to quite often. It was under Muslim rule at the time and a pleasant and peaceful place.

Pope Eugene announced the Second Crusade and decreed that crusaders could capture Muslim territory in the Iberian peninsula and didn't need to go all the way to the Holy Land. Of course, this was a popular decision as it didn't involve so much time and expense, not to mention danger, so a group of crusaders decided to conquer Lisbon and turn it into a Christian stronghold. The self-proclaimed king of Portugal, Alfonso, joined them. The first skirmishes didn't go so well for the crusaders, so they simply laid siege to the city. The city leaders knew what hardship would follow, so the blockade only lasted four days before they opened the gates and surrendered.

Alfonso was officially proclaimed King of Portugal, which would now be an independent Christian state. Some of the crusaders went home, but many carried on to the Holy Land.

Hunter was nineteen in that life and had been restless for some time. To my horror, he allowed himself to be persuaded to join the crusade. He claimed he had no choice as an able-bodied man, but I wasn't so sure. We could have simply left. I tried to reason with him, but he wasn't moved by my warnings of the carnage to follow against people whose only crime was to follow a different religion.

"Hoenir, Christians and Muslims worship the same god. They just do it differently. Priests claim Muslims are evil just because they worship differently and should be conquered and converted—or killed. Most of them know nothing about Islam. And most Muslims know nothing about Christianity. No one should die for holding different beliefs."

"But the excitement, the glory of battle! It is so boring here. I need some action."

"Are you ready to kill babies because they are Muslim babies?"

"Oh, I would never do anything like that."

"You may have no choice. And remember Ragnarok? The misery of losing loved ones, the agony of your wounds? War is not a game."

"This is not at all the same as Ragnarok. You just do not want me to go and have fun."

I gave up at that point. The boy was afire with the promise of excitement and glory.

After he left, I couldn't stay and wait for his return. If he returned. I wandered from one country to the next, unable to settle, and ended up in Norway, where I stayed for a year. There was a lot of trading between Norway and Iceland then as most Icelanders were descended from Norwegian settlers. The King of Norway was determined that one day he would also be King of Iceland, but the Icelanders thwarted him at every turn. As I found out later, they had reason to be content with their lot as they actually practiced democracy even then. Each region had its chieftain, or law-speaker, whose duty it was to memorize the law. There was an annual national assembly called the Althing, where grievances could be heard in an orderly manner and important matters discussed. Punishments were usually fines, a three-year exile, or permanent exile. I'm just giving you a very simplified outline of how it was. Of course, the church was active and most of the bishops and priests were Norwegian and keen on Iceland coming under Norwegian rule, which meant more power for the church.

There were two bishops in Iceland then, one in the north and one in the South—Bishop Pall Jonsson of Skalholt, whom I eventually met. I don't remember the name of the bishop in the north. I never met him and he's not part of the story. These two bishops commissioned many works of art, including many more texts than had ever been produced in Norway. The first was a law book, then there were histories, medical treatises, and many other works of literature, including all the sagas, about 140 of them. They provided the Norwegian court with poets too. This was Iceland's golden age, and the more I heard of these wonders, the more curious I became.

It didn't take long before I became acquainted with a wealthy trader who set me up in a cozy little house in Bergen, where he visited me every Friday when his wife spent the evening playing cards with her friends. I told him I was curious about Iceland and wanted to visit. He resisted at first as the voyage would take me away for months, but after I saw to it that someone whispered something about his beautiful mistress in his wife's ear, he found it convenient to arrange passage.

Even though it was early summer, we endured a treacherous trip. The Norwegian sea is as treacherous as the North Sea, and while I was not affected, the sight and smell of seasick sailors and the few passengers became repugnant. The food wasn't great either. To add to the misery, the captain soon decided I was lonely and needed cheering up—in his bed, naturally. Since I didn't fancy tossing him overboard and dealing with the mayhem that would inevitably follow, I just went along with it. None of his crew was capable of captaining the ship, after all. He didn't bathe often and ate a good quantity of salted fish, which left it's smell hovering around his cabin and clothes. But needs must.

After we landed, I made the uncomfortable journey by cart to the large church in Skalholt, where I found a service in progress. I carried my bags inside and placed them inside the aisle end of the back row pew. Not many were in attendance, so I guessed it wasn't Sunday—I'd lost track of time during the voyage. After a quick glance, no one stared, which I thought a little odd. Even though I needed a bath and clean clothes, I knew I must still look extraordinary. After spending a few months there, I realized that Icelanders are like that. They mind their own business.

It was cold in the church, even though it was early July. I'd come from a warm environ before staying in Bergen, and I still found it hard to adjust. Although Norway has a cool climate, Iceland has a cooler one. Much cooler. I only stayed in the church because I needed to build goodwill and find an acceptable place to live.

When the service ended, the bishop and his entourage progressed down the center aisle. He looked me in the eye as he passed. His bearing was regal, his eyes an extraordinary shade of dark blue that gave me the impression he saw all. I shivered and not from the cold. I found out later that he was descended from a Norwegian king and so bore noble blood. He looked like a king as he walked, even though his fine wool ecclesiastical robes were of muted hues, his mitre snow-white.

I waited until everyone had left their pews before following them out. The bishop shook everyone's hand while exchanging a quiet word or two. He turned to me.

"I see we have a traveler in our midst," he said. "You are most welcome."

I understood his Icelandic but answered in Norwegian. "Your Grace is too kind. I arrived from Bergen today and wished to thank God for my safe journey." I know, shocking hypocrisy.

"What brings you to our midst, good lady?"

"I have heard so much about the great literature and art produced in Iceland, I wanted to see for myself. My husband is participating in the Second Crusade, so I am free to follow my heart as we are newly married and as yet have no children."

"Do you have somewhere to stay?"

"I do not. I was hoping to find a family who might be able to accommodate me. I can pay."

"I am Bishop Pall Jonsson. Please come to my house for dinner. Several of our local citizens will be there. You can stay the night if nothing transpires."

"Thank you, Your Grace. I am Lin Thoren."

I walked beside him for a few minutes until we came to a large wooden house. It was cool outside but not as cold as the church. I hoped his house would be warm.

The great hall was warm because at the end near the kitchen, an enormous fire roared and spat in a most satisfying way. The furs folded on benches at the other end looked as if extra warmth was available. I came to know that those benches were for sleeping—one bench for women and one for men. Both guests and servants slept on them. A very long box adorned with elaborately pierced carvings against one side wall was the bishop's sleeping box—an enclosed box on legs with carvings that protected the privacy of the sleeper (or sleepers) yet provided ventilation. The only separate rooms were for storage, cooking, bathing, and writing. Very different from what I had been used to.

A long dining table stretched down the hall's center. The bishop motioned me to be seated next to what I knew must be his place at one end—the chair looked like a throne. A servant added a log to the fire, poking it with gusto. Gradually, the guests began to arrive, mostly men, although a few brought their wives. A woman with dark hair stepped in alone, wearing a long dark green cloak that she cast aside to reveal a simple shift of pale blue. Bishop Pall spoke to her for a few minutes before bringing her over to sit beside me.

"Lin, this is Margret. She is the best ivory carver in Iceland."

"Good day, Margret. I am happy to meet you."

She looked at me long and hard before pulling out a chair and settling herself next to me. Her pale face was without blemish, making it hard to discern her age. There were faint crow's feet at the outer edges of her eyes, but those green eyes looked clear and bright. She was pleasantly plump and wore an air of authority. She turned so that we faced each other, and I wasn't sure if it was just courtesy or combative on her part. Was she going to be a problem?

"So, why are you here?"

"I have been in Bergen for a year, and people talk about all the literature being produced in Iceland—the art too. It intrigued me so much, I had to see for myself."

"Can you read?"

"Oh yes."

"Good. I'm sure the bishop will let you read some of the works in his collection. He likes people who think and read."

"As do I. Tell me about your work."

"We get most of our ivory from walrus tusks that are brought in from Greenland. Our fishermen provide ivory too, but not enough. Many pieces I carve are used by the bishop as gifts. He has many important friends in Scotland, Denmark, and Norway. He believes in making sure his friends remember him fondly—the King of Norway being one of them, of course."

Her last remark was delivered with a mischievous little laugh. I relaxed and decided I liked her.

She went on. "I've done a few things for the church. Little statues for the niches and so on. The bishop keeps some of what I produce for himself too. He is particularly keen on me making chess sets. That's what his friends seem to cherish. It takes me a whole winter to make one set. Not that there's anything else to do in winter."

"Is winter here very hard? Winters in Bergen were hard, although we could get outside most of the time. I had been living in Portugal before that, so the cold was almost unbearable."

"I understand. In deep winter, we only get about three hours of daylight. We have to make sure we have enough lamp oil set aside to last until spring. The oil comes from sheep, so it smells strong when the lamps are lit from morning to night, but you hardly notice after a few days. Food has to be stored. If the snow isn't too deep, we can get out to slaughter a sheep if necessary, but we need to have plenty of salted fish and other things just in case and plenty of hay for the livestock too. I don't keep cattle or sheep, thank goodness, but the bishop sends food when he can. When it hasn't snowed much, we can visit nearby friends, so that makes a nice change."

"Winter sounds awful. The darkness would annoy me after a while. I like plenty of light."

"Well, it's summer now, so you'll have all the light you like. It hardly gets dark at all at this time of the year."

The food finally appeared, and a parade of servants placed empty platters in front of the guests and huge platters of food along the table. Lamb—or was it mutton?—alternated with bowls of skyr (yoghurt), fresh fish, and dark bread. I had smelled the bread baking. Its delicious yeasty aroma still filled the air.

We ate well, the meat delicious and flavored with herbs, the fish delightfully flaky, and the skyr creamy and mixed with luscious, fat blueberries. We drank ale, and I eventually sat back, sated.

"Well, you were hungry," said Margret.

"You wouldn't believe how bad the food was on the ship," I said.

"Oh, I'd believe it. Would you like to stay in my house for a while? I'm the only one, apart from a servant girl, as I have no family around here."

"Are you sure it's not an imposition? I'd love to see you work."

"No trouble at all. It will be good to have company."

After I had thanked His Grace and accepted gratefully the loan of a vellum book about Icelandic legends, we made our way to Margret's home. This was not a totally wooden house but one made of sod pressed over a wood frame. A fire warmed the room. It wasn't bright as it burned peat, which gave off a pleasant, earthy smell. We entered the side room that served as the kitchen, where a girl sat stirring a pot.

"Ana is making herbal tea, good for general health and well-being." The tea smelled of the essence of summer. "Lin will stay with us. Please make sure there is hot water so she may bathe tomorrow."

"Yes, mistress." The girl stared at me for a few seconds, her face neither welcoming nor hostile, before she returned to her task.

I was looking forward to getting clean. We went back to the main room where Margret showed me the large table where she worked. Several tusks, one much larger than the others, rested at the back against the wall and an oil lamp stood at each end. There were no windows, so she'd have to light the lamps to work, even on a summer day. A few chessmen stood to one side. They looked slightly comical. The knight's feet almost touched the ground as horses were much smaller in those days. Icelandic horses are still small, although very strong. The queen clutched her face as if she had a toothache, and the king looked downright depressed. But they were beautifully and intricately carved. I complimented Margret on her skill. Her answer was a radiant smile.

Margret showed me to a sleeping box, which surprised me.

"But isn't this yours?" I asked.

"No." She gestured to another on the same wall. "I sleep in my mother's. She died in it two years ago. Sleeping in her box makes me feel close to her again."

I was relieved not to be sleeping on a bench. I got in and Margret shut the door. Privacy is nice, but this felt a little too confined. The stuffed mat was comfortable, though, and the woolen blanket warm. I soon slept and was embarrassed to find the sun high in the sky when I emerged. Margret was out, but Ana soon filled a tub in the kitchen with hot water, and I was finally able to clean myself. The warm water felt luxurious, although the draft from the smoke hole made me shiver when I got out. She took my clothes to wash, so I put on a wrinkled but clean dress. It smelled a bit fishy, so I decided to take a walk and air myself. I needed to eat first though. Ana gave me bread and cheese at the kitchen table with a cup of milk. A small bowl of berries followed. It was clear I shouldn't expect a great variety of food in Iceland.

I had just finished my berries and skyr when Margret returned, carrying an armful of flowers and herbs, which she dropped on the table. Ana, who had come in to greet her mistress, took the herbs to the kitchen. She came back with a big jar of water, into which Margret put the flowers, tweaking them this way and that until the effect pleased her.

We had exchanged perfunctory greetings when she came in, but nothing more until the flowers had been properly arranged.

"I hope you slept well?"

"I did. I'm sorry I slept so late, but I was exhausted. I had a good bath, too, and ate well. Thank you for your hospitality."

It was so strange that I was exhausted and needed to sleep for hours. I didn't truly need it, but sleeping had become a habit and it was—well, restful. How far from my origins I'd come.

"You are most welcome. I have to do some work now. What would you like to do?"

"I thought of taking a walk to explore the town a little. I could sit outside and read too. Then maybe watch you work later?"

"Please feel at home here."

I ducked out of the doorway and wandered the streets. Most of the houses were constructed like Margret's, some smaller, some larger. A couple had extensions built onto them, mostly cubes stuck on the back or sides. None had windows, just a hole on each roof with a dark circle around it caused by smoke from the kitchen fire. I realized that winter must be quite an ordeal between the cold and the darkness. Not for me. I walked by the church, which loomed large amongst all these modest dwellings. Margret had mentioned that it was the largest church in Iceland.

When I came to the edge of town, I looked out over a green expanse dotted with wildflowers that offered glorious splashes of color. Basalt rocks gleamed darkly from their nesting places strewn across the land. I walked farther until confident I was out of sight of anyone before breaking into a run. When I run so fast that I become invisible, it tends to upset people.

"This is quite a long tale, so let's finish it tomorrow." Lin swung her feet to the ground and stretched. "I'm hungry."

"I heard Dora tell Auntie she was going to try some Chinese recipes for lunch."

"By the gods, that's going to be interesting. I hope she's not expecting Hunter to eat that."

Hunter got his steak, and the Chinese stir-fry and fried rice weren't bad. Rose had a second helping. I thought that maybe I should take her to a Chinese restaurant.

7

Lin came down to breakfast late and told me she wouldn't be down for our session for another hour or so. She had some phone calls to make. I had everything set up before sitting down to continue reading my novel. It crossed my mind that I should be writing a novel rather than reading one, but in reality that had been a non-existent proposition for a couple of years. Even Auntie had stopped asking about it.

Lin ran downstairs and jumped onto her back on the chaise.

"You're either very happy or very mad," I said.

"I have made some very satisfactory travel arrangements," she said. "I'll let you know sooner or later. Let's get to it. Where was I? Oh yes, I'd set out for a walk."

Tape 2 continued,
Volume 3

I spotted a group of rocks overlooking the river. Not a ship in sight. Maybe it wasn't deep enough. I found a comfortable patch of moss where I could sit leaning against a smooth rock and took out my book. Icelandic is very close to our old Norse tongue. Of course, we didn't use the written word in Asgard, but I took the opportunity to learn during my many visits to Midgard. Most letters are the same as western European alphabets, so I could read it fine, even though Icelandic has a few extra ones. But I managed to figure them out by reading aloud so I could fill in what should be there. I quickly became absorbed in tales of trolls and elves, not to mention the Hidden People.

"No one really knows. It's all just stories."

I just about jumped out of my skin. Only another supernatural being can creep up on me like that. A strange boy edged around the rock until he faced me. He was very tall, and his face was well-proportioned, except for his eyes. They were huge, and so dark they seemed almost jet black. I've seen pictures in children's books like that. Pretty little things with big soulful eyes that were usually blue. His brown tunic set off his sallow skin and yellow hair.

"Who are you?"

"Ah, so you can hear me and see me. You are not one of those then."

"Those?"

"People who live in houses and make things and kill creatures to eat."

"I am a goddess who used to live in Asgard. There are very few of us left. I have learned to live and eat like human people because I have to live with them. Our world was destroyed."

"Our stories mention that terrible time. It is the responsibility of one member of each community to remember all our stories and tell us one every night. There are thousands of them."

"Are you one of the Hidden People?"

"I am. We are Holdur. We live inside and among these rocks. We saw you coming. My name is Bjorn."

"May I meet some of the others? Your parents?"

He laughed—a high tinkle, like a silver bell. "I was obliged to find another community when I turned fifty. There is only room for so many in each outcrop. I thought of going into some of the immense black columns that face the sea, but I decided that a smaller group would be more to my liking. Come with me."

I tucked the bishop's book into my pocket and got up. He took my hand and led me to a gap between two of the larger rocks. It felt like passing through mushy clouds before I found myself in a large hall with at least twenty skinny tall people lounging on colorful mats and cushions lining the walls. Having all those enormous eyes staring at me intensely was disconcerting. So many sconces adorned the place that it looked almost like daylight.

An elderly woman dressed in a diaphanous robe of leaf green approached, her hands outstretched. "Welcome, my lady, welcome. I am Darl."

"Thank you, Darl," I said, looking up at her. "I am so pleased to meet you. I am Lin."

"We are so glad Bjorn brought you. It is not often we have guests."

"I suspect you are not easy to find," I said. She laughed, the bell moving up and down the scale for a few seconds..

Her eyes were huge like Bjorn's but light gray. When I turned to Bjorn, I discovered that his eyes were the same color. Daylight must affect them.

Bjorn showed me to a comfortable cushion before disappearing, only to return with a plate of fruit. I have never seen or tasted anything like those delicacies before or since. There were blue pear-shaped pomes that tasted like lichees, berries that tasted like peaches, and many other delights of all shapes and colors. I only finished half the plate before feeling full.

"You see," said Darl, who had seated herself beside me and soon busied herself finishing my plate, "there is no need to kill anything to eat well."

"Yes, I can see that. But I have never seen fruits like that among humans."

"We cultivated them. We have our own orchards that are hidden from human view."

"Perhaps if you shared them, they would stop killing things."

"We cannot show ourselves to humans. We are the Hidden People for a reason that lies far back in antiquity. It is said that our ancient earth mother tried to hide her unwashed children from God, and that in his anger he said that if a mother tries to hide her children from God, they should remain hidden. That's what the old stories say, but who knows where the truth lies? And which god anyway? While we are outside the world of people, we are happy and peaceful, and that is more than can be said of them."

"So far I have found Icelanders very peaceful."

"Others will disturb their peace eventually. There are always those humans who crave power over their fellows."

"Yes, that can happen with gods too. And once that happened in Asgard, it led to the end of our world."

"We heard tales of the final battle. After many eons, stories change—little things added, others forgotten. Would you mind telling us your account of Ragnarok?"

I told them the sad story, which they seemed to find spellbinding.

Darl patted my hand. "Thank you for trusting us with that sad story. It is different from our account but only in small details. We will be sure to retell it right."

"Humans should learn from old tales that war is futile. No one truly wins," I said.

"Indeed. Please tell no one of our meeting." Concern wrinkled Darl's brow.

"I will not. People are not to be trusted with such revelations."

"You are a wise woman."

"I am still a goddess, although my powers have weakened over the millennia. I am not what I was."

"You are still worthy of our trust."

"Darl, I must return to my friend now. She is a fine artist. She carves beautiful things from walrus ivory." I knew I shouldn't have said that when Darl's face creased with anger. Walrus ivory meant dead walruses.

"I know of her. Because of people like her, so many walruses are slaughtered. It's unbearable cruelty."

"I know. But that is the way of people."

Darl beckoned to the boy Bjorn—well, a fifty-year old boy—and directed him to lead me outside. We embraced before parting, an odd experience, as everything in her felt soft, even where bones should be. I looked deep into her eyes, which seemed to suck me in. I saw her old soul, her love and wisdom. I didn't want to go, but knew I must. Bjorn took my hand again and guided me through the cloud until I emerged once more into sunlight. I turned to thank him, but he'd melted away.

I sat on the same rock once more and thought about my visit. I could not tell any of these Icelanders about it because they'd want to know where and maybe even try to pry apart the rocks. Humans always feel the urge to explore and discover—and conquer. And then there was the church. The existence of Hidden People would threaten their view of scriptural correctness, which meant it was something that must be destroyed. Or the bearer of the story must be. No, nothing for humans to know.

I ran back to the edge of town before slowing to a walk, making my way to Margret's house. I found her and the bishop standing outside conferring anxiously.

"Lin!" she cried when she spotted me. "We've been so worried. Where have you been?"

"I walked a long, long way before sitting on a rock to read the book the bishop lent me. Why? Is it late?"

"You've been gone for so long. We ate dinner hours ago!"

I'd forgotten about the long summer days in this part of the world. "I'm so sorry. I lost track of time. I'm not used to it staying light so long." I held out the book to Bishop Pall. "Thank you for this. I found it absorbing."

"I am glad you are safe, my child," he said, looking into my eyes. He was suspicious, I could tell. "It doesn't do for a young lady to be alone too far away for too long."

"No, Your Grace, you are quite right." I bowed my head. Clergymen love submission. It soothes their souls.

He patted Margret on the arm before walking home.

"I'm so sorry, Margret. I really had no idea of the time."

"That's all right. I'm sure you discovered something interesting." A smile played around her lips before she went inside. I followed after a startled pause. *What did you mean by that?*

Ana warmed me a plate of lamb and greens over the fire and filled a mug with ale. I enjoyed it less than the previous evening's meal. Darl's disapproval of killing animals for food or any other reason niggled at me. But refusing the food would have seemed odd. Even the skyr and berries didn't compare with the fruits I'd shared with Darl. Anyway, this is where I was and where I had to deal with it, at least for a while.

The next morning, I rose just after dawn after a good night's sleep—disappointingly dreamless—and ate breakfast with Margret.

"I must work most of today," she said. "The bishop asked me to finish the chess set I've started as quickly as possible. He wants to send it as a gift to the Norwegian king. I want to get as much as I can finished before we go to Althing. I've made sets for him before, so I'm trying something different. A little comical."

"Ah, I wondered about that. They are comical figures yet very endearing. And what is Althing?"

"Althing is our annual gathering of the chieftains and their clans where the law is read, complaints dealt with, and matters of interest to all discussed. Everyone looks forward to it. You will be welcome, of course."

"It does sound interesting. I'll watch you work for a while, then I might take a walk. I promise to stay in town this time though."

"Good idea. It is hard to judge the passing of time in summer. And the bishop is always worried about the virtue of young women. He keeps a good check on me, I can tell you."

"Surely he doesn't think I was playing around with a man, does he?"

"He probably wonders, knowing him."

"I didn't see a soul out there. I read, dozed a little, and read some more."

"Oh, I believe you. But you know how people like him are so obsessed with sin. I think they find it titillating. And you are beautiful, after all."

"Thank you. I'll be careful."

After Ana had cleared away, Margret went over to her work table. I carried my chair a little closer and at an angle so I could watch what she was doing without making her feel as if I was breathing down her neck.

First she looked over her supply of tusks. "This big one is from an old bull walrus," she said. "They use their tusks to dig up clams, make their way across rocks, and fight for their mates. They have a lot of cracks in them, so I can only use part of it. Luckily, I'm carving small items." She took a sharp knife and scraped it across the surface until white showed through. Then she sawed it into short pieces, working around the cracks. She selected a few tools and started on the smallest piece from the top. After what felt like at least an hour, I could made out a crown: a king or queen. She alternated between chipping and carving with small, sharp instruments and a sure hand. The head began to form. What a painstaking business.

She held up the piece, turning it around for my benefit. "When I get further into the body, I will have to carve deeper, so you will see how the ivory looks different under the surface. Lots of beautiful markings that are much more interesting that the smooth surface."

"Yes, I see. I'd like to take a walk now, if I may," I said, hoping she wouldn't be offended by my leaving so soon. She waved her hand without speaking, so intense was her concentration. "Can I get you anything while I'm out?"

"Ask Ana," she replied without looking up.

Ana wanted some skyr and told me the best place to get it and how much it would cost. I'd walk around before visiting the farm so that the skyr wouldn't get too warm.

There wasn't much to see, just a lot of sod houses. Other people walking on the lanes nodded politely and wished me a good morning, which I reciprocated. I walked through the entire town before arriving at the farm where Ana had asked me to go. I entered the front yard where a young girl in a coarse-woven tunic was filling a bucket from the pump.

"Good morning," she said. "Do you need something?"

"Good morning. I am staying with Margret, the carver. Ana, her servant girl, asked me to buy skyr while I was out for my walk. She said this was the best place."

The girl smiled. "Please come in and sit down while I fetch her usual order."

I followed her into a cool room and sat at the rough wooden table. She placed a mug of ale in front of me before going back out, presumably to one of the outbuildings. I hadn't realized how thirsty I was after my long walk. It was a crude brew, rather yeasty and bitter, but it quenched my thirst. The girl returned with a large wooden bowl covered with a cloth. I had the money ready.

"That's too much," she said.

"A little extra for your hospitality."

She thanked me, blushing with pleasure. I took the bowl and left.

When I got back, I found Margret in the same position. *Did she move at all?* Her back and neck must have suffered greatly. I gave the skyr to Ana and went back to my chair, where I could see the deeper carving had revealed some patterning. The piece was the king, judging by the beard below his doleful face. He indeed looked comical.

Suddenly, she put down her tools and stretched. "I must move around," she said, getting up and walking round the dining table for a few minutes. She rotated her head and bent down to touch her toes several times. "That's better," she said. "It must be time for our midday meal."

Almost on cue, Ana brought out bread, cheese, and fruit before going back to the kitchen for a jug of ale. I reminded myself not to expect any variety in the menu.

While we ate, I asked Margret about her work. "How long will it take you to finish the king?"

"I should finish it today."

"It's going to take a long time to carve a whole set," I said.

"Yes. I can't finish them all that quickly, but the pawns are very simple, so I can usually do four or five in one day."

"The king looks sad."

"Yes, I like to think of them lightening the mood of the players, so he might be sad, but it's funny in a way. Chess is a complicated game that many people take much too seriously." She tore off a piece of bread and alternated bites of it with a piece pried from a wedge of cheese. "You know, it's only two weeks until we have the Althing."

"You seem excited about it."

"It's very important to us. It's the big gathering of our chieftains and the people in their holdings. I think I mentioned that it's where matters of the law are discussed and complaints and quarrels settled. Friendships are rekindled too. We will ride there with the bishop's entourage. Our law-speaker will recite one third of our laws too, so everyone will hear them for themselves."

"And what kind of punishments are handed out?" I asked.

"It's usually a matter of negotiation to make wrongs right. And if the law has been broken in a serious way, the wrongdoer might be exiled. Usually for three years, but if it's very bad, forever. No one has been banished forever for many years."

"That sounds very civilized," I said. "Much better than most countries I've visited—and I've visited a lot."

"Yes, we are a civilized people. This is a harsh country. Our winter weather is dangerous, and there isn't that much good pasture for crops and livestock. We all need each other in order to survive. We can't do it alone. The winters are getting colder too."

Over the next couple of weeks, I walked and ran out into the countryside past farms that had a few good fields and some that would yield a poor crop, judging by their sparse growth, past high pastures dotted with sheep, and higher still where there was barely any plant life at all. I often thought of Hunter in those quiet spaces, wondering if he was safe—alive, even. I missed him.

It was soon time to pack up for the Althing, where we would live in tents for a week. The whole town seethed with excitement, even though many could not attend. Those who did go would bring back stories and perhaps gifts from the crafters who peddled their wares at the event. It was the only time these people had any reason to leave home.

It proved quite a trek, involving bumping along rough paths and forcing horses across fjords that for now ran still and shallow. After three days, we came to a wide meadow where many people had already claimed their spaces and set up tents.

The bishop sailed off to a large tent where he received a loud welcome. Margret and I walked to a quiet area while a couple of the bishop's servants set up our tent under Ana's supervision. That done, she unpacked the sheepskin bags containing our supplies and started a fire. We soon had our meal set before us on a small collapsible table. I sighed. Lamb, skyr, bread, and fruit. At least the ale was good. I knew that after a couple of days, our meals would feature salted fish. In the evening, we were invited to the chieftain's tent, where some good cheese and spit-roasted chicken was added to the menu. The chieftain eyed me with great interest whenever he thought the bishop wasn't watching. A burly man with blond hair and a red beard, he seemed quiet and thoughtful.

A drunken clamor erupted outside, which made Bishop Pall purse his lips. I picked up girlish giggles and boyish shouts too, fading into the distance as youngsters chased each other, no doubt into rocky hiding places where shrubs provided just enough privacy.

"There'll be some babies made tonight," whispered Margret.

"What happens to the girls if they are not married?" I whispered back.

"Oh, they'll get married," she answered. "It's quite normal. It happens every year. It's not always the real father she marries if her father wants a more advantageous union."

What a difference. In most countries, she'd be ostracized or even punished severely. And a good—or any—marriage would be out of the question.

The Althing started the next morning, not very early, as headaches plagued most attendees. I found it impressive. The chieftain, who was the law-speaker, stood in front of the assembly and recited Iceland's laws for quite some time. He would recite a third of them each year, Margret had told me. Then we listened to the first complaint. It was not very interesting—just a land dispute over boundaries. What did prove interesting was that each farmer had to have five witnesses to affirm his side of the story. Elders consulted with the chieftain about possible solutions, and the chieftain finally proposed a settlement between the parties. No voices were raised or insults offered. I couldn't believe how civilized these people were.

Eventually the Althing finished its business, and we all went home. The rest of Europe had a lot to learn from Iceland. The church wouldn't allow it though, cherishing power and obedience as it did. It tried to wield its power in Iceland too, but while the people were Christians, they held firmly to old ways, and most still believed in the old legends. Elves, Hidden People, and trolls formed an unassailable backdrop to their newer Christian beliefs. It must have driven the clergy mad. I suspect Bishop Pall was a little more philosophical, accepting that that was the way matters stood, so why fight it? Just so long as Mother Church kept her foot firmly in the door.

Margret rested the day after we got back. We went herb gathering not far afield and visited a neighbor's small farm, where we heard all the local gossip about who might be married soon (with a wink), who struggled to make their farms pay, and who seemed to be sick. To my surprise, Margret participated with great enthusiasm. I'd have thought her more high-minded than that, but then there wasn't much else to do or talk about. She never mentioned her work though.

Margret returned to her bench and renewed work on the little king. He was taking shape now, a long beard resting on his chest between the folds of his robe, hands grasping what looked like a scroll. I saw how she'd carved the back and arms of the throne, which she continued to work on down the sides in a trellis pattern. Watching the figure come to life was a wonder. She would pick up one small tool, then another, carving out a delicate fold, or a wider facet, smoothing, and shaping. When she'd finished the king, she held it up and rotated the piece, looking for flaws. She made a few minute adjustments before declaring herself satisfied. She then picked up a piece of ivory left from the first few cuts of the new piece. "That's just about big enough for a pawn."

"What do your pawns look like?" I asked.

"Nothing like those from China or India that the bishop has. Nothing fancy at all." By the time Ana put lunch on the table, she'd carved a simple cylinder with a domed top and faceted sides. I found it pleasing in its perfect balance and clean lines.

"Will you be able to finish a set before winter?" I asked.

"Yes, I only have a couple of knights, a berserker, a queen, and six more pawns to complete."

I'd been salivating for most of the morning because I smelled chicken roasting. I stuck my head around the kitchen opening to see where Ana had the bird stuck through with an iron skewer resting between two forked stakes stuck in the dirt floor on either side of the fire. A metal pot hung underneath the chicken to catch the fat.

We sat down for lunch: a perfectly roasted chicken with crisped skin, thanks be to the gods. I'd eaten enough lamb and mutton to last that lifetime, if not several more. I was also sick of the smell of sheep tallow candles. I wouldn't stay much longer. Trading ships were expected to arrive in August. I liked the Icelanders and their culture a lot, but the harsh climate made for a very restricted life. They all complained that the winters were getting colder and that those who used to eke out an existence in higher pastures could no longer do so. I had to get out before cold weather set in.

August came and went with one violent storm following another. No ships came into port, and it was assumed they'd been lost at sea. I was stuck, probably until spring. I couldn't concentrate. I was so depressed at the thought of spending winter in almost permanent darkness that I hadn't been able to settle to anything for a couple of weeks. We surviving gods need blue skies and crave sunlight after the three-year winter that presaged Ragnarok and the near-eternal void that followed. It left its mark—as did our grief at all we had lost.

And what of Hunter? Would he return and think I'd abandoned him? I longed for him. I went back to where I'd met the Hidden People with another book the bishop lent me.

"Bjorn, are you there?"

Nothing. Perhaps they felt once was enough. If they opened the portals too often, maybe others would discover them.

"Were you looking for someone?"

Startled again, I turned to find a handsome young man behind me. "Are you Holdur?"

"No, I am not. Do I look like one?"

"Well, no, you don't. But no human can creep up on me like that. What are you?"

He laughed and laughed until I thought the din would make me crazy as it bounced from one rock to another and skimmed across the river and back before erupting skyward, gradually fading into the wispy clouds. When he'd finished, he put his hands on his hips and looked me up and down. He was three times as tall as I was, with broad shoulders and what I suddenly realized was quite an ugly face with walnut skin and a black beard. How odd that I'd first thought him handsome.

"You first. Who are you?"

"I am the goddess Lin. Lin of Asgard."

"Well, little lady, you're a long way from home. A home you won't be going back to." He looked as if he was going to laugh again, but his remark had annoyed me enough that I jumped high enough to slap his face. His face registered shock before settling into fury.

"Can't you guess what I am?"

"Well, you have the manners of a troll. Not that I've ever met one, but I've never heard anything good about them."

His face twisted until it looked even uglier. "Well, I am a troll. And I can have very nice manners when I want to. When people are nice to me. If they're really nice to me, I don't even eat them. I've never eaten a goddess. You look tasty."

"I'm afraid you will find me indigestible. We are not made like other people. Different blood, power that would make you explode from the inside out. I've never heard of you eating any of the townspeople anyway."

"The Holdur put a spell on me many years ago." He looked sad. "I can't eat people anymore. Only sheep. I'm sick of eating sheep."

"So am I," I said with sympathy. "Have you tried fish?"

"Fish is for weaklings."

"No, not at all. Even the strongest of men eat fish sometimes. It makes a nice change."

"How would I get one? I don't like getting wet."

Judging by his rank smell, I could believe it. "You make a little iron hook and tie it to a piece of thin rope. Then you put a worm on the hook and dangle it in the water. When a fish eats the worm, he can't escape because of the hook. So you pull the fish out of the water. You might have to get your feet wet."

"I don't know about getting my feet wet. The water is very cold."

"If you don't like the cold, whatever do you do in winter?"

"I sleep most of the time. I store enough wood in my cave to last all winter. I store meat in the snow. I have lovely fur blankets."

"I thought you trolls live under bridges."

"How many bridges have you seen around here? That is, bridges big enough for me to live under? And it would be too cold in wintertime. How long have you been here?" He leaned over me, fists on hips. "Have you been through one of our winters?"

"No. I wanted to leave on one of the trading ships, but they never showed up. I'm dreading all that dark."

"Little goddess, would you like to be my wife?"

"But I hardly know you."

"No need to be so fussy. I would like to bed you."

"Well, you'd have promise to take a bath every day. I'm very fussy about that."

"No, no, I can't." He started to pant. "Water? Water every day?" He looked close to panic. "No. Goodbye, beautiful lady." He blew me a kiss. "Goodbye."

I could swear he had tears in his eyes as he gazed at me soulfully one more time. He clumped across the meadow, covering about ten feet with each stride. He turned and waved once before breaking into a run.

I felt it wise to leave too, and ran back to the edge of town before strolling back to Margret's home. I wondered if I should tell her but decided against it. She'd think me mad.

We spent the fall months getting ready for winter and visiting the neighbors while we could, all of whom were more than hospitable. We bought fish that Ana salted. An old man delivered a large quantity of lamp oil. A younger man delivered logs that he split and stored by the door in a roofed space built for the purpose. More was stored along a kitchen wall.

"When food begins to run low, we wait for a day without too much snow and buy meat," said Margret.

It sounded dreadful. The only saving grace was that the bishop lent me a pile of books to occupy my days.

Gradually, the days got shorter and shorter, and snow started to fall. Sometimes only an inch or so but at other times enough to make walking impossible. Margret had a kind of shovel that I used to clear a track so we could get out on clear days. One day, she walked behind me while I shoveled a path all the way to the bishop's house. Everyone marveled at my strength. I took great pleasure in getting out, although we could only be gone for about three hours in midwinter before it got dark again.

Margret carved away and finished a complete set. She took a day off before starting the next one. I read until even my eyes got tired. I found the darkness deeply depressing. Ana cooked, cleaned, spun, and slept. Her woven cloth was quite fine. Margret presented me with a good length of it so that a local woman could make me a new dress. I felt like a princess the first time I tried it on. I wasn't used to being as dingy as I'd become.

No one talked much. Everything outside was silent—no children laughed and cried, and hardly any dogs barked. The thickly piled snow deadened most sound. I couldn't wait to leave. Margret kept on carving, and I finished the bishop's stack of books. Thankfully, I managed to return them to him on a clear day and borrow a few more.

At the end of April, a slow thaw started, leaving huge patches of mud in the streets. The snow hadn't finished with us yet, and intermittent falls again hid the grass that had fought its way to the surface. Well into May, the grass prevailed, people visited, and we got fresh fish and lamb. Lots of lamb, poor little things—Darl's condemnation still got to me. Ana was able to walk far enough to places where she could gather greens, which we'd run out of long ago. They tasted wonderful. My mood rose. One morning, I found her washing some strange dark red roots.

"What are those for?" I asked.

"They are good to eat, but Margret needs these to color the chess pieces," Ana replied.

"Why? They're beautiful as they are."

"Half of each set has to be a different color. You've never played chess?"

I hadn't, but I'd seen others play. "Yes, of course. I'd forgotten."

"The traders will be here soon," Margret said. "I suppose you will leave us. I will miss you."

"Margret, you are like my sister. I will miss you too. But I must find my husband. If he is still alive." Of course the silly boy was alive. No one could defeat him, or so I hoped. He'd lost more of his powers than I had after being so badly wounded at Ragnarok, but he was still stronger than any human. And still immortal. As were the other gods— until they weren't.

The ships sailed into port. I packed my things into a sheepskin bag and went to take my leave of the bishop, returning those of his books I still had.

"God be with you in your travels, my child."

"You have been goodness itself," I told him. "I will never forget my time here with all the wonderful people of this town."

He made the sign of the cross over me before I left, which I found strangely touching. Margret would ride with me to the coast as would the many others who had goods to barter. The local farmers had suffered hardship after missing the summer's trading and had been hard put to buy grain and hay for the winter. I knew the bishop had helped many of them as had a few of the more prosperous farmers.

The bishop approved Margret's latest two chess sets, wrote a letter to the Scottish and Norwegian kings, and had one of his boys wrap and seal them. She would entrust one to a captain going at least as far as the Faroe Islands; from there, it would find its way farther south. There would certainly be a Norwegian trader to take the other to his king.

The beach was absolute bedlam with traders setting up tents and showing their wares. The captains themselves seemed to be trading on behalf of their owners. Margret pointed to one who had his back to me. "He's from Spain. That's near Portugal, isn't it?"

I waited until he had finished with the man he was bargaining with and tapped him on the shoulder.

"Yes?" he snapped before getting a good look at me. Then he asked, "How may I be of service?"

"I hear you are going to Spain. I would like passage on your ship. I can pay."

"What's in Spain for you?" he asked.

"I actually want to go to Portugal. I have been living there for many years. When my husband joined the crusade, I came to Iceland to study their literature and art."

"Oh, a woman who reads! Well, well. Yes, I can take you. As it happens, I'll be dropping off cargo in Lisbon before going on to Spain."

I was so relieved not to have to make my way from Spain to Portugal that I probably didn't bargain hard enough. We settled on a price, and I gave him the coins, which I had ready in my waist purse so as not to show where I kept the rest. He called one of the sailors to show me to my berth. I hugged Margret hard.

"I will never forget you," I said. "You are a true friend. I will write to the bishop so he can tell you my news."

She pressed a little package into my hand. "A knight to remember me by," she said.

She was a true friend, I thought, as I walked up the gangplank. She had no idea what I was, yet showed me every kindness. I stood on deck and waved farewell once more before going down to my poky, smelly little berth for a good cry. I unwrapped my miniature parcel and held the chess piece in the palm of my hand. A funny little ivory knight whose feet almost touched the ground.

The voyage was rocky until we got far enough south that the sea turned from gray to blue and the sun perked up. We moored at several ports. The captain was not that interesting but passable. He bade me a fond farewell before I disembarked. I wasn't really in the mood, but he saw to it that I ate well and had what I needed, so he deserved his reward.

"So there, Mary, you have my story of the knight."
"That's an incredible story, Lin. How old is that carving?"

"Well, I think Margret made it near the end of the twelfth century. You do the math."

"Wow, no wonder you are so protective of it. Did you write to Margret?"

"Yes, via the bishop for many years. Then Bishop Pall told me she'd died one winter. She had been walking home from a neighbor's house just before dark one day at the beginning of winter. The snow was not very deep, but the temperature had dropped, and she slipped on ice and hit her head. Ana went out looking for her when she didn't come home. She called at the nearest house for help, and some men carried her home. She had to be kept packed in ice until spring and they could dig her grave. I wept when I read his letter. I wrote back, of course, expressing my sorrow for his loss as well as my own. I never heard from him again. You know, I named my Margareta after Margret. I don't know why I didn't use the name for earlier daughters. When people wrote about her in later centuries, they referred to her as Margret the Adept. My Margareta is rather adept, I must say."

Lin teared up. But I had to ask.

"Well, what about Hunter?"

"Would you believe I found him at home? He'd taken part in a battle in Spain, which the crusaders won, before raping and pillaging the local town. He'd been disgusted by the slaughter and assault of innocents, just as I knew he would. He said a few of the crusaders had been thrown off a cliff and were dashed to pieces on the rocks below. He threw his tunic and sword down there, hoping someone would recognize them, before wending his way back home, dressed as a beggar, hunching over a stout stick as though weak and sick."

I couldn't help laughing at the mental picture that conjured up. "But wasn't he afraid that people in Lisbon would recognize him?"

"You would have thought so. He was an impetuous young man who didn't always think things through as he should. I deemed it in our best interests to move yet again."

"I loved that story. I had no idea Iceland was so progressive. Very unusual for that time."

"Quite unusual for these days too, in many areas of the world."

"I wonder what it's like now."

"I haven't been back. I've heard it is very advanced—top notch schools, and so on. Up until the second World War, it was still quite undeveloped, but when the Allies began to use it as a base, things started to change."

"I'd quite like to go. Is it beautiful?"

"Very. Anyway, I've decided that we will visit Agna in London in April, then go on with her to Egypt. That will be something quite different for you."

"London and Egypt. Wow! But what about Rose? I can't be away from her for so long."

"She will come with us, of course."

"Is it safe?"

"Don't be silly. Egypt is full of children. By the way, it's only a cold lunch today because Dora is out. Smoked salmon and so on."

"Smoked salmon sounds good to me. Dora is out?"

"Yes. Her boyfriend is taking her on a lunch cruise along the Potomac."

"Hope she doesn't get seasick."

"She will."

I hardly said a word during lunch. I was too excited and a little apprehensive too. What if Rose got sick? What if and what if.

Auntie Peggy followed me and Rose downstairs. After I'd put Rose down for her nap, she asked me, "Are you all right? You look tense, and you've hardly said a word."

"Auntie, I'm so excited. Lin has invited Rose and me to go with her to London to visit Agna, then we'll all go on to Egypt. I really want to go, but I'm worried about Rose. There are all sorts of diseases out there, aren't there?"

"Well, I think you'll both have to get some vaccinations. And only drink bottled water. If you stay in a nice hotel—and I can't imagine Lin staying anywhere else—you should be fine. Those hotels have doctors on call too."

That made me feel a lot better. I'd start surfing the internet and would order a guidebook too.

8

We didn't do any more recording before it was time to leave for London. Rose wasn't too pleased about the vaccinations. She wagged her finger at the doctor after the first shot, telling him that Santa probably wouldn't visit him next Christmas. He did his best to look sad, which Rose found very gratifying. I didn't enjoy the shots either, but it would be worth it to have such an adventure.

When the weather was good, I took Auntie and Rose for walks, which worked well as their stamina was similar. Auntie was fully recovered by the end of March, although her arthritis still began to bother her after twenty minutes or so. But the walks did her good, and Rose loved to hold her hand and tell her stories. She liked to tell "secrets," turning to us, putting her finger to her lips, and saying, "Just between us."

"Cuckoos steal other birds' nests" was one. And "Papa says 'fuck' sometimes" was another, which went down with Auntie like the proverbial lead balloon.

I told Rose we were going to visit Agna, which delighted her. She skipped around the living room singing, "Agna, Agna, we're coming Agna," until it made us both dizzy.

Lin and I went clothes shopping a couple of weeks before we set off for our big adventure. Lin probably didn't think of it as an adventure, but I certainly did. She'd taken me to Italy the year before, and in March, she decided she missed her best friend Agna, a Norse witch who had been the Egyptian Pharaoh Tutankhamun's protector, both before and after death. We'd depart in early April.

"London will be fairly cool at this time of year and probably rainy," said Lin. "Cairo will be hot. We might go to Upper Egypt too, and that will be even hotter. We'd better take two cases, one for each climate."

I already had the clothes we'd bought a few weeks ago, but Lin insisted we get more. We bought mix-and-match outfits. I got a chic three-quarter length red raincoat with a hood, three pairs of medium-weight pants—black, gray and brown—and a selection of tops and jackets that I could wear with any of the pants. I also got a sleek gray skirt that went nicely with one of the jackets and a light gray silk shirt. One pair of black shoes and one brown, and two purses. We were getting to the end of the season, so the prices weren't too horrendous. That completed the London bag.

We went to a really fancy store for the summer stuff. The spring collections were coming in, but we needed a store that catered to those who travelled to warmer climes early. These prices were steep. I already had a few nice things from last summer but not enough—in Lin's opinion.

Lin pulled out an emerald green silky dress with cap sleeves and a vee neckline. "This would look lovely on you." She pulled out a yellow sundress. "And this. Try them on."

They might have been made for me. I still wasn't used to the woman in the mirror. Only three years ago, I'd been mousy Mary from Pennsylvania, just graduated from college, never been anywhere or done anything extraordinary. Now

I was a lover, a mother, a ghostwriter, and I looked stylish whenever I went out.

We bought sandals, a pair each that had thicker soles, and were less open. "For sandy, rocky spots," Lin said.

We could hardly stagger back to the car with all those bags.

"I've only got one old suitcase," I said. "I hope you've got some extras."

"Oh, we've got plenty," Lin said. "Hunter and I are always going somewhere, and so are the children. Do you have decent nightwear and lingerie?"

"Some. I got them a few years ago before Rose came along."

"Ah yes, I remember helping you with that." Lin laughed at the memory of how embarrassed I was when she tried to make me model them for Hunter. I wasn't used to sharing in those days. "We'd better get some more next week. We'll bring Rose. She'll need a few things too."

"You are so good to me. It's more than I deserve."

"Nonsense. You're family."

Yes, I was family. To the extent a mere mortal can be part of a family of gods.

The next week we shopped for lingerie and outfits for Rose, who was very excited with her new clothes. She insisted on showing them off to Hunter, who voiced the appropriately enthusiastic noises. She hadn't quite taken in the idea of traveling overseas. I think she thought it would be like driving down to the family house on the Chesapeake Bay, which we did quite often.

We took an overnight flight to London. I hoped Rose would sleep most of the way and not get fussy. The idea of flying first-class frightened me a little. I hoped I wouldn't commit some awful faux pas.

"Auntie, I'm sorry to leave you behind. I hope you'll be all right."

"Mary, dear, of course I'll be all right. I've got Hunter and Dora, and the children will be home for spring break. I've done enough traveling in my lifetime, and I would find it too arduous these days. You go, take it all in, bring back photos, and enjoy. Take the good things life offers with both hands."

I wondered again about all her traveling, her hints about experiences overseas, and so on. She never discussed them. I knew she had a generous government pension, so she must have held a fairly high rank. I resolved to get it out of her one of these days.

Hunter drove us to Dulles airport and said goodbye with bear hugs and smacking kisses before we passed through to security. If I'd remembered we'd have to take off our shoes, I would have worn slip-ons. Rose insisted on going through the body-scan port on her own, carefully placing her little feet on the right marks and raising her arms as she'd seen Lin do just before. Everyone around watched, enchanted. Then she insisted on being patted down afterward, again as Lin had been. The security guard kept a straight face as she did it, remarking that such a cooperative passenger deserved a lollipop, which she happened to have in her pocket.

"I like this place," announced Rose as she turned to watch me. I didn't get patted down. "I don't think you'll get a lollipop," she said.

"Oh, well, they don't give them out every time, you know. Lin didn't get one either."

Lin led the way to the first-class lounge, where we found a corner with two comfortable armchairs. I got Rose settled in one with her book and teddy, corralling our hand baggage so we could keep an eye on it.

"We need another chair," Lin said. "Ah, there's a spare one." With that, she strode over to an armchair next to a family of four, lifted it over her head and dumped it next to ours. Our end of the lounge went quiet as a number of mouths gaped. "Oops, I forgot myself," she murmured. A waitress soon came for our drink orders.

In the chaos of leaving the house, while Rose just had to go back several times to kiss the anxiously circling Sam goodbye, I hadn't realized how early we were.

"Lin, why did we leave so early? We've got a two-hour wait."

"I thought it would be easier to eat dinner here rather than the plane. Otherwise it would be very late for Rose. They won't start serving until about an hour after we take off."

"I didn't think of that. Maybe I'll eat too."

"I recommend a snack to keep you going. Rose might doze off onboard while we eat and enjoy our champagne."

I liked the sound of that. Rose enjoyed her discussion about the menu with the waitress as she placed her order. She ate very well, having chosen two appetizers instead of an entrée: smoked salmon with thin triangles of buttered brown bread and prawn cocktail.

Lin and I each had tiny cucumber sandwiches and another glass of white wine. I'd read that it was better not to drink on long flights but never mind. This was my adventure, and one doesn't go on adventures to be sensible.

I didn't realize that planes could be so big—the one we'd taken to Italy had been quite a bit smaller. Rose had no idea we would actually fly. To be honest, I didn't fully comprehend how such a huge beast could possible get off the ground. It worried me. But they did, somehow, and what's more, they did it every day. Each passenger had their own seat, no rows. I needn't have worried how Rose would take being across from me rather than next to me. A flight attendant brought her a coloring book and crayons as well as a lovely picture book. The captain came through and pinned a badge on her. "You've earned your wings," he said. "You can tell your friends that the captain made you my very important passenger."

"And you are my very important captain," Rose said. He laughed and blew her a kiss. So far, so good.

We took off—left the ground and leveled out, despite my skepticism—and as it was dark outside, Rose probably thought we were just driving along the runway. After about half an hour, her eyes began to droop. While I held her, our flight attendant made the bed and covered her with a blanket after I settled her down. Champagne arrived while dishes and silverware discretely pinged each other. Dinner was excellent, and soon after, I was ready to sleep myself. Some passengers read or watched TV, but I was out.

The lights turned on as we approached breakfast time. Of course, it was still the middle of the night for us, but I somehow took it all in stride. We all had our beds returned to upright, and Rose came over for a cuddle until breakfast was served.

Somewhere behind us, a shriek and a crash scared the heck out of me. A male flight attendant soon appeared to reassure us. "Everything is quite all right, ladies and gentlemen. Another passenger ran into one of our staff, knocking the tray out of her hands." His eyes scoured the floor as he spoke. He went back to wherever he came from.

Out of the corner of my eye, I saw what had probably occasioned the shriek. A little field mouse emerged from under Rose's seat and sniffed the air. Rose spotted it too. "You're such a pretty mousy. Come and see me. I have something you'd like." She bent over her armrest, holding out her hand. I wasn't afraid of mice and didn't object. The mouse jumped onto her armrest and scampered over her lap to her table where it sat on its hind legs grooming its whiskers .

She placed a few crumbs of buttered toast in front of the little creature. "Eat up like a good boy now." The sliver of cheese that followed disappeared in no time.

When the approach to Heathrow was announced, all was cleared away, and the attendant raised Rose's blind. The mouse had wisely concealed itself on the other side of Rose, who turned to look out of the window. "Oh, oh! We're up in the air."

"Airplanes fly, and that's how they get to other places fast," I said. "We flew all the way across the sea. We'll be in London soon. In a country called England. Remember, I told you we were going to visit Agna? She lives in London. In a week or so, we'll get into another plane to fly to Egypt."

Rose nodded sagely, as if fully understanding everything, but didn't utter a word.

Raised voices clashed behind us.

"Madam, you cannot use the first class facilities. Please go back to your seat."

"There is a mouse around here. It could be anywhere. I'm not using a lav that might have a mouse it in. Get out of my way!"

A stout woman carrying a tote that must have been at the outer edge of hand baggage limitations barged through, intent on using the first-class bathroom. The startled mouse leapt from Rose's seat to the back of the next passenger's seat. The pushy woman sounded as though she had been put to the rack, rather than catching sight of a minute rodent. The bathroom forgotten, she threw her arms in the air, which catapulted her bag in an arc that culminated in knocking the passenger in front of Rose sideways. Her bag ejected candies, tissues, cosmetics, at least two pairs of black panties, toiletries, a passport, a red wallet, and a full pink bottle of Milk of Magnesia that exploded on contact with a man returning from the bathroom. Barely stifled giggles emanated from Lin, in front of me, which set me off.

The large woman seemed on the verge of fainting, and two male flight attendants manhandled her back through the curtain, presumably back to her seat as she wept, more quietly now. The innocent bystander was being wiped down with paper towels by an apologetic attendant. The poor man was a mess, dripping with pink goo, to which stuck bits of paper and other small items. Another attendant bustled around picking up the detritus and stuffing it back into the woman's bag. I picked up the passport by my seat and handed it to her.

The man's clothes were in ruins. When he started to curse the "crazy bitch," I recognized his voice. Only last week we'd watched the movie he'd starred in. He'd been the victim of a much worse assault in that, and to my amusement, he gave much the same speech. Lin's giggles got louder, and I couldn't hold mine back anymore. Rose started to cry. "Where's my poor little mousey?"

"Never mind, honey. He always finds a safe place for himself."

I suspected he might not survive the wrath of the crew but rather hoped he would.

Finally, we had to put our seats upright and buckle up. The landing was smooth, and the actor was invited to leave first. I expect they'd wait for his baggage so he could change. I assumed they took the troublemaker off early too.

When we got up to leave, Rose stood in front of me. I notice a little bulge in one of her pockets. A bulge that moved. We entered the walkway to the terminal.

"She's got the mouse," Lin whispered.

"I know. We can't take it through customs."

"Why not? There's no body scan on this end."

"Oh. All right then. But I'd better take her to the bathroom." I thought of letting the mouse go in there, but the thought of more shrieks and chaos didn't appeal.

Going through immigration wasn't too bad, despite the long lines. We'd disembarked first from our flight, but there had been several others. At least they had plenty of officers on duty. Customs was easy. We loaded our cases plus Rose onto a cart and wheeled it though the "Nothing to Declare" door. Officers stood watching passengers as they filtered through, occasionally picking one to take their bags to long tables by the wall, but they left us alone.

Agna was waiting, and warmly embraced us—although Rose turned away. "I got a little mouse in my pocket. Hugging might squash him." Agna looked incredulous but shrugged her shoulders and turned to lead the way to where her driver had parked the car. The airport had flowerbeds dotted all over the place. Leaves showed their fresh tips, but flowers were a long way off.

"This is a lovely place to let mousey go," I said. "They need to be free."

Rose looked tearful but nodded. "I know," she said. She reached into her pocket and withdrew her friend. She squatted to set him down under a rose bush. He sniffed the air and scurried away. "He didn't even say goodbye." The tears flowed.

"He was very scared by that woman on the plane. He thought only of hiding in a safe place," I said, hugging her. "I could see he liked you a lot and was very grateful. Now, let's get into Agna's car and go to her house."

"So she really did have a mouse in her pocket," said Agna. "Can I have my hug now?"

Rose obliged before climbing into the back seat. After ten minutes or so, she leaned against me and nodded off again.

I gazed out of the window as we wove our way through London's morning rush hour to Agna's elegant house in London. The outlook improved as we got closer to the city since the area we drove through at first was far from attractive. After I'd travelled more, I realized that was true of most drives from the airports of major cities.

The driver took our cases inside, and Lin carried Rose to a sofa where she gently laid her down. I was thankful I'd taken her to the loo before we went through to immigration. That silk upholstered sofa wasn't one that little girls should pee on.

"I'll make tea," said Agna.

That did sound good. My mouth was dry and didn't taste too good. Too much wine and champagne. I could have brushed my teeth on the plane but shoved the courtesy bag they handed out into my tote.

Lin and Agna chatted happily while we sipped our tea. Sometimes they slipped out of English into what I supposed was their old Norse tongue, which sometimes sounded guttural, sometimes musical, and somehow magical.

"Is there anything special you'd like to do here, Mary?" asked Agna.

"I hardly know where to begin after hearing all Lin's stories," I said. "The Tower of London, certainly. The Lewes Chessmen at the British Museum. That would be a good start. I can't do too much at once because Rose is so little. Is the New Forest very far?"

"The first two are easy. I think we could take a couple of days for the New Forest. Maybe stay in one of the old hotels in the forest. What do you think, Lin?" said Agna.

"Why not? We should take her to one of those old pubs in the forest. I want to see at least one show while we're here too. Maybe the Royal Ballet."

"Yes, I haven't been to the theater since Christmas," said Agna. "I'll pick up the show mag while we're out."

I couldn't believe my ears. Everything I dreamed of just falling into my lap. The Royal Ballet.

"I think we should go out as soon as Rose wakes up," Lin said. "That way you'll both get over the time difference faster than sleeping the day away."

Rose woke disoriented, forgetting where we were. "I miss Sam." A few tears rolled down her cheeks. We assured her that Sam was well taken care of by Hunter and Auntie, and that he missed her too. We'd go home soon.

It was noon by that time, so we ate a robust meat pie and salad before setting out for the British Museum. I knew we could only see a little because Rose wouldn't be able to manage. We entered, walked up the steps, and there were the chessmen in a glass case front and center set out on a red and white board. I examined them carefully while Lin held Rose and made up a story about the kings and queens, the knights on horseback, and so on. I examined the figures, remembering Lin's stories, trying to put myself in that place and time. Finally, I straightened and thought about what else we should see. Not the Egyptian exhibit because we could see all of those things in Egypt. The Elgin Marbles were famous.

The Elgin Marbles were splendid but not something that held my attention for long, and they were not at all interesting to a three-year-old.

"You should really see the Rosetta Stone," said Agna. "That's how Egyptologists were able to finally decipher hieroglyphics because the stone showed three versions of the same text: hieroglyphics, cursive in the everyday language of ancient Egyptians, and Ancient Greek. That gave historians a window into the culture of ancient Egyptian civilization."

The stone was indeed impressive, although once I looked at it and acknowledged the historical breakthrough, my interest quickly waned. "Maybe we should have a look at China," I suggested.

"I'm hungry," Rose whined.

"Good timing," Agna said. "They do a lovely English tea here."

And it was. Three three-tier cake stands presented tasty little sandwiches, cakes, and scones along with pots of jam and clotted cream. All the plates and tea pots were made of matching pale green and white porcelain. Rose loved it all, as did I. We didn't leave a crumb.

We decided to go home after that. Rose and I were just too tired to appreciate anything else.

After a good night's sleep, we took a taxi to the Tower of London. Agna stayed home. Rose was enchanted by the ravens and especially the squirrels that jumped on the beefeater guide's shoulder so he could feed it peanuts. She was quite taken with the crown jewels, to my surprise.

"I want one like that," she said, pointing to King Edward's crown.

"I'm afraid only the Queen of England is allowed to wear that," I said, laughing. "It's very old and very precious. Even the Queen only wears it on the most special occasions."

"Well, aren't little girls allowed to wear crowns at all?"

"They sometimes wear tiaras, but only if they're a princess."

"All right then, I'm going to be a princess when I grow up."

"I'm sure you are." What was the point of arguing? Especially with an appreciative audience.

We went out to dinner at a Chinese restaurant. The food was very different from my previous experiences. To my surprise, we could order half-dishes, so we chose lots of different things. Lin ordered sweet and sour pork. I was expecting the usual bright red goo, but it was fairly light, both in texture and color, not very sweet and quite tangy. Delicious. Then there were the bean sprouts in a delicate sauce. We had various concoctions of fish, shrimp, and beef. I really tucked in as did Rose. I was a little worried she was overdoing it, but she merely leaned back and said, "That was the best dinner ever." She went to bed soon after our return and slept like a log until eight the next morning. I woke with a mild headache as we'd stayed up drinking champagne until I gave up at eleven. I heard Lin and Agna still giggling and chatting downstairs as I fell asleep.

Later in the morning, we took a train to the south coast. We got off in Brockenhurst as they had a few years before. This time, though, we went to a hotel right in the New Forest. Rose was so excited about the ponies she saw wandering all over the place. We checked in and went to our rooms to unpack before going to the dining room for lunch. Purple rhododendrons flowered profusely, and moorland stretched beyond the trees that lined three sides of the hotel grounds. Dense forest stretched back from one side.

Lin and Agna suggested whitebait for "starters" (appetizers). I wasn't sure but went along with it. What a treat it turned out to be. Tiny fish deep-fried to a delicious crispness! Rose tried one of mine, then another until she'd wolfed down half of them. They had a child's menu that included fish and chips, so Rose had that, and I decided on the adult version. Fish and chips is a really English thing, so I felt compelled to try it. I don't remember what Lin and Agna ate. I know I didn't talk much as the fresh fish in its delicate crisp batter alongside fries made from fresh pota-toes held my attention. Then there was treacle pudding to follow. There was no way to pass that up, but no way I'd be good for anything for the rest of the day.

"We're not going to eat dinner too, are we?" I finally asked.

"Oh, we can just have a snack. A couple of hours after tea," Lin replied.

"I think Rose will need a short nap. I may join her. What do you want to do today?"

"We plan to visit an old haunt," Lin said. "We'll be back in time for tea. We'll see you here at four-thirty."

She looked a bit grim. I suddenly realized they were going to the ruined cottage where Loki and his nurse had imprisoned Lin's daughter Margareta a while back. "Be careful," I said.

"See you later." She pushed back her chair and stood up, stalking out of the room as Agna followed.

"Where's Lin going?" Rose asked.

"There are some things she has to do. We're going to take a nap."

Rose and I sat in the dining room at four-thirty, but they didn't come.

"We don't take orders after quarter to five," said the waitress.

"If I order for them, can my friends' portions be held?"

"No, I'm afraid not, madam. They can have a pot of tea in the lounge, though."

I wasn't sure what to do. Maybe we should all just have a light dinner.

"We'll take a pot of tea, milk for my daughter, and a couple of slices of strawberry cake, please."

"Certainly, madame."

The strawberry cake was dotted with fresh strawberries, both in and out. Rose and I would put on a good deal of weight if we stayed here much longer.

"I think we should go for a walk," I told Rose as went back up to our room. I was really worried by that time. We put on our jackets and went down again to explore the grounds. There were lots of pathways and a chicken coop where Rose held a conversation with a fluffed out red hen—she played both parts—and a fountain featuring a little boy peeing, which fascinated the child.

"What's that little thing he's peeing out of?"

I really didn't want to use the word because previous experience had taught me she would repeat this new word *ad nauseam* at the most inopportune moments. "Boys are made a little differently than girls. That's all."

"Oh. Well, the girl shape is prettier."

That was the end of it, thank heavens. I looked at my watch. Seven.

"Let's go back and see if Lin and Agna got back yet. If they're not, we could see what's on TV"

They were just hurrying into the lobby as we got back.

"Lin!" called Rose. "Mama was worried. I could tell."

Neither of them looked happy. "I'm going to my room for a bit. We'll meet for dinner at eight." Lin hurried to the elevator.

"It wasn't a good idea," Agna said. "We'll discuss it later tonight."

She followed Lin, who was holding the elevator, tapping her foot impatiently.

"She didn't hug me," said Rose, pouting.

"She feels very tired," I said. "She'll be better after dinner. Let's go upstairs and wash our hands. There's time for a little TV."

"Mama, now we are in England, we must call it telly."

"How do you know that?"

"That's what Agna says. And I heard other people say it."

"All right. We will watch telly."

We ate a light dinner of sole and baby potatoes with peas. Rose had a child's plate of it too. She had something called strawberry blancmange for dessert and loved it. I had a taste, and it was just a pudding but quite good.

"Let's go upstairs," said Lin. "Call me on the house phone when Rose falls asleep."

It didn't take long before Rose dropped off. "Come over. I ordered wine." I didn't like to leave her, but I didn't want her to hear whatever Lin had to relate. They were only next door.

"I'll have to keep checking in case Rose wakes up and gets frightened," I said as I entered their room.

"Oh, I'll keep my ears pricked," Lin said.

I'd forgotten her godly hearing.

"So, something must have happened. You went to that cottage that blew up, didn't you?"

"Yes. And it was quite an experience."

"Loki is still hanging around?"

"Strangely, no. Do you remember how Agna talked about ghosts?"

"Of course. It really stuck in my mind."

"Well, I ran and Agna flew. It didn't take long. The ruins are still there. No one has cleared them or tried to build on the property. We walked all around and back where the front door was. All of a sudden, a sort of whirlwind blew up, raising a column of dirt and debris. It came swirling toward us with a quiet sort of roar, dancing around us, hopping back and forth, tossing out jagged bits of stone and brick while it arranged itself into a form almost human. It was Loki's nurse who burned before the explosion. Remember how Agna said that hate can cause a ghost to materialize?"

Agna broke in. "There was so much hate. We felt it searing hot and icy cold. I shut it out of my mind and pushed it back with all my strength. I knew Lin did too. It fell apart into a shower of dirt that scattered within what was left of the cottage walls. She was powerful, trying to destroy us through our minds because she knew our bodies were too strong."

"But we overcame its force," said Lin. "If there had only been one of us, I'm not sure we would have prevailed."

Agna said, "The battle took over three hours. That's why we were so late back."

"I'm so glad you overcame her," I said. "What a terrifying ordeal."

"We thought it was all over now Loki has gone," said Lin. "Maybe that's part of her anger. Losing Loki. He obviously left soon after. He was only using her."

We moved to lighter topics after that. Lin ordered another bottle of wine and we had a merry time as we sipped and laughed. They both seemed back to normal.

"What shall we do tomorrow?" I asked. We were to leave the day after that.

Agna said, "We can order a car and go all around the forest. The Rhododendron Walk should be a sight. We can look for wild ponies, and maybe have lunch somewhere near the sea."

Rose hadn't woken, to my relief, and I crept into bed much too late.

The next day, our driver took us to where he knew we'd see ponies. Rose was so excited. She wanted to pet them and feed them, but the driver said no. Feeding them was not allowed, and because not everyone followed the rules, they were apt to bite if you held out your hand. He explained to her that they were not the kind of horses people keep to ride, like pets, but they were wild. Wild creatures need to be left alone to live their own way.

"Like my little mousey," said Rose. The driver looked confused.

"Yes, like your mousey," I said.

The driver suggested a pub for lunch, but Lin said she hadn't liked it much when she went a long time ago, so maybe somewhere different. He suggested another, very pretty, he said, and surrounded by forest. It was a picturesque thatched building with gardens that must have been glorious in summertime. It was a little chilly to sit outside, but they weren't busy, so allowed us to bring Rose in. Lin invited the driver to join us, but he said he'd rather have a sandwich in the public bar and watch the cricket.

The adults opted for individual fish pies, which were delicious: cod, shrimp, and smoked haddock in a white sauce topped with creamy mashed potato with browned ridges. Rose had fish fingers.

Then the big thrill for Rose arrived. I spotted a couple of ponies ambling through the open garden gate. I took her by the hand and followed them.

"You will see some ponies," I said. "You must stay very quiet."

We stood at the gate and watched as they cropped grass and nudged the grid over the fish pond.

"What's that thing on the pond, Mama?"

"The owners cover the pond with a metal grid to prevent horses from drinking the water and slurping up the fish along with it."

"What if they're thirsty?"

"They can find plenty of streams to drink from."

She was spellbound. One of them, a handsome white creature, turned its head to stare at Rose. "Hello, horsey," she said. It whinnied. "He said hello back," she whispered, beside herself as she shifted from foot to foot and squeezed my hand. The ponies obviously felt there was no good reason to stay and headed back to the gate. I wanted to leave, but Rose dug in her heels. We stood to one side as they passed, the white one again turning to Rose and whinnying. "Goodbye, horsey," she replied.

We went back inside. Rose couldn't talk about anything else. I had to remind her to eat with her mouth shut. Lin listened attentively. "Animals like you," she said.

We went to Lymington after that. It was an old fishing town, once a smuggler's haven. The marina was choc-a-bloc with moored boats of every type and size. Rose had never seen anything like it, even near our house on the Chesapeake Bay. Farther out, enthusiasts braved the stiff breeze and sails of all colors billowed and bowed. We shopped a little and found Rose a book about the New Forest ponies. Then it was time for tea. The waterfront was lined with lovely period houses. The tea room we chose served a traditional English tea, which I was beginning to find addictive. Enjoying a spectacular view of the harbor along with it made me feel supremely content.

We went back to the hotel and rested in our rooms until dinner. Tomorrow, back to London.

Rose did not want to leave, and neither did I, although I refrained from whining about it. The New Forest area seemed to invoke enchantment—forest, rolling moors, sea, beautiful cottages and hotels, wonderful fresh food, and cheerful people whose vowels and pleasantries rolled softly off their tongues. I vowed to return.

The one day we had left in London we spent shopping. First we went to a famous toy store on Regent Street. I told Rose she could buy one thing. She was so overwhelmed by the selection, she couldn't make up her mind. I have never seen anything like it. They had everything a child could dream of but of top quality rather than mass produced plastic. The sales clerk finally showed her a toy pony that came with a saddle, a blanket, and a rein. That made up her mind fast. I wondered if this would lead to demands for riding lessons.

We visited a number of boutiques and got a pretty dress each at the last one we went to. Rose didn't complain as she sat herself in a corner and played with her horse, making up all sorts of stories that she told herself in a whisper. While I was grateful for my fantastic experience, I couldn't help regretting that we didn't go to the ballet.

Next day, we went back to the airport for the start of a new adventure.

Agna called a taxi to take us to Heathrow for our flight to Cairo. There was a special lounge for first-class passengers that we entered from the check-in area and would lead us directly to the plane. I could get used to this sort of thing. I reminded myself sternly never to take anything for granted. Everything changes, sometimes with shocking rapidity.

We had a snack and a glass of champagne. Lin went to sit at the bar and started a lively conversation with the bartender. Our flight was called and off we went. Rose napped a little after lunch, and Lin and Agna talked while I read. Immigration and customs were fairly organized, although crowded. A car waited to take us to the hotel.

Over the next couple of days, a guide took Rose and me sightseeing. I guess Lin and Agna had seen it all. I didn't linger too long in the museums, although the guides tended to expound at length. Rose wasn't that interested, except for the mummies. I was fascinated, and she stood gazing at each one for some time.

"They don't want to be here," she announced. "And they want their stuff back."

"How do you know?" I asked.

"They told me."

"I see. I expect they'll get used to it."

She said nothing more. I enjoyed her imagination, always so lively. The guide looked uncomfortable and sidled away from us.

At the pyramids, she perked right up.

"Donkey or camel, missy?" asked the guide.

"First donkey, then camel."

The guide looked at me for guidance. "I'll wait here while she rides a donkey. Then we can ride a camel together."

She sat up straight on the donkey. The guide wound a headdress around her head and furnished her with a whip. He walked alongside the animal as they headed toward the open desert. Suddenly, she whacked the donkey's haunch with her whip, and it took off.

"Go after her!" I yelled. Rose was still astride, leaning low over the creature's neck. The guide mounted a skinny horse and couldn't seem to goad it into more than a trot while the poor, broken-winded creature wheezed and snorted. The donkey slowed down and turned around before ambling back to base. When Rose alighted—without help—she gave the donkey a smacking great kiss on its nose. It whiffled and watched her for a few minutes.

"Wow, that was so exciting!" my brat exclaimed. "Now for the camel."

The guide returned when he saw them coming back. "Not good, missy," he told her. "Bad things out there." Rose smiled at him beatifically until he stopped frowning.

The camel sat while we clambered aboard, Rose perched in front of me while I held her around the waist. No funny business this time. The camel rolled alarmingly as it lumbered to its feet, but I managed to hold on. We rode to the biggest pyramid and back.

"We have to go back to the hotel now," I said. "It's lunchtime."

Rose chattered about her sweet donkey without stopping as the car pushed through the clogged city streets. Wasn't she afraid of anything?

The next day, we took a taxi to the riverfront where our cruise ship was moored. We would sail down to Luxor and tour the Valley of the Kings, then to Aswan before taking a short flight to the temples of Abu Simbel. It would take seven days.

The cabin was small but well appointed. The sofas would be turned into beds in the evening. There were about twenty passengers, mostly older Americans. After dinner, belly dancers took the floor in the main lounge. I'd heard of them, of course, but up close I could appreciate their skill. Every now and then, they'd tie a sequined hip band around a passenger's waist and invite them to dance. It was clearly a lot harder than it looked as the ladies tried to jiggle their hips but ended up jiggling things they'd rather not draw attention to. One of the dancers approached Lin, who danced like a professional. I wondered where she'd picked that up. Then Agna had her turn and also excelled. Each was rewarded by a round of applause.

Finally, Rose had had enough. She marched onto the floor and held out her arms so they could tie a band around her. She couldn't quite get the fast hip movements, but she gamely tried, moving her arms, hands, and feet in a very creditable imitation of the dancers. When the music ended, she received a long and loud round of applause. Pink cheeked and very pleased with herself, she climbed onto a bar chair and fanned herself with a menu. The bartender placed a glass of juice in front of her, for which she thanked him graciously. I felt at once proud and alarmed.

There were several entertainments during our voyage to Luxor and sumptuous meals too. When we disembarked, we were separated into two groups with a guide assigned to each. The temples were mind-boggling, and I took so many pictures, I felt I wasn't looking at things hard enough. On the other hand, I wanted to remember. I came to a stall where thin books of captioned photos were on sale. That solved my problem, and I only took photos of Rose after that.

We went out early because of the heat. After lunch, Lin said, "Agna and I want to visit King Tut's tomb this after-noon. It closes at four, but we can find a way in. Do you want to come? We'll use our own transportation."

"What kind of transportation?"

"I'll run with you, and Agna will fly with Rose. We'll be invisible to human eyes, so it won't cause problems."

"All right, we'll come. After all I've heard, I'd like to see it."

I wanted to see the place, although it was probably no more than rubble. And I wanted to experience going so fast with Lin.

"Rose, Agna is going to take you flying this afternoon. It'll be fun. Lin will take me along very fast. But you mustn't tell anyone. They wouldn't understand. They might not believe you, either, and think you tell lies."

"I know. There are all kinds of things about us I don't talk about."

"Good girl." *And too smart for your age.*

The two of them looked almost like twins. They both wore simple caftans and headscarves that almost covered their braided hair. Lin was taller and had a more athletic build than Agna, and her hair was the color of pale honey. Agna was only slightly shorter and wirier and was a white blonde. I felt dumpy next to them, despite Hunter's protesta-tions that he loved my English fair coloring and complexion.

We went down the gangway and behind a closed office building. Agna tucked Rose under her arm, muttered a chant, and away they went, invisible but for a faint breeze. Lin hoisted me over her shoulder and started running. The landscape became nothing more than a stream of dirty yellow. I started to feel travel sick and closed my eyes. That worked for a bit, then I had to open them again, fearing I might toss my lunch. Lin slowed down and there we were on the valley floor facing a domed structure with a door that stood about ten yards away. I lost my balance and landed heavily on my rump.

Rose came dancing over. "That was so much fun," she said. "I could see everything on the ground and very far away. I can't wait to do it again."

I just smiled and nodded. I felt weak and disoriented as if I'd been in bed for a month. "Sit down for a few minutes," said Lin. "It takes some getting used to."

I tried to sit straighter and took some deep breaths.

Agna asked, "Ready? I have the key."

"Is there anything left inside?" I asked.

"No, but I want to see if I can feel my boy's presence. I keep hoping he'll come home to rest, and I'll find him again."

"How did you get the key?"

"I bribed the guards. They've gone inside their hut to take a nap."

Agna led slowly and softly as we approached the tomb. Could it be getting dark already? I shivered and looked up. A cloud had covered the sun. I felt Agna's tension—the air hummed with it—and it made me grip Rose's hand harder until she protested in a hushed squeal. Even she knew this was a haunted place. Agna stopped and raised her hand.

"Tut has not returned. But another waits."

A faint roar rose from the rocks behind the entrance. It grew louder when a swirling column of sand soared as it gradually blackened.

"Mary, Lin, take Rose and run. Now!"

Hearing Agna's urgency, I didn't stop to think, sweeping Rose into my arms and running as fast as I could over the shifting sand. I cradled her to my chest, leaning forward to protect her from whatever might rain down from the sky. Suddenly, we were surrounded by the maelstrom, which carried scorpions, small snakes, and stones that battered my head and arms. Rose started to wail. "I can't breathe, Mama! Let me get down." I felt her pull away. No, she was being dragged away. I held on for as long as I could, screaming, "Leave her! She's only a baby. Only a baby." She was gone, up and away, I thought into the tomb. I sank to my knees, keening and pleading, to whom, I didn't know or care. I felt Lin's arms around me, her tears falling into my hair. She drew me to my feet. The black cloud had gone. As had Agna.

"Agna leapt into the cloud when it snatched Rose," Lin said. "Agna will get her back. You'll see."

"Where are the guards? Call them. They have to do something."

"They've been watching us through their hut's window. They all ran away when they saw the cloud. There was nothing they could have done anyway. All we can do is wait."

"Why didn't you pick up Rose and run?"

"I couldn't move. This thing was more powerful than me."

Lin walked me over to a flat rock, which she inspected closely before we sat down. I couldn't stop shaking, couldn't stop weeping, couldn't stop the terrifying images that coursed through my mind—scorpions, snakes, evil spirits doing terrible things to my lovely little girl.

"It will be so dark in there," I wailed.

"She's never been afraid of the dark," Lin said.

"But that was when she was safe at home. Not here, not in the clutches of evil spirits."

We sat holding each other for what seemed like hours until the sun sank behind the outcrops. I felt numb as I sat there, wondering if I'd ever see Rose again.

"Look," Lin said, nudging me. "Something is coming. Something good, I think."

A moving cloud, its crest lit by starlight, gradually rose from the tomb's entrance. It rolled toward us and evaporated, showing Agna holding my sleeping baby—but wait... asleep or...? Dread filled me anew as I stroked her cheek. Her warm cheek. She stirred. "Good man now," she murmured.

Lin had moved behind Agna, holding her close, her cheek resting against Agna's snowy fall of hair. "Let's get out of here," she said. She grasped me, and I shut my eyes from the start. "Don't worry. Agna and Rose are just above us," she called.

We dusted ourselves down as best we could before entering the boat. Judging by the looks we got, we hadn't done a very good job. Upstairs, Agna lay Rose on her bed.

"She'll sleep deeply for hours," she said. "Let's take our showers, order room service, and I'll tell you all about it."

"I can't leave her on her own, not yet. Maybe not ever," I said. I was still shaky.

"We'll come back to your room," said Lin. "I don't want to leave her either." She went over to Rose and kissed her face. To my surprise, her eyes were red and wet.

They left and I showered before changing into pajamas and lying down beside my precious daughter. A rap on the door got me to my feet. Dinner. I went to my purse to look for a tip. I only had dollars as Lin had told me not to bother changing money. She and Agna had all the Egyptian pounds we needed. I held out a five dollar bill. I turned to the waiter, who hovered expectantly by the table he had set the dishes on. And an ice bucket with champagne, I was happy to note. I showed him the money. "Okay?" I asked.

"Yes, madame, very okay." He flashed a broad smile and left, standing deferentially to one side as Agna and Lin entered, each wearing bright blue silk caftans with white embroidery creating swaths down the front.

"Good, I'm starving," Lin said. "Let's eat before we talk."

To my surprise, I was starving too. We ate a strange garlicky green soup followed by roast lamb, okra with a fragrant thick meat sauce, and rice. A couple of glasses of velvety red wine relaxed me considerably. A variety of little pastries were prettily arranged on a large round platter. I looked at them wistfully.

"I'm full," I said.

"We can have the sweets later," Lin said. "Time to pour the champagne so Agna can tell us what happened."

We settled into the arm chairs in my sitting area, clasping our full flutes, and looking eagerly at Agna.

"First of all, your daughter is a heroine, Mary. She has a lot of her father in her. Godly qualities."

I didn't know how I felt about that. "Go on."

I set my phone on "Record."

Tape 3,
Volume 3

When I saw him take Rose, I had to go too; otherwise, we might never have seen her again. We were set down in a chamber I never knew existed, far behind where Tut's sarcophagus and his burial treasures lay. Two tiny sarcophagi lay in one corner. My archenemy Ay sat on a massive throne, glaring down at us.

"So, I've got you at last, witch. You will spend eternity as miserable as you rendered my last years."

"You killed the Pharaoh Tutankhamun," I said. "And many others. You were a tyrant, eaten by your lust for power."

"Silence!" he bellowed.

I looked down at Rose, who had remained so quiet. Had shock rendered her mute? She stood quite still, regarding Ay quizzically, her head tilted to one side. He followed my gaze.

"What are you looking at, girl?"

"I am looking at a very unhappy man," she said.

"What?"

"You are so angry all the time that you have forgotten to be happy. Are you going to feel so bad forever? I'm very sorry you can't be happy."

"How old are you?" Ay asked, his voice quieter.

"I am three and three-quarters," Rose said. "That's quite big, you know."

To my surprise, Ay started to laugh. I saw an opportunity. "You know, she is right. We suffer during life for many different reasons, but aren't we entitled to make ourselves better and happier after death? Otherwise, what is the point? I grieved for my boy for hundreds of years before I realized I was wasting my life. I loved him, you see. Have you ever loved and been loved?"

Ay's head sank onto his chest. He groaned. "I knew nothing but my father's stick as a boy. My mother was not allowed to see me anymore after I turned ten. She loved me. I made myself forget how that felt. I pushed it away."

"Think about your mama a lot and how much she loved you," Rose said. She went up to him and patted his hand. "You can be a good and happy man now. I know so."

Ay smiled at her. "I am no longer a man but a spirit. I exist only in people's worst dreams. I will be truly dead if I no longer enter the minds of the living, live in their dreams. But it has never brought me peace. I yearn for peace. Perhaps I will leave people to dream their dreams the way they want. Perhaps peace lies in true death after all."

He rose and circled the chamber, his hands clasped behind his back, breathing deeply. He bent to caress the two little sarcophagi before returning to his throne.

"Children?" I asked.

"My two cats. My servants killed them for me when I died."

"Don't you think they are waiting for their master?"

"I cannot cease to exist. Touching the minds of men is better than not being. I can't let go. I can't. The embalmers took out all my organs to place them in the canopic jars so I may use them in the afterlife. They never remove the heart though. I feel as if it still beats within my chest when I am truly angry." He put his hand over his heart. "It doesn't beat now."

He sat down heavily on his throne.

"Do you love being angry?" Rose asked him.

"I have been angry as long as I remember."

"Don't you want to see your mother again?"

"Little girl, we put all these things in our tombs to help us in the afterlife. All the things in my tomb are still there, never found by grave robbers. But they have not helped me move to my higher plane. I am not sure I believe in all that anymore."

I broke in here. "They have not helped you because you do not want to be helped. Is this your tomb? I see no treasure."

"It is very far back in a maze of chambers and paths that seem to lead nowhere."

"Give them a chance, Ay. Close your eyes and let go of the pain."

He lay back his head and closed his eyes for so long I wondered if he'd fallen asleep. He straightened his head and looked at Rose. "Your sweet words are like honey. I feel my soul pulling away from this place. I have sent my anger and hate rising above the hills, blowing away into the void. I will also rise to my eternal sleep by my mother's side."

He looked at me. "Take this little girl back to her mother. She is wise beyond her years. I will not harm her. Or you."

I picked up Rose. She blew Ay a kiss as we floated to the valley floor where you waited.

I could hardly believe it. "Tell me, how could Rose touch Ay when he was a spirit?"

"Because she believed he was real. So he became real for her," Agna replied. "She truly is remarkable."

"Thank you. Now I come to think of it, she reminds me of Margareta. She has godly qualities too Lin."

Lin nodded. "Yes, she does. I don't know if she's aware of it. But she is stronger in many ways than her human peers. And more resilient."

I looked over at my Rose, my darling. "Hunter will be so proud when he hears about this."

"Uh, not a good idea," Lin said, her brow creasing. "We shouldn't have put her in harm's way. He would probably fly into a rage—not something any of us would enjoy."

"You didn't know what would happen though," I argued.

Agna broke in. "It's my fault. I didn't think Ay would come after me in daylight and in the presence of others. And I definitely never imagined he'd take a child. But I knew he was still dangerous. I shouldn't have gone anywhere near that place, especially with you. I'm so sorry. I know how terrified you must have been."

"Yes, it was harrowing. But it's over now. Rose doesn't seem to be suffering any ill effects, and I know you didn't mean to harm her." I did feel resentful but saw no point in airing it.

"I cast a spell on her to banish the memory and induce sleep. She will remember nothing."

"Oh, the bottle's empty," Lin exclaimed, holding it upside down. "Time for another."

We made merry until midnight when I said I really had to go to bed. I was bone tired, drained more by fear for my daughter than anything else. Rose slept late the next morning, to my relief, because I had quite a bad headache and certainly didn't feel like facing breakfast.

Later that afternoon, we boarded the boat that would take us down to Aswan, from where we'd take a small plane to the renowned temples of Abel Simbel. Another adventure, hopefully less scary than the last. I felt that Egypt pulled its past closer to the surface than other cultures.

I took the precaution of buying a couple of books filled with photos and descriptions of the monuments we visited in Egypt. I'm glad I did because the memories would have become fuzzy as we saw so much in a relatively short time. The grandeur and scale of these ancient edifices was astonishing as were some of the fresh-looking wall paintings I saw inside them. I also bought a papyrus showing my favorite temple painting. In the temple, the bright blue design was painted up the wall, over the ceiling, and down the other side, but the painting had to show a different perspective. It was still handsome. Rose was a little trooper, only getting whiny when she got too sleepy or hungry—or both. I will never forget it. Any of it.

Once we disembarked in Cairo, Rose demanded to ride a camel again.

"Tomorrow," said Lin. "The camels are having their dinner now, and then they have to go to bed."

Agna and I exchanged amused glances. Lin had always been sweet with Rose but a little distant too. I think the fright at Tut's tomb had made her realize just how much the child meant to her. She was becoming more hands-on. Like a grandmother, although I wouldn't dare say so.

Early the next morning, Lin and I took Rose to the pyramids, where she insisted on having her own camel instead of sitting in front of me. I watched nervously as the animal got to its feet, but she held on to the pommel, and the guide held his hand ready to catch her. Lin mounted her camel with an ease that garnered confused expressions from her guide, which she answered in Arabic. I don't know what she said, but he found it funny. We enjoyed a good wander into the desert before heading back to the herd. Lin jumped off her camel while it was still standing. After Rose's camel lay down so she could scramble off, she went around to its head and gazed into the heavily lashed eyes. The guide tensed, moving slowly to her side. I guess they can bite. I sat very still on my mount, hoping she'd move away soon. "You are a very nice camel. Thank you for giving me a lovely ride." The camel made a funny little noise. She patted it and came over to me.

My camel slumped so I could slide off. Then it turned around, made a loud noise like a suddenly unblocked drain, and spat into my face a mixture of vomit and saliva. God, how it reeked. Lin poured her bottle of water over my face. It only felt slightly better. I wanted nothing more than to take a shower. Rose, of course, thought it hilarious. She approached my monster and wagged her finger at it. "You are a very naughty camel," she said. Again, the funny little whimper. No spit for the princess.

It was lunchtime when we got back to the hotel. I'd packed the night before as we had to leave for the airport by two. The flight was blessedly uneventful. I consulted the aircraft magazine to decide what I wanted to do during our last two days in London.

Lin made the decision for me. Shopping. And my goodness, I wasn't sorry. Agna took Rose to the London Zoo one afternoon as shopping for grown-up clothes wasn't interesting for a child—I heard later that she'd had a long conversation with a gorilla. We had never gotten around to taking her to the zoo in Washington, so it was a great treat for her.

We shopped in Harrods before moving on to Fortnum & Mason for afternoon tea and more shopping. Harrods has an unending chain of boutique areas full of beautiful objects I'd never imagined. The array in the Fortnum & Mason food court was full of colorful and appetizing things I'd never heard of but would really like to try. Lin ordered several delicacies to be delivered to Agna's house. Both stores possessed a befuddling, dreamlike quality to a working class girl. We ate well that night, courtesy of Fortnum & Mason. Rose and I loved the escargot, mostly for its buttery and garlicky sauce, which the French bread sopped up very satisfactorily. I was a little taken aback to discover during the course of conversation later that we'd been eating snails. I didn't mention it to Rose.

There was much hugging, kissing, and weepy promises to see each other very soon before the hired car whisked us away to Heathrow. The flight was smooth and mouseless. Seeing Hunter waiting for us outside the Dulles customs hall lifted my heart. "Papa!" shrieked Rose as she hurled herself at him. Lin and I waited for our turn, which never came since Rose clung to his chest and wouldn't let go.

We ate a light dinner at home before I put Rose to bed. Sam settled next to her bed. Hunter had to sit on the other side of her bed until she fell asleep. Far from feeling put-upon, he basked in her adoration. We watched television for a while until I couldn't stop nodding off. When I groggily went to check on Rose, I found Sam fast asleep beside her. Well, why not?

It took me a week to get back to normal. Rose was perky from the next morning.

A few days later, Auntie and I sat on the sofa while I showed her my picture books and told her what we had seen and done—omitting the Tut tomb event—and she was fascinated. When we'd come to the end of my account, she dropped another truth bomb.

"I'm so pleased you had this wonderful experience, my dear. It changes you when you experience other cultures. We Americans tend to be so insular. Of course, part of that is being so far away from most other places. I really didn't see much of Egypt. I had a job to do, you see. There was a war on."

"Auntie, I'm beginning to realize you have led quite an adventurous life you hardly talk about. My parents never said anything about your work."

"They didn't know anything about my work," she said. "And I really can't discuss most of it. I've said quite enough as it is."

Subject closed.

10

A couple of weeks after we got back, Joe and Helen came over for dinner. It was always nice to see them. As usual, we ate early so Rose could join us and sit next to her Uncle Joe.

Dora had cooked chicken with lemon, paired with rice infused with thyme, and finely chopped carrots and peas. She looked frazzled, unusual for someone who produced magnificent meals as a matter of course.

"Do you have any plans for the summer?" Lin asked Joe.

"Well, yes." He looked at Helen, who blushed.

"We decided to get married next month," she said. "We don't want to wait any longer."

"That's wonderful news," said Lin.

"Well done," said Hunter. "It is about time."

"You are invited, of course," said Joe. "It's going to be a small wedding. We've left it too late to find a good venue, so we thought of making it very informal. The registrar, then dinner at a restaurant."

"What about the honeymoon?" asked Lin.

"We've already booked it. Italy. The Amalfi coast."

"That sounds dreamy," I said. "Very romantic."

"Give me the date," Lin said. "I insist on doing your wedding here."

"Oh, no, that's too much for you. We couldn't possibly..."

Helen's protests went unheeded. I had a feeling she really wanted to keep things simple, but Lin had the ball, and she was bent on running with it.

"I don't know what to say," said Joe.

"Then say nothing. That's always the best policy."

After dinner, I took Rose down to get her ready for bed. Joe soon came down with the new Flower Fairy book she was counting on.

"They're talking weddings," Joe said. "It's too much for me."

"I know what you mean," I said. "But you know Lin. It's a project, and she'll do it superbly. Like she does everything."

"Uncle Joe. My story."

Lin was fully preoccupied as she had three weeks to pull off a wonderful wedding. After a while, I tuned out of most of the endless discussions between Auntie and Lin. Dora didn't participate. She looked downright peaky. Do Greek nymphs get sick? The next morning, I had my answer.

Hunter looked thunderous at breakfast. "There is no steak. Auntie is cooking eggs. Where is Dora?"

"I'm afraid she's not feeling well," said Lin. "She said the smell of the raw steak nauseated her."

"What the hell? Since when do nymphs get sick because of steak?"

"It is certainly very odd," said Lin, who had never been sick in her life.

"Humph."

I knew at once what was going on. I went to the living room after he'd finished his eggs and about eight pieces of buttered toast. Hunter usually disappeared into his study with Rose at that time. As they rose from the table, Lin shrugged and said, "What the hell?" At least it lightened his mood, particularly as Auntie wasn't there to hear it. She was tidying up in the kitchen, where Lin and I joined her.

"You realize what's the matter with Dora, don't you?" I said.

"No, I've never see her sick before." Lin looked puzzled.

"When humans get pregnant, they often get morning sickness. Different smells and foods can make them feel bad."

"Pregnant!" Lin sank onto a chair. "Well, you didn't get sick."

"I was one of the lucky ones. I think there may be a second wedding soon."

"By all the gods."

"I'll go and see if she needs anything," Auntie said.

The day before the wedding, things amped up. Furniture got rearranged, flower arrangements were installed everywhere, a huge tent erected in the yard, wine and glasses delivered—there was no end to it. Auntie happily bustled around taking orders from Lin. I took Rose out to lunch and a kid's movie to keep her out of the way, and I don't think Hunter emerged from his study all day.

Dora managed a simple dinner in the evening. My rooms had been left alone, so we all gathered there.

"Such a bother," Hunter groused. We finally gave up and went to bed early.

I spent a good hour getting Rose ready for the wedding. She wanted her blonde hair loose down her back. I wanted it up in a high chignon, through which I could thread the rosebuds that matched the petals she would strew in front of the bride as she walked down the aisle. I settled on a compromise. I drew up hair from the sides to a chignon and let the rest flow. It did look sweet, I have to admit. Her pale blue dress highlighted her blue eyes beautifully. Hunter huffed and puffed while he waited to drive us all to the church. Auntie sat in my living room, wisely keeping her own counsel.

The bellowing organ filled the church anteroom, setting the tone for the majesty of ritual. Rose held my hand tighter.

Helen was already there, standing patiently while her maid of honor—her daughter Toni—fussed with her veil. A frowning man, who I assumed was her father, paced back and forth, annoying in such a small space. He ignored us.

Helen noticed Rose's nervousness. "You look really beautiful," she told her. "Don't worry. All you have to do is walk ahead of me and throw a few of these petals on the floor to make it look pretty. When you get to the end, you will simply go to your mother. You will be perfect."

Rose looked happier. "Yes, that does sound easy. I can make the floor pretty."

I added, "Goodbye for now, Rose. I'm going to take my seat now so I'll be there for you."

Auntie had saved me two spaces on the aisle in the front row, so Rose would have no trouble finding me. Joe stood with his best man as if bracing for a high wind. He didn't look at anyone. It was comical in one normally so in control.

There were many guests on the bridegroom's side, mostly colleagues, I guessed. On Helen's side, the entire board of the Salton Symphony had come. A good-looking woman in a royal blue matching dress and jacket, most likely her mother, sat next to an older woman dressed top-to-toe in black and several younger women, perhaps from her law school class. And us.

It wasn't long before the wedding march rang out. The congregation stood and turned to the bride, who looked like a princess. I glanced at Joe, who looked more relaxed, his face suffused with adoration.

Rose managed so well, I couldn't have been prouder. Hunter made a sort of *aww* sound deep in his throat until Lin kicked him. She tossed the petals this way and that in a remarkably spaced out fashion. I had to remind myself to look at the bride. Helen looked as radiant as all brides should. She and Joe didn't take their eyes off each other. Eventually, Rose reached the front and walked to me. Helen passed her bouquet to Toni.

Weddings always make me teary. I'm not sure why. It's not as though I ever dreamed of one for myself. It would never happen now, and I didn't mind a bit. Maybe it's the romance of it, the result of childhood conditioning for little girls. Anyway, I had to brush away a tear or two.

Then we got to the "or forever hold your peace" bit

"She is my wife." A disheveled man reeled up the aisle.

Bride and groom whipped around.

"Pat!" Helen gasped, her face the color of her dress.

"Dad!" Toni gasped.

"We are divorced. You are not my husband," Helen said shakily, albeit loudly.

"Until death do us part. Remember that?" the man growled.

Thank goodness most of Joe's friends were cops. About six or seven of them arranged themselves behind the drunk and dragged him out of the church as he screamed profanities. Hunter followed. I knew Helen wouldn't hear from Pat again. It wasn't long before we heard police sirens.

Joe mopped Helen's and her daughter's tears with his breast pocket handkerchief. Helen's father scowled in situ. The mother sniffed into a tissue. The woman in black smiled. I looked at Rose, wondering if she'd been frightened. She shrugged. What a strange reaction for a child. I'd ask her what she thought later.

A sonorous voice cut through the buzz. "I am sorry, my dears. Very distressing. Shall we continue?" The vicar cast a stern gaze over the whispering guests until all was quiet once more. He glared at the smiling toad in black.

The ceremony came to a close, and the processional, which should have been joyful, showed the strain. Joe smiled graciously at his guests, and Helen did her best. Her daughter still looked on the edge of tears. How embarrassing to see her father act that way in front of everyone.

Back at the house, I took Helen and Toni downstairs to repair their make-up. "I'm so sorry he spoiled your wedding," I said.

"He always tries to spoil everything," Toni retorted. "He's angry because I won't see him. He accused Mom of stealing me, turning me against him. The judge asked a lot of questions about his behavior and why I didn't want to see him. I told the judge exactly why. Now he doesn't want to see me either, thank goodness."

I needed to get them back on track. "Helen, this is your and Joe's special day. Don't let him take that from you. It's all about you two—not him. Enjoy."

Lin came in at that point. "Hunter warned him off. You won't see him again. He is nothing compared to Joe. Put him right out of your mind."

"You're both right." Helen lifted her chin. "Come on, Toni."

And up they went, followed by Lin and me.

Lin had outdone herself. The flower arrangements were profuse and fragrant, the tent in the garden beautifully arranged with tables and a buffet, extra food and drink was available in the dining room, and waiters and waitresses darted around making sure the guests had enough of everything. Joe and Helen circulated among the guests, making sure they welcomed everyone. Helen's mother mingled with the guests too, without her husband and sister-in-law. She was soon surrounded by her former friends from the Symphony as was Helen. I wandered around taking in everything, ending up in the living room. Helen's father sat alone in one corner with a glass of Scotch. The woman in black sat the opposite corner with her hands clasped to her waist. No one approached them until Helen and Joe came in.

"Dad, can we get you anything to eat?" Helen said. "You need to eat."

"I'm not hungry. Just thirsty."

"Thank you for coming, sir," Joe said, holding out his hand, which was ignored.

"Mother insisted."

Helen looked on the verge of tears again. They moved to the other corner.

"How are you, Aunt Barbara? Thank you for coming."

"That husband had a point," she answered grimly. "You were married to him in the house of the Lord."

"Let's go," Helen said, her voice tight. "I've had enough of these miserable characters."

Aunt Barbara's face took on a furious grimace as bride and groom swept out. I left too. Their antagonism sucked the energy from the room.

I was touched to see Toni spending most of her time with Rose, taking her around to chat with the guests. I finally decided to eat and found Auntie sitting at a table with Helen's mother.

"Mary, this is Helen's mother, Letitia Gandy. Letitia, this is my niece, Mary."

"Very nice to meet you. Helen and Joe are great favorites in this house," I said. "I'm going to have something to eat. Can I get you anything?"

"Not for me," Auntie said. "We've eaten. I'm saving space for the cake."

"Same here," Letitia said. "I understand that the precious flower girl is your daughter. She is so lovely and so mature for three."

"Thank you."

I was soon back with a plate of smoked salmon and various salads. I didn't feel like tackling roast beef. Maybe it was the white wine that killed my appetite for anything heavy.

"I understand you're a writer."

Letitia didn't phrase it as a question, but she clearly expected an answer. "Yes, that's right. I'm writing a novel, although when I had Rose, it got put aside for the time being."

"Yes, I can understand that. Is your husband here?"

"No, we are no longer married. Life is too precious to waste around toxic people, don't you think?"

"Maybe you're right." Her face fell and she looked down into her lap. "But some don't have much choice since they have no way of supporting themselves. Do you see?"

Poor woman. I saw only too clearly. "Yes, I know, it's not always that easy. I've been fortunate, that's all."

I beckoned over a waiter with a tray of wine. "Why don't we have our own toast to the beautiful bride and her groom?"

That eased the tension, further eased by Toni and Rose joining us at the table. Soon it was time for the speeches, so champagne was poured for everyone by the small army of waiters. Neither Helen's father nor her aunt appeared. Hunter spoke, welcoming everyone and saying a few words about the happy couple and Helen's lovely mother, Letitia. We toasted. Joe's best man spoke, joking about Joe's determination and perseverance as a detective being employed to win the hand of his bride. The cop contingent cheered, and we toasted. Joe spoke briefly about the happiest day of his life and so on. We toasted yet again. To my shock, I suddenly realized that Toni and Rose were also participating in the toasts. I gasped and grabbed Rose's glass.

"Don't worry. It's fizzy apple juice," Toni said, laughing. "Mine is too. I don't want to be like Dad."

Whew. Alcohol could be dangerous for children. And she would have had a terrible headache. Like I probably would.

"Oh look," Letitia said. "The cake."

It had been rolled in front of the head table. Helen and Joe walked around to hold the brutal-looking knife and cut the first piece. Everyone clapped as Joe gently fed a slice to Helen and she did likewise for him. I hated it when the couple shoved it in each other's face. So crass. This was sweet and tender.

"I'm going downstairs so I can help Helen change," I said. "Won't you join me, Letitia?"

"Oh, how sweet of you. Of course."

I had already laid out Helen's things on my bed. Her pale green dress hung over my closet door. Lin and I would take the wedding dress for professional cleaning and packing next week.

We sat and waited for Helen.

Letitia cleared her throat. "That thing you said. About toxic people. Is it true, or did you say it for my benefit?"

"I'm sorry. I'd just come from the living room where your husband and his sister—I assume—were very unpleasant to Joe and Helen. I couldn't understand how a nice person like you could live with someone like that."

"The sister lives with us. She came to us while we still lived in Salton, then persuaded my husband to move into the family home in Pittsburgh. She rules the roost. My husband has always been frugal, but now, he makes sure I have no access to money."

"The courts would make him pay you alimony."

"He can afford the best lawyers. How would I pay for one?"

"There are ways. People to help. Does Helen know?"

"She must know I'm unhappy. We've never discussed it."

"Then I think you should visit her in a couple of months and talk to her."

"I doubt Wilbur will let me come."

"I'll buy you a plane ticket."

We both turned, startled. Helen stood at the bottom of the stairs.

"No, I can't possibly…"

"No, I will drive up and get you, Mother."

"Oh, Helen, I didn't mean you to hear all that."

"Dad and Aunt Barbara are despicable people. I didn't know you wanted to leave. I should have guessed. You were happier when you lived in Salton before Aunt Barbara moved in. Dad was always difficult, but his sister seems to have so much influence on him. She's evil."

"This is your day, Helen," Letitia said as she got up. "Let's get you ready for your honeymoon. We can talk about this in a couple of months."

Poor Helen. Too many dark cracks in her happy day. "Where are you going?" I asked her. Joe had already mentioned it, but I knew she'd love to talk about it.

"Amalfi! I'm so excited. I've never been to Italy—or anywhere else, for that matter."

"It sounds dreamy," I said. "Perfect for a honeymoon."

We all threw silver streamers as they walked down the front steps. I think Rose was a little jealous; she ran to Joe and insisted on a big hug and kiss. He was happy to oblige. "I'll bring you back something pretty," he told her. Rose was gracious enough to blow Helen a kiss.

The guests gradually dwindled as afternoon turned into evening. I didn't see Helen's family leave. Auntie told me later that Letitia had said a hurried goodbye because Wilbur was keen to get on the road. When she spotted Lin, she rushed over with a breathless goodbye and thanks. "Wilbur doesn't like to be kept waiting."

The staff cleared and cleaned for several hours before driving their vans away. We settled into the living room. I leaned back and closed my eyes, reveling in the sweet smell of roses.

"Poor Letitia," Auntie said, sighing.

"Her husband is really quite dreadful," Lin said. "He hadn't even the grace to greet us or say goodbye. And that creature in black. Who was she?"

"His sister," I said. "She lives with them. Letitia is miserable, but she's not allowed any access to money, so she doesn't know how to leave. She wants to. She feels trapped. We were talking downstairs, and Helen overheard us. She's going to get her mother out."

"Good for her, and we can help too."

We unwisely opened another bottle of champagne. We all woke up next day with a headache, even Auntie.

11

"**H**unter, we've got to deal with Dora." This was the third time she had retired to her room while cooking Hunter's steak. "She is going to have a baby. I expect she and Stan will get married."

"What does he do for a living?"

"He's an army veteran," Auntie said.

"Yes, but what does he do now?"

"He works for the country parks department, maintaining plantings and suchlike."

"Do we have space for both of them, Lin?" he asked.

"Yes, Dora's apartment over the garage would work. It's already got a queen-sized bed."

"Well, then, in return for living here, he can maintain our garden."

"Perfect. I'll go and tell her."

"And I hope this sickness in the mornings is not going to last for a long time."

"It's usually only for about three months," I said. "And she's ten weeks gone. So, not long."

"Half of a month." Hunter sighed.

"I can manage your steaks," I said.

"I'll help," Auntie added.

Lin rubbed her hands together. "Now, we have a wedding to plan." We all groaned, Hunter loudest of all.

As it turned out, the wedding really would be simple this time. Dora didn't know anyone except us. Stan only had his mother in the area. He had moved to the area to be near her after retiring from the army and had made very few local friends, none he'd care to invite. Lin invited him for lunch one day to discuss the matter. Dora prepared the lunch but sat with us, stiff as a board with awkwardness. For the most part, Stan only spoke when spoken to. I sensed a certain wariness in his demeanor. He was likely from a working class family like me and not used to being in such classy surroundings.

In a hiatus after discussing the wedding, he blurted, "You will have to excuse my mother. She speaks her mind, often when she shouldn't. She's Irish and small. Feisty."

"That's quite all right," said Lin. "We are all a little strange around here."

The wedding was to be held in a registry office but not until Dora got over her morning sickness. Stan moved his few things and himself into her apartment the weekend after the dinner. He started tidying up the garden right away, as Hunter had canceled the contract with his service in June because he wasn't satisfied with their performance and had not yet selected another. The garden had become quite messy after the earlier big clean up and planting for Joe and Helen's wedding.

Eventually, Dora started to feel better. They got their license, and they both stood in front of a bed of roses in the garden one morning while the officiant performed the ceremony. Lin had persuaded them to do it at home. Sven came, but Margareta couldn't get away.

Dora looked attractive in a pale blue dress with an orchid boutonniere. Stan wore his army uniform and stood ramrod straight. His mother was an oddity, for sure. Only about four feet tall, she wore an orange dress topped by a green hat that sprouted a yellow feather. Shiny black Mary Janes and a massive patchwork cloth bag completed her outfit. She arrived at the last minute, so hardly spoke beyond a perfunctory greeting ahead of the ceremony. Rose stared and stared until I whispered an admonition into her ear.

Dora got a little teary while saying her vows, so Stan patted her hand. She looked up at him adoringly. Auntie sniffed beside me. Everything seemed right, except the mother, who stared at Dora without blinking. Unless we'd both blinked simultaneously.

We all went to the living room afterward. Lin had hired a caterer to handle lunch. Dora protested, but Lin insisted. "You are not going to cook on your wedding day. It's your special day, and you will be treated special."

Hunter and Sven served the drinks, first pouring champagne to toast the bride and groom. Lin gave a little speech, making Dora blush with her lavish praise. Hunter also spoke briefly. The mother still had not opened her mouth.

"To Dora and Stan," Hunter called out, and we all drank. The mother knocked hers back at one go. Hunter gallantly refilled her glass, which was emptied just as fast.

"I can see yer all different," the mother suddenly blurted out. "Well not all of you. Not her, or her, or him." She pointed to Rose, me, and Sven. She pointed at Dora. "I don't know what she is, but she's not of this world. I'm different too. One of the little people, yer know. We can always tell."

"Now then, Mother, we don't need to get into all of that," Stan said, squirming with embarrassment.

"You are small compared to the other grown-ups. Is that the only thing different?" Rose asked. She'd been uncharacteristically quiet until then.

"No, lots o' things different."

I closed my mouth, which had been hanging open far too long. *Little people as in leprechauns? Leprechauns are a thing?*

One of the caterers entered and whispered in Lin's ear.

"Let's go in to lunch, shall we?" she said smoothly and led the assemblage into the dining room, which was adorned with flowers and silver. A beautiful cake decorated with real flowers sat on the sideboard.

Hunter pulled out the mother's chair—I still didn't know her name—and she jumped backward into it, leaving her feet dangling. "Well, son, I think you've found the end of your rainbow."

"Mother, just stop." Stan looked at Lin apologetically. She patted him on the shoulder.

"It's fine. Just enjoy yourselves."

The meal passed without further inappropriate comments from Stan's mother, and Auntie did a sterling job of keeping the conversation flowing pleasantly.

"What time is your flight leaving?" asked Lin.

"Five-thirty," said Stan. "I'm taking Dora to Alaska. The weather is pretty nice this time of year. Maybe we'll see whales. I've arranged for a taxi to take Mother home and another to take us to the airport."

Normally, this is where someone would break in and insist on giving the guests a lift, but apparently, no one felt up to it. They could hardly offer to take the newlyweds without offering a similar courtesy to the mother.

After a long silence, Auntie chimed in. "I will be happy to take your mother home."

"No, no," said Stan. "I've already paid for it. But thank you."

The cake was cut and more champagne poured. Lin took photos. The taxis arrived promptly at two-thirty and the three of them left. Stan said a heartfelt thank you to his hosts, as did Dora, who handed her bouquet to Rose—who had become quiet again. The mother just nodded her head.

Rose blew kisses to Dora and Stan before coming back inside. "Is there any cake left?"

"I think you've had enough," I said.

"But I couldn't enjoy it properly with that horrid lady looking at me. I don't like her."

"All right, just a small piece."

"She is different, for sure," said Lin. "I mean, really different."

"What do you mean?"

"She's from leprechaun stock. I got to know one quite well once. They're not all fun and quaint games. I'll tell you the story sometime. But she missed the right boat when it came to brains and looks."

Dora and Stan returned after a week. Stan made Rose her own little flower bed where she planted a few marigolds and radish seeds. I didn't think she'd like radishes, but she'd love the quick results. Stan seemed to talk to her more than anyone. I kept my eye on them, just in case. Motherhood induces paranoia.

12

Rose and I came upstairs one morning to find Auntie and Lin cooking breakfast.

"Where's Dora?" I asked. She'd been working her normal hours since the morning sickness wore off, and she'd returned from her honeymoon.

"She and Stan went to stay overnight with his mother. She isn't feeling well and she's getting on in years," Auntie said.

"Oh, too bad." I couldn't be too upset about an unpleasant woman I hardly knew.

Lin told me she'd be down in a little while, and I was pleased. This year's volume would be rather slim if she didn't give me some more stories. Perhaps I could turn my own experiences into stories. I didn't know how Lin would feel about that.

When she came down, I said, "Didn't you once tell me there were no such things as leprechauns?" I asked.

"I might have said something of the sort. There are all kinds of strange beings that pass for humans. Not just gods and nymphs."

"And witches. Do leprechauns really get ill?"

"Oh they do, and they're not immortal, just long-lived. Two hundred or so. Let me tell you about my interaction with one."

The Knight, the Gnome, and the Fox

"Oh they do, and they're not immortal, just long-lived. Two hundred or so. Let me tell you about my interaction with one."

Tape 4,
Volume 3

There was this funny little cobbler where I used to live out-side London in a small town called Ruislip. I lived there for about eighteen months after we had to go through rebirth sometime in the late 1800's. London is one of those places I went back to again and again, like Lisbon. When you have to keep moving, it's nice to go back to a familiar place. Sort of familiar. I've never seen a city change so much so quickly from century to century. Anyway, I decided to opt for peace and quiet this time so looked for a small house that was within walking distance of the shops, away from the din of city life, but near enough to visit. I didn't yet have a nanny, and Hunter was a handful, so I needed to make things as easy as I could.

I found a maid quickly enough, thanks to a note pinned on the board of the local newsagent. Newsagents in England sell papers, magazines, candy, and cigarettes, and there's one in every shopping area. Dolly was an obliging soul who fitted in with our relaxed routine and tolerated Hunter and his shenanigans.

I didn't get to know my next door neighbor for about a year until we came face to face outside my gate. Mildred was a sweet soul, the widow of a businessman who had been "something in the City," whatever that meant. She had been rather distant with me until I recounted my sad little tale of sudden widowhood due to an unlucky fall from a horse in Cornwall. Fortunately, he'd left me well provided for. I wore an expensive diamond wedding ring, which helped my tale ring true. That reassured her that I was safe to know.

Mildred said she would ask around to find a nanny. My maid had said she didn't know anyone—rather too quickly. I think seeing Hunter in action had put her off exposing her friends to such a challenge. "We'll start with the church," Mildred said and insisted I join her the next Sunday. I went with her several times. St. Martin's was a lovely old church. The stained glass windows cast a soft glow over the altar and congregation, which together with the mellow tones of the organ soothed the soul.

One day, she came to me with good news. "You know the cobblers on the high street? Thomas & Sons?"

"I've passed it, but I haven't needed his services yet."

"Well, he has a sister, just over from Ireland. She nannied for a family over there for years until their children grew past that stage. She decided to join her brother and is looking for employment."

"That could be good. Especially if she is a mature woman, rather than a girl."

"That's what I thought, my dear. Hunter needs a firm hand."

"Indeed he does."

Mildred invited us to tea soon after we got into the habit of chatting over the garden fence. It did not go well. Hunter loved her cat, but her cat did not love Hunter, possibly due to the one-year-old's violent shows of affection. I'd told him several times to leave the cat alone. The cat, stretched to its limit, suddenly bit and scratched, and Hunter screamed with rage before smashing one of Mildred's Dresden figurines—which seemed to make him feel much better. I scolded him and took him home.

I was thoroughly fed up with parenthood. I wanted to visit London and have fun. I didn't have any friends there anymore but craved nights at the theater and opera. I wanted to get some chic dresses, too. And I needed to buy Mildred a lovely Dresden figurine. I knew just the place.

Mildred invited the cobbler's sister, Miss Colleen Allister, to tea at my house on a Monday afternoon. She was quite short, thin as a rake, and had the face of a bulldog. Even Hunter was intimidated when she fixed him with a stare.

"Is this the young man in question?" she asked without the usual preamble of, "Good afternoon," and "Nice to meet you," and so on. She clasped her hands at her waist.

"Yes, this is Hunter. Hunter, say hello to Miss Colleen."

Hunter hung his head, and said nothing.

"Hunter. Your mother asked you to say hello. Say hello. Now."

His glance slid up to and past her face as he did as he was told.

"He is quite forward for his age," opined Miss Colleen. "Walking and talking. One year old, you say?"

"Yes and two months. He is big for his age and yes, rather forward."

"Well, plenty of fresh air and a strict routine should keep him in fine fettle. When do you want me to start?"

"Don't you want to ask me any questions? Or see your room?"

"I can see you are a respectable household. There is nothing more to it."

"I need to be in London for a week soon. Is that acceptable to you?"

"Of course. I will supervise your maid and the household will run smoothly."

That was the strangest job interview I ever conducted. However, I felt she would be able to deal with Hunter better than anyone.

She moved in the next day and took over. I didn't have to do a thing. Hunter hated her. Resentment would build until he had a massive tantrum to which she responded with—nothing. She ignored him, stepped over him, and continued whatever she was doing without acknowledging his presence. He soon wore himself out and calmed down, usually falling asleep right where he was.

The maid hated Miss Colleen because she subjected her to stern discipline regarding the preparation of nutritious meals and the correct method of cleaning just about everything. The wonderful week I spent in London didn't help. I had a quiet word with her.

"You know, Miss Colleen has you so well trained that by the time six months is up, you'll be able to work anywhere." Somewhat appeased, Dolly saw my point. I wouldn't stay there much longer. I'd had about enough of small town life and peace and quiet. I knew my city lifestyle would not suit Miss Colleen, although Dolly might like it.

One evening, when Hunter was in bed, Miss Colleen came to the living room. "I need to speak to you," she said.

I put aside my book and motioned her to sit down. I never saw her after dinner. She either stayed in her room or went to see the cobbler, so I knew it was serious. I didn't want to lose her.

She sat on the edge of an armchair and clasped her hands on her lap. "My brother Tom is in some difficulty. I know you are different, so wanted to ask for your help."

"Different? How so?"

"My brother and I are different too. Not human. Like you."

I was shocked I never picked up on that. Yes, she was unusual but hadn't struck me as not human. "How can I help?"

"We are leprechauns. There is a man who is after my brother Tom. He means business. The man almost trapped him last week. He wants to kidnap Tom for his gold. Not that he has that much, you understand, but every leprechaun has his own stash. As the legend goes, if you catch a leprechaun, he has to give you his gold."

"How did he try to trap him last week?"

"He is Irish. He invited him to a party to meet other Irish people. There was no party. Tom walked into the house to find it quiet. 'Over here,' his new friend said, opening the door to a small room. The walls of this room had hundreds of shamrocks pinned to it. Leprechauns are drawn to shamrocks, and it was this man's plan to lure him in and lock him up. My brother said he was tempted to rush in and bury his face in the shamrocks, but he resisted. He guessed it was a trick. Tom ran away and back to his shop as fast as he could. He lives above his shop, you know."

"What can I do?"

"I wondered if you could keep an eye on the place after closing time for a few days. For leprechauns, it's a catastrophe to lose their gold. They don't spend it on fine things. They just have to have it. It's like part of their soul. And what's to stop this man from killing poor Tom once he gets his hand on the treasure?"

At last, a mission. "Of course I will. Starting now."

Miss Colleen rewarded me with the most frightening smile. If you imagine a smiling bulldog, pointy teeth and all, you get the picture.

I ran upstairs and changed into loose black pants and a black sweater. Miss Colleen looked askance at me when I came down. A woman simply did not wear trousers in those days. Since I didn't have to hide myself from her, I left her at the front gate and ran to her brother's place in under a minute. I can't look back when running at that speed, but I'd have loved to see her face when I disappeared from view halfway down the road.

There was a small yard at the back of the property, so I jumped the fence and looked around. I noticed a line of crumpled newspapers against the back door. Maybe his assailant would try to smoke him out. I removed them and threw them over the fence into the alley. I stayed there all night, moving between the back and front of the building at regular intervals. I saw a man in a long coat approach, not exactly tiptoeing but close to it. When I walked toward him, he turned back and quickened his pace. I should have followed.

I reported back to Miss Colleen in the morning. She had Dolly prepare me a breakfast with extra bacon and sausage. I couldn't help loving those things, especially British sausages, but sent my silent regrets to the pigs that suffered on my behalf. Hunter liked them too. I noticed he seemed to be more comfortable with Miss Colleen. Maybe strict routine really was the way to go.

The next night, I returned. This time, I sensed a presence in the back yard. I climbed the fence silently, peering over the top to see what was going on. A man was replacing the newspapers and had set a tinder box at his feet. I leapt over the fence to land in front of him. He jumped back and pulled a knife, which I snatched from his hand with a speed that dumbfounded him.

"What are you doing here?" I asked.

"None of yer business."

"Oh, but it is. After a pot of gold, are you?"

He looked scared. "Don't be ridiculous. What does a runt like that want with gold?"

"Yes, I'm sure you'd use it better. Why are you trying to set fire to his place?"

"Am not."

Tom opened the back door. "What's going on?" He didn't seem to notice me, only the man in black. "God, it's you." He slammed the door and shot the bolt. When I turned toward Tom, the intruder seized his chance to knock me over the head with a brick and flee through the back gate. After a moment's dizziness, I gave chase, and it was only a matter of seconds before he was down. He punched me in the head, which I felt was overdoing it, so I slammed his head on the ground. Too hard, it seemed. A crimson pool spread down to his shoulders. At least it wasn't on Tom's property. I ran back to the cobbler and knocked on the door. Tom called out of an upstairs window. "Who is it?"

"I'm coming up." I scaled the wall, then climbed through the window. The poor leprechaun shrank away from me, trembling. "Don't be afraid. I am your sister's employer. She asked me to help you. The intruder is no more. You will not be bothered again. Did you know him?"

Tom let out a great sigh of relief. "He once befriended my brother, Liam. He caught my brother and stole his gold. Liam died of a broken heart. What can I offer you in return?"

"Nothing. Your sister is very good with my son, and I appreciate it. I am glad to help."

"You have some funny white stuff dribbling down your forehead."

"Don't worry. It's fine."

"Colleen said you were different. I saw you in action. You are truly different."

Are we ever! White blood instead of red, for a start. You don't need to know. "As are you," I said. "Tell no one."

I left and went home to bed. Next morning a velvet package sat on the dining room table in front of my plate. "What is this?"

"I think it's a little present from my brother," Colleen said.

It was a little gold pin in the shape of a shamrock. I have it still.

"Did you move shortly after that?" I asked.

"We did. To Florence this time. And Miss Colleen came with us. She was marvelous with Hunter. But after a couple of years, Tom got ill, and she had to return to London to look after him. She kept in touch. He recovered but was never quite the same. They went back to Ireland. Tom had to find a wife to bear him a son so that he could die. Every male leprechaun must leave a son. A daughter isn't enough."

"Do you think Stan's mother is a leprechaun?"

"I'm not sure. I don't think Stan is, so his father would be fully human. He's too big, for a start. And too quiet. All leprechauns have the gift of the gab. I was sorry I never took the trouble to know Tom better. They can be very amusing."

"The women don't seem to be at all amusing."

"Irish tradition has it that female leprechauns don't exist. But I know differently. Miss Colleen was the only female one I met apart from Stan's mother—I think. I'd like to ask him, but I don't think he'd welcome us prying into his family background."

"No, especially if he doesn't realize you are 'other.'"

Lin frowned. "His mother came right out with it and said we were different. Her behavior was very odd. He seems to be the type to accept strange things without comment."

"I can't wait to see the baby." *A little friend for Rose.*

"I just hope it's normal."

Normal was in short supply in this household.

in came down the next Monday morning. "These weddings reminded me that I never told you Hunter and I
have to get married quite often."

"Why?"

"For the marriage certificate. We have to get birth certifi-
cates made each time, which is a nuisance, but the marriages
with witnesses makes things easier if we decide to have children in that lifetime."

"Do you have big weddings?"

"No, of course not. Just a civil ceremony these days. In
some places, in some cultures, in some eras, we had to have
a religious ceremony, but we'd rather not."

"You must have attended lots of weddings. Do any
stand out?"

"I told you about the weddings of Gyr's daughters. But
there's one I particularly remember that didn't ever happen."

"That sounds intriguing."

"Turn on the tape, and I'll tell you about it."

Tape 5,
Volume 3

You may recall that time during the rule of Oliver Cromwell we had to leave London in a hurry after Hunter made fun of the Roundheads in a tavern one evening. Most taverns had been closed, but this was one of the last hangers-on. I don't know what happened after we left for the New World, but no doubt the spy who reported him ensured its demise.

Anyway, before that, we lived in the outskirts of Northampton, a bedrock of the Parliamentarian cause. We were lying low after another unfortunate misunderstanding in Wales. We seemed to hop all over the place in that lifetime, mostly due to Hunter's wild streak. I don't know what got into him. He calmed down after fifty, thank heavens.

Anyway, Hunter was working for a wealthy merchant who traded in cloth and owned a number of weaving establishments. Hunter wanted to learn the business before striking out on his own, paying the weavers above the norm, and treating them better too.

This merchant, John Gatt, was a nasty character—miserly and harsh. His wife died in childbirth during Hunter's time there, and he immediately set about finding a new wife to take care of the newborn and his five other children. No one liked him, and no one wanted to betroth their daughter to him. One day, he caught sight of the daughter of one of his weavers.

Ella was fifteen and very pretty in an English rose kind of way—clear, fair skin, big blue eyes, and fair hair that fell naturally in ringlets. The weaver protested that she was too young, but he lived in tied housing, and John Gatt threatened to throw his family out on the street if he didn't comply.

We went to the church because the bridegroom would have taken it amiss if we did not. Churches were required to go by a different prayer book during that time. They had to hire a registrar to record marriages and refrain from unseemly displays of extravagance. That was just fine with John Gatt, of course. The small church had a few stained glass windows behind the altar but was otherwise unadorned. Not a single flower lightened the gloom, and the woman I took to be Ella's mother sobbed into a rag. The minister and registrar stood waiting before the altar. There was no best man. I'm not sure if that's a modern custom or if they usually had one in those days. I don't remember.

Loud footsteps clomped down the center aisle as John Gatt arrived to claim his bride. He faced the small congregation without acknowledging the minister, whose lips curled in disgust. The bridegroom cast his eyes over the congregation before settling on the mother, who was drying her tears and trying to control herself. His glare carried the promise of retribution for failing to be properly grateful for the honor he was doing her daughter.

The minister said, "Please rise."

We all stood and turned to the bridal procession of two. Ella wore a plain dress of gray with a white collar and carried no flowers. Her grim-faced father held her arm in a vise-like grip, almost dragging his daughter down the aisle. The bride was a picture of misery—her puffy eyes studied the floor, her lips would have trembled had she not clenched her teeth so tightly, and her free arm hugged her waist as if she had the colic. John Gatt bared his teeth in what passed for a smile as he stared at his prey.

When they reached the altar rail, the bride's father released her arm and pushed her toward the groom. She refused to look him in the eye, merely drooping a little more and making fists.

As the minister opened his mouth to speak, another voice sounded from the back of the church. "Ella, come on!"

Ella whipped around and ran like a hare out of the church doors with a young man. The sound of hooves galvanized John Gatt out of his numb disbelief.

"After them!" he roared. "You'd better find your slut and get her back here if you want to have a living," he yelled at Ella's father. Then to Hunter, "Go on, get her."

We both ran out of the church. As I run much faster than Hunter, I gradually increased my speed so that those around me wouldn't notice when I disappeared around the first bend in the road. I soon caught up with the couple. Their cart had lost a wheel in the mud by the riverbank where it had recently overflowed. I pushed it so that it toppled into the water, its wheels just showing above the surface. The boy had unharnessed the horse before they ran into the woods. I slapped its haunch to make it run too. It made for open ground.

I ran into the woods, listening to their footsteps and panting breaths. They were running toward the general area of our house. The footsteps stopped. They were sprawling under a tree, trying to catch their breath when I found them. They jumped up in horror when they saw me.

"Don't worry. I'm here to help," I said.

"Your man works for Gatt," Ella snapped, "Is this a trick?"

"No, no, we don't like him either. Hunter is only learning the trade so he can start his own venture. He wants to hire weavers and treat them better than Gatt does."

They still looked at me askance.

"You are not far from our house," I said. "I will lead you there. You will be safe until we can get you a long way from John Gatt. We have money."

"We don't have a choice, my love," the young man said. His name was Matthew.

"We never have a choice," Ella answered sharply. "My own father sold me to that horrible man."

"He didn't have a choice either," I said. "Gatt threatened to throw your family out into the street if he didn't agree. No home, no job. He only did what he had to."

"I suppose he did," she said in a lower tone. I didn't point out that the family would be poverty-stricken now.

I led them to the edge of the woods closest to the back of our house. It would be hours until dark. Should I risk running with each of them in turn, thus alerting them to my "otherness"? Or should I wait until dark?

"You will have to conceal yourself until dark," I said. "Either Hunter or I will come to take you to our house. We have a spare room you can use."

They looked at each other shyly. "We are not yet..."

"You are not yet wed, Ella. Do you intend to be wed?" I asked.

"Oh, yes," they said in unison.

"Very well then, no harm done. I managed to tip your cart into the river, so I'm hoping they'll think you drowned. With all the flooding we've had, the river is quite deep there, and the current runs swift."

"Yes, I did not expect the lane there to be so muddy and slippery," Matthew said. "I should have. We have had so much rain, the river burst its banks in many places."

"You were racing to get Ella away from a terrible situation," I said. "You must not blame yourself."

Ella stroked his back. "You are my hero, Matthew." He puffed up, no longer downcast. It didn't take much.

"I will see you tonight. There will be a good dinner waiting for you. Our woman goes home before dark, so she won't see you. She will cook our dinner first though."

"Go on. Hide yourselves in case anyone comes looking," I said.

When they were out of sight, I ran home, letting myself in through the back door. To my surprise, I found Hunter sitting at the kitchen table, drinking ale from a massive tankard.

"What are you doing here?" I asked.

"Gatt dismissed me."

"Why?"

"I got to the river ahead of the others. I saw the upturned cart and realized what happened. The skid marks in the mud by the riverbank made it clear. There was no sign of the horse or the couple. Very sad." He looked upset. "Poor girl."

"And then?" I prompted.

"Several others finally came, including the girl's father. Gatt eventually caught up. He went mad, shouting at us all, firing us all, including Ella's poor grief-stricken father, and laying about us with his stick."

"What did you do then?"

"I grabbed his stick, broke it across my knee, and threw it in the river. Then I told him that the girl had gained a happy release from a loveless marriage to a heartless miser. He will never hire me back now, even if he might have reconsidered."

"Well, I have good news," I said. I explained what had happened, which lightened his mood considerably.

Later that night, Hunter went looking for the happy pair. He also has godly hearing and sight, although not as good as mine, so it didn't take long to find them and guide them to our back door. They were cold, wet, and starving by that time, so almost rivaled Hunter with their intake of beef stew and potatoes. I sent them off to bed after dinner. I thought they may as well get on with it. Of course, I can't shut off my sharp hearing, so I dragged Hunter upstairs not long after.

As I lay in the dark later, I pondered our next move. The maid would be back tomorrow. What if she recognized the couple? I'd have to hide them away while she was here. In the shed, maybe. I must get them away. And Hunter had no job. We didn't need the money, but in that life, I had to keep him busy if we wanted to avoid indiscretions. Perhaps we should all move. It's not as if there was anything to keep us in Northampton. Puritanism was hardly my strong suit. Cromwell had turned everything drab and colorless.

London appealed to me. Cromwell had certainly left his mark on the city but not quite as much as up here, where there had already been a strict Presbyterian streak in the populace. London wasn't a wool town, though. Would Hunter be able to ply the trade from there? I was quite sure he could. It was the largest port in the country, after all. The center of the universe according to contemporary belief.

I rose before dawn because I had to deal with Ella and Matthew before the maid arrived. I went down to the shed and looked around. A couple of trunks and some packing boxes were about all. They needed a good dusting, but I'd leave that to Ella. I needed to find some blankets, a pitcher of water, some bread and cheese, and a duster. A chamber pot too. I rushed to get all those things down there before the nosy neighbors would be able to watch and wonder. Then I knocked on the happy pair's door and practically frog-marched them down the garden path.

"Sorry, my dears, but no one must see you. I'll fetch you after dark."

They didn't look too unhappy to be locked up all day. Now I had to tackle Hunter. I slipped back into bed. The maid wouldn't approve of me being such a lay-abed, but there were important things at stake.

"It's time to leave Northampton," I whispered.

His eyes suddenly opened wide. "What? Why?"

"Think about it. The town has become very boring. You have no job. We can enjoy life more in London, don't you think? And you could start trading wool cloth there. We could pack up and take Ella and Matthew with us."

"What will Matthew do there?" he said. "He's a country boy."

"You will employ him in your new firm," I said. "He will be your most loyal employee."

Hunter lay back and closed his eyes. I knew he wouldn't go back to sleep but would lay there worrying all these things around his brain like a dog tracking a scent. I got up and dressed so that the maid wouldn't give me that narrow eyed look I noticed occasionally when my extravagance or leisurely ways were at odds with her rigid code of conduct. I really didn't like these people. Their god was all about restriction, punishment, Duty (with a capital D), and joyless existence.

When the maid arrived, I told her that my husband had been called to London to assist his uncle with his business affairs. His uncle was a churchgoing and church-contrib-uting Presbyterian and the most honest, plain-living man I'd ever met. I could tell she approved of that by the self-righteous nod of her head. I mentioned a going away gift of two month's wages. She approved of that too.

When Hunter came down, he recognized that we were moving anyway and seemed to have come to the conclusion that it was the right thing to do. He simply looked around and went out for a walk.

We had packed up by the end of the day. In the afternoon, I left the maid to finish up and rode into town to notify the landlord. I gave him the rest of the money due under our contract and told him he'd find the key in the shed. We already owned a covered wagon in preparation for Hunter's business venture. That evening, Matthew helped him load everything. We would leave at dawn.

Ella and Matthew hid behind the boxes until we were well on our way. A small band of men halted us as we were about to leave the city limits.

"We are looking for a maid who has run away from home. Young, fair of face, light hair. Have you seen her? She might be traveling with a lad."

We said that we had not and were moving down south to help Hunter's uncle. We didn't mention London, that den of iniquity. They didn't try to detain us.

It was a wretched journey. The spring rains had been heavier than usual, so the condition of the roads alter-nated between slippery mud and excessive ruts. We were exhausted when we came to our first stop at a roadside inn that looked well kept. We claimed the young ones as my young sister and her husband. They looked happy and content. Matthew could ride alongside Hunter now, and I would lounge in the back with Ella.

We were on our way down the narrow and uneven death trap of the inn's staircase when I heard a familiar voice. Gatt. I pushed everyone back up after raising my finger to my lips. I then crept down again to eavesdrop. The stairs lay behind a wall, and I was able to creep through a door to a closet where travelers could leave their cloaks while they ate and drank. Peeking through a couple of thick wool cloaks that had never been cleaned or aired—the same probably true of their owners—I could see the man sitting at one of the rough long tables and shoveling food down his throat. It looked like the meat and carrots we'd had for dinner.

"Ungrateful little slut," he was telling the landlord, who did his best to look interested and sympathetic. "She'll pay if I catch her. And that boy... She thinks she got away clean. But no bodies washed up."

"Yer know, good sir, with all these rains, the currents in that River Nene are something wicked. They coulda been washed right out to sea fast enough."

"Hmph. Well, if you see a girl that looks like what I said, there might be something in it for you."

"Yessir. Course, sir."

"I'll be getting back now. Business calls."

"Yessir."

Gatt got up and came over to retrieve his cloak. I scrunched myself as tiny as I could behind the remaining garments. He flung it over his shoulders and strode to the door.

"Er, sir. A little matter of payment, if you would be so good."

"Oh, really, you charge everyone for leftovers?"

"Course we do sir. Can't be throwing away good food."

Gatt's protruding lower lip betrayed his displeasure. He pulled a coin out of his purse and threw it on the table before storming out and slamming the door.

I showed myself. The innkeeper cocked his head to one side and smiled. "I didn't say anything," he said.

"Thank you. The girl was being forced into marriage with him. He's a terrible man. You will be rewarded well for your discretion. I don't think you will ever get much out of Gatt. He is known for his miserly ways."

"He short-changed me for the meal, right enough."

"I'll call the others down for their morning meal then."

We ate well, paying the innkeeper what he asked and adding a gold coin. He beamed as he wished us Godspeed. Ironic, eh?

We got to London without further ado and rented a decent sized house with room for our wagon and our two young charges. To cut a long story short, Hunter did start his trading business, ordering from a firm in Northampton that Gatt had quarreled with over bills due and dropped without payment. The business went well, but Hunter got bored and turned it over to Matthew. The country boy adapted well to city life and thrived, as did Ella and their two children. They extended an invitation to Ella's family to join them, and soon the business gained a reputation for fine woven cloth.

I was sad to leave them without saying goodbye. Fortunately, we had moved into smaller lodgings when Ella's babies started to come. They needed the space, and I needed peace and quiet. I loved the children but in small doses. Putting up with little ones is different when they're your own. Hunter didn't feel that England was stable at that time and didn't want to buy, so we entered another rental contract. The landlord might possibly go after Matthew for the money after we skipped town, but he could afford to pay. We never contacted them to explain. Cromwell's spies were everywhere.

"So, a potentially horrid wedding story turned into a happily ever after story, Mary."

"Did they ever get married?"

"Not at the time we left. They might have been punished severely for fornication, so who could they ask to marry them? Different times."

"It's still like that in some places."

"True enough. Not here, thankfully."

14

I'd just brought Rose upstairs for dinner when the doorbell rang. Sam performed his usual song and dance routine—barking, wagging, and circling. I was closest, so I opened the door. Sam dropped and growled. The strangest little man stood there, his thin lips spread into an improbable stretch. He was about eighteen inches shorter than I, and I'm not tall. His face and neck were lined like a drought-blighted riverbed, his large ears stuck out at an angle suggesting he was ready for take-off, and greasy gray hair stuck out at all angles beneath his tweed cap. Finally, I remembered my manners and stopped gawping.

"May I help you?"

He looked nervously at Sam, who emitted a steady stream of humming growls. "Do I have the pleasure of addressing the lady of the house?" he asked in a Cockney accent, which I was acquainted with thanks to television.

"No, I am a guest."

He barged into the foyer and set down an old brown leather suitcase, its corners worn white. "Get me either Hoenir or Lin, would yer, luv?"

"Wait here," I said, uneasy. *Hoenir? He knows the old name. Who is this fellow?* I looked down at Rose, who led me toward the kitchen, closely followed by Sam, who kept looking back at the stranger. Uncharacteristically, she hadn't said a word.

I found Dora in the throes of setting out dinner on the sideboard. Lin was already in the dining room.

"Lin, this strange little man just came to the door. He's English and knows Hunter's real name."

"'allo, Lin! Bootiful as ever, I see."

We both pivoted to the doorway. The cheeky guy had followed me.

"And who might you be?" said Lin, her voice signaling the possibility of unpleasantness.

"You won't remember me. I'm Nisse. My friends call me Nick, now."

"Why are you here?"

Nick gestured toward me and Dora, who had deposited the last dish and stood staring at this apparition. "I assume they know about you two."

"Yes, but we have another guest, who will be down any minute, who does not."

Lin was referring to my Auntie Peggy. While I had told her about Lin and Hunter, they still didn't know I'd tattled.

"Well, to cut a long story very short, I got free from my prison after Ragnarok because there were so many rockfalls—Ragnarok and rockslides, that's a good laugh—because the mountains got shook up bad."

"That's not funny," Lin said in a low, hard voice, moving closer to him.

Nick took a step back. "Sorry, luv. It was a long, hard way of life until there was something I could get out to. I was going ter use that nice little treasure trove. But you two got there first. I was hiding in a fissure of the cave wall when you got in."

"What do you want?" Lin didn't sound as if she'd be sympathetic to whatever he wanted.

"I want a nice place to live and a nice chunk of change to go along with it. I been in ol' Blighty for a few 'undreds, but I've been in the good old U.S. of A. about a year now. I know about the IRS. I know about the FBI. I know how Americans think and behave towards the weirdos. You don't want me to start gabbin', do yer?"

Lin looked ready to commit murder then and there. Fortunately, Hunter made his entrance, closely followed by Auntie Peggy.

Lin turned to Hunter. "Let me introduce Nick. He is visiting from England. He knows us from the old days."

Hunter glared at him. "I remember you," he said.

Lin broke in, "And these are our guests, Mary and her aunt, Peggy Lambert."

"How do you do?" Auntie said.

Nick swept off his cap and bowed deep, which induced an embarrassed simper from Auntie. I had a good view of the grime lodged in the creases of his neck, so was less amused.

"It is my honor (pronounced with an aspirated "H") to meet such a charmin' lady.

"Dora, set another place please," said Lin.

Dora usually sulked at such requests but was clearly excited to watch this extraordinary turn of events.

Eventually, we all served ourselves and sat down. Nick hardly stopped talking while Lin and Hunter remained silent, as did Rose. She stole a glance at Nick from time to time, but when he tried to get a laugh out of her, she turned her head up and away, pursing her lips. Auntie and I tried to be pleasant, although it didn't work.

"So, Nick, I understand that you have spent many years in England. What brought you over here?" asked Auntie.

"Oh, this and that. Friends, 'amburgers, you know the sorta shit." He went on to expound on the virtues of various barbecue sauces. Then it was jeans and how difficult it was to find his size. I noticed Rose taking notice of what he was saying all of a sudden.

"Why do you not shop in the children's department?" asked Lin.

"Well, it's a bit awkward, you know." He glowered at her. Then he went on about all the big houses around here. "Do you know lots of your neighbors, Linny?"

I stiffened much as Lin did, expecting a meltdown. But she kept her cool. "No, we don't know most of them. And kindly refrain from calling me anything but Lin."

"Sorry. Lin."

"Shit!" said Rose.

Nick laughed as if she'd just told the wittiest joke ever. I distinctly heard a snort from the kitchen. And Hunter dabbed his lips and coughed for much too long, his eyes teary.

Auntie Peggy was not amused. "I don't want to hear you say that word again, young lady," she said in the tone of an outraged schoolmarm—one she'd never had call to use on me. Rose looked startled at this rare rebuke from her doting Auntie.

"Rose, that is not a word a little girl should ever say," I said. "Don't encourage her, Nick."

Nick stopped laughing like a crazed donkey but kept the residual smirk. We ate quietly until Auntie decided she should break the silence.

"So, Nick, what did you do in England?"

"Oh, this an' that. I nearly went on a crusade once."

"Goodness me," Auntie said, skepticism clear in her voice.

"Let me tell you all about it."

Lin cut him off. "After dinner."

Once the apple strudel and cream had been cleared away, Hunter rose. "Lin and Nick, please join me in my study. Auntie Peggy and Mary, please feel free to enjoy the television."

I was dying to join them, but it would have been intrusive. Lin would tell me about it later. Hunter knew I was aware of his and Lin's godly status, but he didn't know about the memoir Lin was having me write, so had no idea how much I knew about them. Secrets within secrets.

Auntie and I put Rose to bed. Auntie read her a story while I went into my sitting room to see what was on BritBox. I loved having my own TV, although I usually spent my evenings with the family. I was in the mood for a British mystery, and Auntie always enjoyed them. We'd only seen a few seasons of "Murder She Wrote," and we always enjoyed it. I selected the next episode and put it on pause.

"Whatever is Nick doing here?" Auntie asked when she joined me. "That is a very strange little man, indeed. Even Rose doesn't seem to like him. He's not quite the thing."

"That sounded rather British, Auntie."

"Well, I spent quite some time there because of my war work, you know."

"No, of course I didn't know. You never talk about your work."

"Well, it's all in the past now. Nothing worth talking about. What are we going to watch?"

More secrets.

"We're in the living room," Lin called down.

"I think I'll stay down here in case Rose wakes up," Auntie said. "I really don't care to listen to any more of this little man's preposterous yarns."

I went upstairs and sat down. Nick was clearly raring to go as he fidgeted and waggled his crossed leg. I noticed that Hunter was absent.

He cleared his throat and sat straight. I turned on my phone recorder. Nick cleared his throat dramatically and began.

Tape 6,
Volume 3

I were working at a fair in Ferminster one autumn, helping a family of folk from the west to prepare their horses for sale. Some had to be altered a bit—you know, change their color and so on—and others needed gingering up to make them seem younger. One afternoon, I were rubbing down a mare when I noticed a man watching me in a corner of the yard. Well dressed, he nevertheless looked on the rough side with his scarred face and big meaty hands. I didn't rightly know what to make of him. Or why he were watching me. After about half an hour, he strode over. I backed up, but the wall stopped further retreat.

"You'd better come with me," the man said.

"Why? I haven't done nothing." I tell you, my knees were knocking together by this time.

"My Lord is in search of someone like you."

"Like me? What about me?"

"Small. Stupid looking. Only, you're not stupid, are you? You know how to doctor horses."

Well, I were fair gobsmacked by that. What impertinence. "I don't want to work for someone who insults me like that. Go away."

With that, he grabbed my arm and marched me over to his mount. He were that strong, I couldn't help meself. He tied a rope around my waist, jumped on his horse, and trotted off, dragging me be'ind. I tripped a time or two before I got the hang of it, and he just laughed. I was panting like a dog by the time we reached his master's estate.

It were a big spread. I hadn't never seen a castle before, but this place looked like it might be one. Big walls, guarded gates, lots o' people goin' about their business to and fro, soldiers playing about with their swords. Master Baxter— for that was what he said he were called—dismounted and some young feller took away his horse to be seen to. It were covered in mud and muck. I were too, and you wouldn't believe the pong. He untied the rope and grabbed my arm again, pulling me around to the back—which took a fair while, it were so big—and in through a door. Up and down corridors, we went until I were right dizzy.

We came to a big hall where a bunch of men sat at tables stuffing their faces with dinner. The meat and stuff didn't half smell good.

"What have we here, Master Baxter?" bellowed a man at the head of the table. He rose and was just about the biggest man I ever seen.

"I found you a fool, my Lord."

The Lord (Carvon, as I found out later) came around and looked me up and down. "He stinks" was his conclusion.

I'd had it by that time. "So would you if you'd been dragged through the muck and mire behind a horse whose arse exploded like a cannon with a grudge."

Everyone in the room rollicked with laughter, holding their full bellies.

"He'll do," said Lord Carvon. "Take him away and have someone give him a bath. You have done well, Master Baxter."

I was dragged away again and taken out to a corner of the stable yard. Baxter yelled for a maid, who was told to bring a bathtub and hot water. After a good time, while I sat against a wall, a couple of maids appeared carrying a tub between them. More soon arrived with hot water and some cloths.

"Take off your tunic and get in," Baxter commanded.

"In front of everyone? I don't think so."

"Either you will do it or they will," he replied with a nasty smirk.

So I dropped everything, folded my hands in front of my privates and tried to climb in. Only, the sides were high so I tripped and fell in on my back, my legs stuck in the air, my privates waving in the fresh air for everyone to see. They were all highly entertained, and more people gathered to see what the fuss were all about.

"You'd think it'd be littler," chirped a maid while they all giggled and craned their necks.

I finally managed to sit properly and soak.

"Wash with this," said the maid who'd seen fit to comment on my person.

"I have business to attend to," Master Baxter said in a more cheerful tone than he'd shown until then. "You girls watch him. See that he doesn't run away. And fetch him something to wear. Throw his old tunic away."

Well, that added insult to injury. But I couldn't rightly run away in that state, so I washed and got myself clean as I could what with the water being so dirty now. The soap smelled of animal fat in those days, too.

"We'll have to rinse him," said one of the maids. "That water's ever so dirty."

Two of the maids disappeared, soon to emerge from the back door hauling a couple of pails each. I knew they'd have cold water in them. I don't like water much at all, but cold water is the worst. I forgot my modesty, rose suddenly, and climbed over the side of the tub. The two maids who'd remained grabbed me soon enough, laughing as I struggled and cursed. Those wenches were strong. Suddenly, they fell away, and I had a pailful of cold water slung over me. I yelled and danced, only to be soaked again. And twice more. One of the maids started to rub my hair with a cloth. She then went to work on my back and chest.

"You'll feel better when you're dry," she said.

She meant well, but I felt pressed to grab the cloth from her before she started below the waist. I was past being embarrassed by my naked state, but there are limits. Finally, she popped a new tunic over my head, and my ordeal was over. Well, that particular ordeal, anyway.

A groom arrived on the scene. "I have come to take you to your room, sir," he said, bowing and indicating the way with an outstretched arm. *Well, that's more like it*, I thought. The maids' fresh onslaught of giggles should've warned me. We arrived at the stables, and he opened the door to the room where they keep all the bridles and such. "Your room, sir. You'll find your mattress in the hayloft." He sauntered away whistling. I would have to find out where he slept. I wanted to kill him or at least do him a major mischief.

I still didn't know what they wanted of me. I did notice a lot of military drilling going on in the courtyard, so something must be up. All I could do for now was have a kip, so I went in search of the ladder to the hayloft. When I got up there, it seemed quite cozy. Why not sleep up here? I fluffed up a loose bale and lay down. The horses whinnying was like a lullaby. I swear I'd hardly got my eyes shut when an unearthly screech woke me, and I was treated to the sight of a cat bounding across my chest with a not quite dead rat in its mouth—as if I wasn't even there. I realized a hayloft would be rich pickings for rats and other varmints, so maybe I should go back to my assigned lodgings. I gathered a couple of armfuls of hay and threw them to the foot of the ladder before climbing down after them. It wasn't quite dark, thank heavens, so I didn't misstep and hurt meself.

Settling in a corner that had the fewest bridles hanging down from wicked-looking iron hooks, I closed my eyes. It was almost dark. I would find a way to escape on the morrow. When said morrow arrived, a boy shook me roughly.

"Get up," he said. "Master Baxter wants you."

A horde of boys followed him to collect saddles, bridles, and all the other things they needed to dress a horse, including what was hanging over my head—and not being too fussy about where they were standing.

I felt a bit groggy but stood up in a hurry and went out looking for a place to relieve myself. The back of the stable seemed to be the only place. I was just rearranging my tunic when a mighty slap to the side of my head send me sprawling.

"You scurvy little toad," yelled an old man, who looked as if he'd been pickled in brine an' hung out to dry.

"Sorry," I mumbled. "Didn't see a good place."

"Well, this ain't it. Bugger off!"

"I'm to see Master Baxter. Do you know where I can find him?"

"They all be in the courtyard waiting to set off fer the Holy Land."

"What? That's an awful long way away, isn't it?"

"Too right, my lad. You'd better make haste, or you'll miss all the fun."

God save me, I didn't want to go to war. I couldn't give a shit (pardon me, ladies) who ruled said Holy Land. But as far as I knew, there was nowhere to run. Ferminster wasn't all that far away, but I could hardly go there. They'd be bound to find me. The only thing to do was to join them and escape when we got to whatever port we were supposed to sail from.

"There you are, fool." Master Baxter had come up behind me.

"What's all this then?" I asked.

"Haven't you heard of the Crusades? A holy war to free Christian lands from Muslim rule."

"I remembering hearing about something of the sort. But what's it got to do with me? Look at me. I'm no soldier."

"Your job will be to raise the mood of the men before battle commences with jokes and songs."

Well, that didn't sound too bad. Unless the other side won. "I don't know any jokes. Or songs, neither."

"And then you will ride up and down the lines encouraging them and cheering them on."

Now that was not on the books. "I can't even ride a horse."

"But I found you working with them."

"Doesn't mean I can ride the bloody things!"

"Well, you've got a thousand miles to learn. And think up some jokes and songs. See that boy on the charger?" He pointed at a horse nearly as tall as the castle wall with a scared looking boy perched atop. "We take some spares just in case. You get up behind him."

"I'll need a frickin' ladder to get all the way up there."

He beckoned to a groom. "Get him up behind young Tom over there."

The groom hoisted me over his shoulder without so much as a by-your-leave and dumped me on the horse's back. The horse objected, bucking and twisting until he'd succeeded in dumping both his passengers, to the audible amusement of the company at large.

"Now, now, Star, that wasn't nice," the groom cooed into the monster's ear, patting him to calm him down. "Now then, let's try that once more."

He held the horse while another groom did the honors. All was well when the boy was set on his back, but when the groom hoisted me up, he started to stomp around until the first groom whispered and caressed it to a standstill. I kept as still as I could, though my shoulder hurt. The ground in the courtyard was compacted and hard as a rock.

Finally, the order to move sounded. I hadn't heard a word from my companion.

"What's your name?" I asked, although I'd heard Master Baxter say his name.

"Tom."

"Mine is Nick."

No reply.

Although his legs could hardly grip the sides of the massive beast, the boy seemed to be able to steer the horse with the reins. I gripped him around the waist. I felt him stiffen, but damnit, what was I supposed to hold onto?

My bottom was right sore by the time we broke for a meal. I managed to slide down on my own. When I extended a hand to help the boy, he ignored it and jumped, disappearing immediately. I didn't know what the hell to do with the horse, so I left it grazing and wandered over to the cooking fires. I'd had no dinner the night before, nor any meal since. I were weak from lack of nourishment. I sat down under a tree and could have wished for a softer cushion, given my saddle soreness, but at least I were in reach of food. I thanked my lucky stars I weren't asked for songs and jokes yet. My mind couldn't get around to it with all the things that happened to me since yesterday.

One of the cooks looked askance at me. "Hungry, are we?"

"Yes, no morsel has passed my mouth since yesterday breakfast. I were taken against my will from my place of work and kept in the castle stables. Not a crumb was offered."

"I'll see you right," he said. He gave me a generous portion of mutton and bread. I were grateful for it and told him so.

"Dartmouth be a busy place," he said. "A man get lost there easy if he don't know his way." He winked.

"I get lost easy," I said and winked back.

Tom and I were lifted back on the devil's back without undue disturbance this time, and we were soon off again. After what seemed like hours and hours, after which I knew I would probably never be able to walk properly again, we came to Dartmouth's port. It were good to see the sea again. It'd been too long.

"Do we get off?" I asked the boy. He shrugged, maneuvering the horse to the edge of the crowd hawking their wares and waiting for passage. We had ridden at the back of the procession. I scanned the company. All eyes were fixed on the ship that would carry us across to France. It already flew the crusaders' flag of a red cross on a white background.

"I have to stretch my legs," I said. "I must find a place to relieve myself too."

Tom shrugged.

I slid off on the side where the crowd looked thickest and zig-zagged around people who were bent on moving in the opposite direction. I spotted a blue cap fluttering into a corner and quickly retrieved it. From the back, I would look like a boy. When the crowd thinned, I ran. I traversed filthy back alleys, avoiding major thoroughfares. After an exhausting trek, I came to a market that was just packing up.

"Need any help?" I asked a farmer's wife, who was toting bags of potatoes onto a wagon.

"Yes, I could do with someone lifting this lot. You up to it, are you?"

"Oh, yeh, I'm stronger than I look."

"What do you want? I don't have much. Custom weren't so good today."

"I need a ride out of town. Do you live far?"

"Happens our farm is a ways out. In trouble, are you?"

"Sort of. I was taken against my will to go on the Crusades. I ran away at the harbor. Can you help?"

"Well, I heard of such goings on. Any good with horses, are you?"

"Well, yes. I was working with horses when I was taken."

"We buy them and sell them, you see. They need looking after and doing up. Know what I mean?"

I couldn't help grinning. "I most certainly do."

I helped her load the cart, and we drove out of town. I lay down in back and covered myself with a sack until we were clear of other travelers, then sat up beside her. I amused her with my patter, and we got along famously.

They had a decent sized farm, big stables, and quite a robust business. The farmer took against me at first because of my looks, but he warmed up when he saw my skills preparing the horses for market. I worked for those people for nigh on three years before I came across a couple of buyers at the market from London. They agreed to let me ride with them in exchange for help with their purchase of two mares.

And so it was that I arrived in the famed City of London to make my fortune.

"And did you make your fortune?" I asked.

"Off and on. It's a long story." Nick looked shifty. There was no need to take it any further.

"Time to go, Nick," Lin said firmly.

He looked disappointed. "I've got lots more stories."

"Time to go. Hunter has started the car."

"Bye, all," he muttered as he stomped off.

"Hunter's taking him to a motel," she told us. "He will give him strict orders to smarten himself up."

"Glad to hear it," said Auntie. "Bit of a pong, as he would say."

Lin laughed. "He's rather a disreputable character," she said. "We'll get rid of him sooner or later. But he's a relative, so that complicates matters."

"Yes, family can make things difficult," Auntie replied.

Hunter didn't come into the living room, although I heard the car return. I tried to enjoy the mystery, but that phrase, "get rid of him sooner or later" worried me. I didn't like the little man but still.

The next morning, Lin came downstairs. "Why don't you go and see if Dora has any cookies?" she said to Rose. "Papa is busy this morning."

"Nick will be here for lunch, but I wanted to explain a few things," she said to me.

"I will go to Dora now. I do not like Nick," Rose told Lin, wagging her index finger at her. She climbed the stairs, one at a time, followed by Sam.

"That's a very perceptive little girl," said Lin, who had tried to keep a straight face at Rose's adamant statement. "I want to explain where this character came from."

"Okay. Coffee?"

"No thanks. It's too soon after breakfast to have more coffee."

"Too soon after breakfast to eat cookies, too."

"Well, sorry, but this is not for her ears. She often seems to understand more than we expect her to."

"True enough."

Lin made herself comfortable in a corner of the sofa, as did I at the other end after turning on the machine.

Tape 7,
Volume 3

"Nick, or Nisse as he was known in Asgard, is a gnome."

"Good grief, another survivor!" *How many more?*

"Yes, they do seem to be adding up. I never came across him, but Hunter saw him when he was with of the dwarves who presented Thor with his famous hammer. He stood out from the others because he was quite a bit taller. He didn't realize then that Nisse was a gnome, not a dwarf. Hunter heard from Thor that the chief dwarf told him a gold ingot had gone missing. This was an ingot Odin had given him so he could make a magical necklace for Freya, one that could transport her anywhere she desired just by touching it and visualizing the place or speaking of the place. Odin was furious. The dwarf promised he and his trusted council would search high and low until they found it. They hadn't told anyone about the loss. They searched in every sleeping nook and storage place until they found the ingot as well as several smaller items they'd missed. It was well concealed in a space created by pushing aside a rock that sat between two others and covered by a flatter, wider one. Dwarves can almost smell gold, you know. They have a sixth sense after working their magic with it for so many thousands of years.

The dwarves concealed themselves for two days near the stash. Nisse finally made an appearance, pushed the cover aside, and pulled a gold chain out of his pocket to add to his treasure. The watchers seized and bound Nisse before dragging him before Odin. Odin, pleased that both the culprit and his ingot had been found, merely sentenced him to one hundred years in prison without food or water. The dwarves locked him into a cave deep in the bowels of their mountain, secured by an iron gate. And that, presumably, was where he found himself freed by the convulsions of Ragnarok."

"Sam knew he was no good," I said. "It pays to take notice when a friendly loving dog like Sam takes a dislike to someone. And Rose didn't like him either. Maybe she took a cue from Sam. But didn't you tell me that gnomes were rich and lived underground? That sounds more like the dwarves."

"Did I? Yes, I meant the dwarves. Gnomes lived near humans, usually in barns."

"It's all very confusing. But did Nick, or Nisse, steal that stuff?"

"Of course, he tried to say he was framed because the dwarves were jealous of his height, but we know better. He was a thief and probably still is. He is threatening to tip off the IRS, suggesting they audit the source of our finances. That really hit a sore spot with Hunter. He also threatened to start rumors about us. He demanded to stay here. We said that we will get him new clothes and so on, then he can stay in a decent motel. He demanded to eat with us. We said lunch only. So, that's the situation. We're stuck with him until we find a way to send him packing."

Send him packing? Permanently?

The bell rang. "I suppose that's him," said Lin.

"How did he get here?" I asked.

"Probably walked. The motel is only five miles away. He'll ask for a car next."

16

Lunch was as awkward as yesterday's dinner. Everyone dispersed as soon as their dessert plate was clean, except Lin. No doubt she felt he should be watched. I took Rose down for her nap.

"Poppet asleep, is she?"

Nick leant against the door jamb, his grin in full stretch. Rose shot up. "I got to sleep now. Go away. If you come back, I will go to the beach house."

I kissed her forehead and laid her back down. Then, I left the room, motioning him out. "Upstairs," I said.

"Just wanted to get the lay of the land, yer know. Beach house?"

"Yes, they have a place on the Chesapeake Bay. Why do you need to get the lay of the land?"

"'spect I'll be living 'ere one of these days."

"Do you really?" I hoped not. When we got up to the foyer, I called Lin. She came downstairs.

"You were supposed to leave. I heard the front door close. Why are you still here?"

Nick said, "Just makin' conversation with your guest."

"He came downstairs to Rose's room," I said.

Lin strode over to Nick and hoisted him under her arm. He struggled before getting dumped outside.

"Yer should be nicer to me," he called from the bottom of the steps. "I want ter go to the beach house."

"You are not going anywhere except back to your motel. If you know what's good for you, you will mind your step," Lin replied, her fury making her voice as sharp as a boning knife.

"We'll have to do something about him and soon," she said after she'd slammed the door. "How does he know about the beach house?"

"Rose told him that if he comes back, she's going there."

"Good plan."

"He doesn't know where it is though."

She stomped upstairs and I retreated to my room for a quiet read and a cuddle with Sam. Auntie must have been napping, which she had been in the habit of doing after lunch for the past few months.

We saw Nick every day. He had given up talking to anyone, so lunch had become a dreary, silent affair. After about three weeks, he seemed unusually tired after he'd finished.

"Lin, I need to take a little nap before I walk all the way home. I'm ever so tired."

"I'll drive you," she said.

The same thing happened about a week later.

"What do you do all day, anyway?" she said. "Not work, that's for sure."

"I'm pretty busy in the evenings," he said, nudging Auntie in the ribs with his elbow.

"That's rather forward," Auntie said, her color and dander high.

"Sorry, luv, just a little joke," he said, his expression not at all sorry.

"I will take you back to your motel today," said Hunter, his voice only just above a growl.

Nick looked a little apprehensive, I was happy to see. The gnome made everyone uncomfortable. His bonhomie was a veneer coating a venal little con man. I knew it instinctively, even without hearing Lin's story.

The next day, I heard Nick leave after he'd used the wash room next to the front door. Lin suddenly rushed in there and shouted, "I'll kill him!"

Hunter and I hurried toward her.

"I took off my rings to wash my hands and forgot to put them on again."

She ran out of the front door and soon got up to top speed so she could no longer be seen—a godly ability I envied. In a few minutes, she was back. Hunter went down the front steps to relieve her of her burden, who shrieked and hollered as if he were being murdered. Maybe he would be. He should have known better. I wondered if anyone had heard him as Lin whisked him along the road. Hunter disappeared around the side of the house. I didn't follow. I didn't want to be a witness.

Auntie had gone to the kitchen to make herself a pot of tea. Now that I knew how much time she'd spent in England, I understood where she got that habit from. I followed her. My stomach clenched. "Auntie, I thought Rose was with you and Dora."

"Oh, she was, dear. She went to join Hunter outside."

Oh, God, what was she seeing? Rose pushed open the side door. She was doing that lovely trilling, her little girlie laugh. "Nick is in the twash," she said. "Where he should be."

My stomach clenched yet again. What had they done to him?

"Come an' look," she said, taking my hand and pulling me to the door.

I didn't think I wanted to. But it was spectacular. A pair of short legs with knobbly knees kicked and waved from the can—a very large one. His baggy pants had evidently fallen around his ears because the curses and cries for salvation were mercifully muffled. Hunter and Lin stood and watched, their arms folded, wearing looks of grim satisfaction. I noticed she was wearing her rings again.

"How long are you going to leave him there?" I asked.

"Until I feel like removing him," said Hunter. "He has to finally learn his lesson. Stealing is bad enough, but stealing from us? He stole from his fellow gnomes, and now from us. He must learn."

"Well, a one hundred year prison sentence didn't do it," I said.

"Yes, but he knows it will go much worse for him if he does it again," Hunter replied. "I feel like taking a nap."

"Me, too," said Lin.

I wasn't sure it was all right to leave Nick like that. Lin saw I was worried. "Don't worry, Mary. You're forgetting he's not human." And off they went.

"Ah, yes, I had forgotten. Well, that's all right then. Come on, Rose. Nap time."

Later that night, Hunter got Nick out of the can and sent him on his way. He didn't come back.

Joe and Helen came to dinner one evening a week or so later. They were such nice people and a joy to be around. Normally guest dinners were held at eight, although dinner for the family was at six. We kept to the family schedule that evening because they were keen on seeing Rose before she went to bed. Joe delighted in reading her a bedtime story. He had bought her all the British Flower Fairy stories, bringing them one by one, which delighted her. The pictures were enchanting—paintings of flowers and their guardian fairies. I looked them up on Amazon and found there were twenty-seven of them, dating back to the 1920's. Rose ate well, eager to get downstairs and enjoy her new book with Joe.

"How is work going?" Lin asked Joe.

"We've got a series of burglaries to deal with at present," he said. "It's a strange case. The burglar targets big, isolated homes, which is no surprise. He manages to sneak in when people are watching TV or otherwise occupied in the early evening before they've set the security alarm for the night. He either finds a back door unlocked or uses a skeleton key. And he only takes yellow gold. No watches, pearls, or other gems unless they are set in yellow gold."

"Yellow gold?" I asked. "Isn't gold always yellow?"

"No, there's white gold," said Joe, "but he's not interested in that."

"And he's never been spotted?" asked Hunter.

"Only once. And here's the oddest part. One of the teenaged sons of the homeowner saw him going out the back door. He gave chase but couldn't catch up, despite being a high-school track champion. He said the burglar was small, like a child."

Lin sat straighter. "Tell me more," she said.

"There's nothing more to tell. I wish there were," said Joe, sounding dispirited.

"Time to get into your jammies," I told Rose.

Hunter picked her up and carried her downstairs in front of me. He was frowning. "What's the matter?" I asked.

"I will tell you later," he said.

I got Rose changed before leading her out to the sitting area.

"Ready," she called up.

Joe and Helen hurried down and Rose snuggled between them on the sofa to hear the latest story, exclaiming over each picture. This usually resulted in Rose demanding a real flower of the same kind the next day. Sometimes I could do it, sometimes not. Not all English flowers flourished in Virginia and certainly not year-round. If I couldn't oblige, we usually drew one with crayons, which sometimes looked vaguely like the original, but often she did not even use the right color. But if Rose wanted to get creative, why not? Forcing a child to color within the lines and norms could only stifle her artistic soul. I liked the idea of my daughter having an artistic soul. Hunter had no feel for aesthetics. I'd thought I did in the writing arena but found out otherwise. I'd done all right in college with my short stories, though. Maybe the challenge of writing a novel had paralyzed me, and I should stick with the short form. I'd try again when I found a spare moment.

Rose got her usual kiss good night from Joe and Helen before happily trotting off to her room, the new book held firmly under her arm. She would go through the pictures with the help of her night-light, murmuring to herself until she fell asleep. I'd rescue the book later.

When I went back upstairs, everyone was sitting in the living room, some drinking coffee, and others, like Auntie, herbal tea. I went to the kitchen and got a glass of water before joining the others.

"Well, I have an early start tomorrow," said Joe. "Thank you so much, Lin and Hunter."

"Thank you," said Hunter. "Rose was thrilled with the book."

"Oh, she's a delight. I love to make her happy."

"How did you know about these books, Joe?" I asked. His knowing about English fairy tales seemed odd.

"My grandmother was English, and she read them to my mother. She read them to my sister and me, too. My sister reads them to her daughter. The books are old now, but the children love them. I pretended to disdain them when it occurred the me that they were girly. But when I first saw Rose, I knew I had to get them for her." He blushed a little.

"I'm enjoying them too," said Helen. "I hope we'll be able to read them to..." She broke off, embarrassed.

"You are so good to her," I said. "She really loves you both."

After hugs all around, they left, and we all sat down again. Hunter was frowning.

It was Auntie who broke the silence. "A burglar the size of a child?"

"Quite," said Lin.

"Aren't you going to tell him?" asked Auntie.

"It's awkward," said Hunter.

"I don't see why. It's not your fault."

"It's complicated," Lin and Hunter said in unison.

We didn't even watch TV but went to bed soon after. How could I not have cottoned on at once? It was so obvious. A burglar who only wanted yellow gold, a burglar the size of a child. I could see the complication. He'd start blabbing if they caught him. Lin and Hunter would probably stay up all night concocting a good back story.

Lin came downstairs right after breakfast the next morning.

"What's the story?" I asked.

"Nick is not actually a relative, but the son of the cook of an old friend in London. Both friend and cook passed away a few years ago. We have a name, and Agna will supply the paperwork. He has always been troubled and lives in a world of fantasy. He thinks he is short because he is a gnome who can make magical things out of gold. That's why he thinks he has to acquire it. He has some very strange ideas about us too. We put him up in a motel because we didn't want him in the house and didn't quite know what to do with him. We will suggest that Joe search his room."

"That sounds plausible," I said.

Lin added, "I doubt he has a visa. They'll send him back, I hope. We're going to see Joe now."

Things didn't go as planned. To Joe's fury, the driver of one of the police cars converging on the motel turned on his sirens. Nick, ever fleet of foot, escaped through a back window, hot-wired a yellow car in the back lot, and drove sedately away. The car was found abandoned in Falls Church near the hospital. Another stolen car report soon came in, so they knew they were looking for a white Toyota Corolla; how many thousands of those were out there?

Joe had recovered most of the missing jewelry, although Nick must have grabbed a handful before he escaped.

Lunch was fun again, full of happy chat. We all wondered when the nasty gnome would pop up again but enjoyed our reprieve. Rose's birthday would soon be here, and we looked forward to celebrating at the Bay house. I'd been buying little gifts, a few at a time, and hiding them in the pantry.

Joe and Helen couldn't join us, and neither could Reema, Lettie, Margareta, or Sven. Dr. Ayre wanted to come. She loved the place, saying the sound of the sea brought her peace. Auntie Peggy came too. Lin hid the little gifts in a cooler and off we went. I'd bought her a couple of jigsaw puzzles as she was becoming very proficient putting them together. It was uncanny how she seemed to spot just the right pieces.

We unloaded everything while Hunter took Rose down to the beach since she just couldn't wait. He'd retrieved her bucket and spade from the shed first. There was a warm breeze coming off the water, and I reveled in the fresh feel of it. I noticed the ospreys were still in residence.

Dora was busy making sandwiches for lunch and organizing the groceries. I went down to the beach to tell Hunter and Rose to come back up, knowing the protest that would bring about.

"Lunchtime," I called.

"No, Mama, it is not."

"Oh, yes it is," said her father, sweeping her upside down in his arms as she giggled and shrieked. Before she knew it, she was on his shoulders and nearly back at the sliding glass doors.

When we got in, no one was sitting at the table, but standing around as if a death had been announced. What now? Dora was red-faced and teary, and Lin was pale with fury. Dr. Ayre, who had just arrived, looked her usual unflappable self.

"What's up?" I asked.

Lin answered. "Dora went to her room and found her bed has been slept in and the window was open. Someone has been using the house."

"What about the kitchen?" I asked.

"She opened all the cupboards and found an unwashed frying pan in one, and the dishwasher full of dirty dishes."

"Why didn't the security system didn't go off?" I asked.

"I have no idea. It was armed when we walked in," Lin said.

She turned to Hunter, who hadn't yet said a word. "We use the same security code here as we do in Salton," he said. "Nisse must have seen us set the alarm at some point."

"I don't know when," said Lin. "He came unannounced. There was always someone at home when we drove him back to the motel."

"No," I said. "Remember that time I took Rose to the doctor after lunch, and Hunter had a meeting with his accountant? Dora had the afternoon off to meet her boyfriend. He must have memorized it when we all left. I remember how he hung back, and you shooed him out before the alarm went off."

"I'll call Joe," said Lin.

Hunter said, "How did he know where our house was?"

I replied, "Well, Rose mentioned the house, but I didn't say it was in Maryland. He probably spent hours in the public library doing property searches on all the Maryland and Virginia counties on the Bay until he found your name."

"What a scoundrel," said Auntie Peggy. "A nasty piece of work if ever I saw one." She went to the kitchen to help Dora and offer sympathy.

Joe was with us in a couple of hours, having notified the local police of the possible presence of a wanted criminal. An investigator dusted the house for prints, leaving a sooty mess that irritated Dora no end. She whipped off her bedclothes to wash them as soon as the tech cleared it.

"Contaminated!" she hissed.

17

"That damn gnome is a menace. We'll have to do something about him,"

Lin had come stomping into my room after lunch. Clearly, she'd been stewing for a while. Even being by the Bay hadn't soothed her like it usually did.

"Hunter just told me another story about Nisse. Even worse."

Tape 8, ## Volume 3

Hunter told me about what Nisse did before the final straw when he stole Odin's gold. He was a disreputable character from the start. I dimly remember hearing something about a renegade gnome but don't remember the details.

Gnomes at our time mostly lived in households, usually in one of the barns. They mostly helped, unseen, with difficult lambings or blighted crops. Sometimes, the younger ones played pranks on someone in the house but never did anything harmful.

Nisse was the exception. He was given to playing mean tricks on his household, like putting salt in the flour or cracking eggs so they spoiled. He bored holes in the roof once, which caused havoc with the family home. Their newborn almost died of cold. When the chief gnome heard of this, he complained to Odin, who banished Nisse to live with the dwarves. Not that they wanted him, but Odin gave them no choice.

Nisse learned quickly, for he is a highly intelligent individual. He loved to work with gold, although it took a dwarf to instill magic into the piece. This angered him, so he often sneaked out of the mountain caves to find a wise one to solve his problem. One day, a rat sprang onto his shoulder just as he emerged into the moonlight. Nisse was startled and tried to brush it off, but it clung on and whispered into his ear that he knew where the wisest of the wise ones lived.

"What will you give me?" asked the rat.

"It depends if the wise woman tells me the secret I want to know."

"If she tells you what you want to know, you will become rich," said the rat. "What will you give me then?"

"How do you know what I want from the wise woman?"

"You have been asking everyone and everything you pass if they know of a wise one. You even asked the rock under which I have my den. Of course you want to know what will make you rich. You are no different from men in that regard."

"I will give you a bag of gold that will buy you enough food for the rest of your life."

"I want a crown that will make me king of the rats."

"All right, I will make you one."

"She lives in a mountain behind the one in which you live with the dwarves, halfway up in a long cave that penetrates almost to the other side."

Nisse immediately started to walk to the next mountain. It took him two days and a night to get to its base, which presented a sheer, slippery slope that rose as far as he could see. He had no hope of surmounting that side of the mountain so set off to explore a spot that would be easier to climb. When the sun began to rise above the peak, its beams reflected off the jagged edges of an area not far from where Nisse had slumped in exhaustion. He had eaten nothing but berries plucked from bushes along the path and drunk only a few sips from little pools that seemed to be fed from a trickle between the rocks. He jumped up and soon found purchase in the ragged terrain. When he came to a flat surface that seemed to ring the mountain like a collar, he walked carefully, glad of the light the sun provided, for the drop to the base was terrifying.

After many hours, he came to a stone that blocked half his path. He peered over the top and could just see the entrance to a cave. His heart thumped with excitement. But he had to get around the stone, which called for the kind of courage he was short of. He sat with his back against the mountain, furious about being prevented from realizing his dream. Greed won the day.

He hugged the stone as he slunk around it, finding little pits in the surface that allowed him a shaky grip. He thought his breath might run out, and his heart might stop before he got all the way around.

He finally planted his left foot onto the solid surface in front of the cave, needing only to hitch his other leg round beside the first. His feet were too far apart. He might stumble and fall all the way down to a base of sharp rocks. There would be no chance of survival, only an agonizing demise. He stopped and took some deep breaths. He was stuck now. Flattened against a stone nearly as tall as him, danger in each direction. His hands were getting tired. He took a deep breath and swiveled his foot—toe in, toe out—until it reached the first. He was still perilously close to the edge. He flung his left arm around the side of the rock and walked his right hand along to join it. He threw himself into the cave entrance. He tottered from side to side, back and forth, only regaining his balance by a supreme effort of will. He walked a little way into the cave before sinking to the ground, which he found was covered in warm moss. He placed his head on his hands and fell asleep.

By the time Nisse awoke, the sun was sinking. His spirit sank with it. The cave would be cast into impenetrable gloom. And, he realized, if he found the wise woman, he would still have to make the same perilous journey back. He stretched and stood, peering into the cave. Was that a light? He walked toward it. The light brightened as he went. He didn't know how long he walked, only that his eyes started to ache from the strange glow, sometimes orange and sometimes purest white. At last, he could bear it no longer, sat against a damp wall, and rested his aching eyes, covering them with his palms.

The sound of scampering feet roused him. He opened his eyes and slowly adjusted to the gloom, slightly lifted by a mercifully soft glow. He jumped up. The scampering feet were those of rats, hundreds of them. Some white, some black, and some brindle. They all suddenly stopped their frenetic zooming and sat in orderly rows against the opposite wall, staring at him with radiant orange eyes. He stared back, not knowing what else to do.

A voice behind him asked, "What do you want here?"

He pivoted to see a very old woman sitting on a white rock, her head resting on her hands, which, in turn, rested on the head of her cane. She was entirely blanketed in layers of green gossamer. A light seemed to shine from within because he could see her sagging breasts that looked as if they had suckled an army of children.

"You look at my breasts. Yes, I have borne many children. You see them behind you."

She laughed when she saw his look of horror when he turned and saw there were still only rats behind him.

"Now, what brings you here? How did you know where to find me?"

Nisse, nervous and appalled, cleared his throat. "I have been asking people, trees, stones, birds, animals, if anyone knew where to find a wise one. I am in need of good counsel. A rat jumped onto my shoulder and whispered your secret abode."

The old woman grunted. "Kark, a wayward boy. He strays too far from us and commits all kind of mischief. What do you want that you brave this mountain?"

"Odin sent me to live with the dwarves in their mountain lairs. I have learned their trade very well, but I cannot infuse my work with magic properties like they can. Can you help?"

"I suppose you think it will make you rich. You are greedy, like men."

"I just want to be able to make something remarkable," Nisse replied.

"Liar. I will grant you your wish. But you will be immortal thereafter."

Nisse was beside himself with joy. "Thank you, dear lady. Thank you."

"Do not imagine that immortality is easy. You are a wayward character. You will often be poor, the gold you need out of reach. You will spend time held against your will. You may find riches for a while, but you will not keep them. You will wander the world forever." She held out her arm, palm flat toward him. "Go now. One of my children will show you an easier way down the mountain."

The cave turned black as basalt, and Nisse shuddered as a little body crept up his tunic and jumped onto his shoulder. "Walk straight ahead," it said in a squeaky whisper. The atmosphere got lighter so that the way ahead became clear enough to walk without bumping into walls and stray rocks. On they went, turning sometimes to the left, at others to the right, and always slanting downward. Nisse was almost at the end of his endurance when they came to a rockfall.

"What do we do now?" he asked.

"You climb over it, where you will find the way out. I will leave you now." The rat took a flying leap off Nisse's shoulder and scampered away, the sound of its claws on the stony path quickly fading away.

Nisse started to climb, his hands and knees getting scraped and cut by the sharp edges of these rocks that seemed wrought from a different material from the rest of the mountain, almost as if forged for cutting. When Nisse got to the top, his eyes streaming and his nose dripping, he couldn't stand the idea of the painful climb down. The cave entrance was right ahead, the sun had risen again, and the path looked smooth.

Nisse jumped, tumbling over several times, his joints horribly abused. He had rolled out of the cave into the sunshine. He lay quite still, weeping with pain once more, as he moved his various limbs gently, trying to assess the damage. His right ankle hurt badly, his shoulder too. His hands were cut but not otherwise damaged, and they were the most important concern. He got up and limped a little farther to see how far down he still had to climb. To his relief, the mountain rose behind him, and he stood in the valley. The rat had brought him all the way down. Now he had to find his own mountain. He limped along the rocky base, squealing every time a stone caused his ankle to roll. A stand of trees stood not far away. Perhaps he could find a stout stick to steady himself with.

The wood lay closer than he'd thought. He entered the cool shade gratefully as the day had become hot. After all the time he spent in the mountain, he wasn't used to hot weather anymore. A long stick, its top a wedge shape, leaned against a tree as though it waited for him. He grabbed it, finding that it fit under his arm and helped relieve the weight on his damaged ankle, although it made his shoulder ache. He turned to go back toward the mountain. He couldn't move his feet.

He tried many times to lift his feet, ending on the ground with a bump that knocked the breath out of him. He turned back to face the dark interior of the wood. He found himself able to move again. He was frightened now. He was stuck in an enchanted wood with no chance of finding his mountain again. No working the gold that would make him rich with the magical properties he would infuse into his creations. Nothing but leaves and soil. Cool and damp. Well, cool and damp he had in plenty in the mountain. But no gold. That was unthinkable.

"You need to rest," a childish voice called from above.

He looked up and saw a little girl all dressed in green sitting on a high tree branch.

"Who are you? Be careful. You're too high up. You might fall and hurt yourself."

"Oh, silly, we all climb trees. Sometimes we sleep up here too."

"Oh. Well, who are you?"

"You are in Alfheim now. We are elves. You are not allowed to leave until our big father says so."

"Why?"

"Because you need to get better. And no one who is not an elf leaves Alfheim on their own. And once they leave, they will never find their way back. Who are you, anyway?" She started to swing so fast on her branch that Nisse felt dizzy.

"I am Nisse, a gnome. I live in the next mountain with the dwarves. I was visiting a wise woman in the mountain behind me and hurt myself getting out."

"You must have been very naughty to be made to live with dwarves. What did you do?"

"Enough of your questions, girl."

A man almost as tall as Nisse—which wasn't saying much— had materialized in front of him. He was quite old as his hair was white in places and dark gray in others. His wrinkled skin had a greenish tinge, accentuated by a green cloak and hat.

"I am Saldo, chief of this small community. We welcome you. You will remain with us until you have healed. Then we will take you to your home."

"Thank you." Nisse was relieved to get help, although not happy about the delay in getting to work. Maybe they'd even give him food. If elves ate, that is.

Saldo led Nisse to a little stone house with a bright yellow door. The building seemed to lean against a tree.

"You don't build your houses of wood, then?" Nisse asked.

A sudden wind roared through the canopy, causing a flurry of leaves to fall around them.

"Heavens no, the trees are our friends. Come inside."

Nisse had to duck his head to pass through the door. The furniture was small but not too bad, given he only topped Saldo by a head.

"My wife has prepared a meal for you. After you have eaten and drunk your fill, she will treat your injuries, and you will sleep."

"You are most kind." Nisse could see he had no option. Besides, he was hungry, thirsty, tired and in pain, so why not take advantage of the situation?

Suddenly, a plump woman with curly white hair appeared in front of him and placed a steaming stew of roots and fruits on the table.

"I am Brit. You need a good meal. Eat. Saldo will pour wine shortly."

Nisse thanked her and ate like a starving wolf. Saldo did not partake. At last he sat back, fully satisfied.

"Allow me to pour you some wine. It always makes one feel better."

The wine, fragrant and floral, soon made Nisse irresistibly sleepy. He felt his eyelids droop, and through blurry eyes, he saw the two old elves looking down at him, grinning as if they had won a game. He knew no more until he woke next morning in a comfortable bed. His shoulder didn't hurt any more. His hands, covered with grease of some sort, didn't either. He moved his ankle. A twinge but not too bad. It felt as if it had been bandaged. He sat up and swung his feet to the ground.

He looked around the small room with its rough white-washed walls and furniture that seemed to be woven out of twigs and thick grasses.

"Ah, awake, I see. I will get you some breakfast." Nisse jumped. Brit. He hadn't noticed her in the corner. "Your clothes are clean and on top of that chest."

Nisse looked down at himself in horror. He was naked, save a white bandage on his right ankle. Feeling his cheeks flame, he looked up at her. She'd left. He walked over to the chest and got dressed as fast as he could. He never knew when and where these people might show up. He noticed he walked quite well with only a mild ache in his ankle. He'd be home soon.

He left the bedroom and found himself in a maze of corridors. The house hadn't looked that big on the outside. He heard voices and worked his way toward them. Three little elves sat around the table eating their breakfast. Their mother—grandmother?—stood over them, helping the littlest with her spoon, and admonishing the others to mind their manners.

"Good morning, Brit," he said.

"Ah, good morning, good morning. Your breakfast is in front of the chair at the end."

Nisse thanked her and sat. It looked a little strange, but Nisse picked up a spoon and discovered a sort of grain soaked in hot milk. It filled him fast. A mug of juice stood to the right of his plate. It tasted like apples or pears—he couldn't decide which.

What was he going to do all day?

"You will stay one more night," Brit said. "By tomorrow morning, your ankle will be healed well enough to return to your people."

"Thank you. That's wonderful news. Not that I haven't enjoyed my stay here, but I need to get back to work."

"Saldo and the children will take you on a picnic a little later, and you will see something of our neighborhood. Most elves do not live so close to the mountains, but we like it well enough. Our queen doesn't like us being here, but Saldo is her uncle, so she leaves us alone."

"How interesting. Where is Saldo?"

"He had some business to take care of. He will be home soon."

Nisse wondered what sort of business elves could possibly have. "I think I'll take a little walk, if that's all right."

"Yes, please do. But don't go deep in the forest where the trees stand very close and dark. It isn't safe for strangers."

"When I was at the foot of the mountain, I only noticed a small wood. You say there's a forest?"

"Yes. In Alfheim, things are rarely as they seem."

Nisse suddenly realized that all the children had disappeared. They hadn't exchanged a word. "Where are the children?"

"They'll be playing in the trees somewhere," Brit said.

"Even the little one?"

"Oh, he'll just climb the low branches. You can't start them too soon."

Nisse ducked out of the door and looked around. Another cottage stood amongst a beautiful garden some distance away. He could smell the flowers from where he stood. He had to get over there and inhale those scents. Mindful of his ankle, he walked slowly, but it was as if the house was moving away from him. The farther he walked, the farther away the house seemed. Disappointed, he turned back to Saldo's home. Why hadn't he noticed the beautiful flower garden around the house he'd just left? Again, he could smell the alluring scents. He almost ran toward them, cupping his hands under a blood red bloom the size of a platter, and inhaled.

Next morning, he awoke in the familiar bedroom. He felt himself under the covers. Naked again. He pulled the coverlet under his chin and looked around. The room was empty. He spied his clothes hanging over the chair back and got dressed.

"Breakfast is ready," said Brit, right behind him.

"Thank you," he said, gulping. He was very hungry. There had been no picnic yesterday and no dinner. He remembered the way to the dining room, noting that his ankle didn't hurt anymore. There were no children there today, only an incredible array of dishes. Saldo sat in the large chair Nisse had occupied the day before. He waved Nisse over.

"Come and sit down," he said. "This is your farewell breakfast. You are well enough to go home now."

Nisse sat while Saldo filled his plate with a little of everything. Nisse wasn't sure what he was eating, but it was delicious, so he didn't really care.

"We have enjoyed having you," said Brit at his shoulder.

Nisse coughed on the fruit he'd swallowed the wrong way when she spoke. "You have been very good to me. Thank you. And my ankle feels strong."

"Drink your juice."

Nisse awoke at sunset, propped against the entrance to his own mountain. He rubbed his eyes. Had he dreamt it all? Alfheim, the cave, the wise woman, the rats?

He walked into the workroom to be met with angry recriminations.

"Where have you been?" they asked.

"I can't remember anything."

"Drinking the bane of men, no doubt. To bed without dinner for thirty days," pronounced the chief dwarf. "Now, get to work."

He did, and he was able to create a few small pieces with magical properties. He kept this from the dwarves, however, hiding those pieces in what he thought was a safe place, together with whatever other gold he could steal.

Lin stretched and sat up.

"How did you know all these details? Surely he didn't tell anyone so much."

"The chief dwarf took him before Odin and his sons. When Odin gazes into your eyes, you have to tell everything. Hunter was there too. He has a good memory."

Will Hunter remember me when Rose and I are long gone?

18

Vixen snuffled the air. A new scent hung above the usual scents of the Chesapeake Bay—seaweed, gull guano, and pine—and a dangerous one that caused her to flatten in her hollow. She'd noticed a flash of gray fur weaving through the woods toward the swamp a moon ago. Too dark and too big for her mate. There it was again, a whiff from a different spot—the sign of a dangerous, stealthy creature best to be avoided. Her woodland den was too far away to risk dashing for it. The burrows under the human place, dug by ground hogs, was near enough if she moved slowly. It was not quite dark. She must not let the humans see her. They were dangerous.

"Kill the people."

She sprang up and looked behind her. Where did those people sounds come from? She didn't understand the words, but she understood the urge they conveyed because that was how she ate. She killed the ground hogs to take over their den and make it a home for her and her kits. *Kill people?* Too big, too tough.

Vixen suddenly realized she had exposed herself. She stretched low again. The scent wafted her way once more.

Closer now. She padded as fast and as low as she could before reaching the edge of the woods closest to the humans. She lay down again, her snout pointing toward a small human who gathered strange colored things that filled her arms.

"Kill her."

That voice again. The human was quite small. If she went for the throat first... A very, very big human, probably a male, came out of the house, took some of the things from the small one, and they disappeared back inside.

She did not understand where this voice came from. It had started immediately after she ate that cooked bird the humans left on the beach. There must have been something bad in it. She had felt restless, not normal, full of wanting to do something but not knowing what. Even her eyes felt wrong. The voice kept telling her to kill. It sounded loud, but the humans had shown no signs of hearing it.

The light was gray enough now that she risked streaking under the human place. She was hungry. She should have kept one of her kits close. Their meat was young and tasty. She did not know where they were now. Maybe that creature with gray fur ate them. She would look out of the burrow at dawn. That's when the rabbits usually started to nibble the grass and some of the plants growing in hard round things near the burrow. That was always a good time to catch them.

She slunk deep into the burrow, curled up, and slept.

At dawn, she crept to the opening closest to the growing things the rabbits found so tasty. Sure enough, there was a nice fat one with its paws on the side of the hard thing, enjoying a feast. She eased herself into the open and pounced. She killed it with a tear to the throat so quickly that it didn't utter a sound. She needed to drag it into the burrow at once so as to not draw attention to herself. But some madness came upon her. She tore out the throat, tore at the abdomen, and ravaged what was there. She could not stop pulling and tearing, chomping and swallowing. Exhausted, finally, she left the meager, bloody remains and went back underground to lick the blood of her paws and face. She must not allow the scent to attract flies and other animals. She slept until the sun was sinking below the horizon.

She had felt the urge to explore, to see the other world—the world beyond the wood. Soon after the cooked bird feast, she made her way through parts of the wood she had never before explored. Why would she venture beyond home and food? But she felt she had to. She traveled for two moons before sinking to her stomach in the clear space in front of the trees from which she'd emerged. Human plants and living spaces, some atop a hill, and some along a wide path where humans ran huge noisy things when they wanted to get somewhere fast. She'd soon gone back into the undergrowth. One day, she found a brown crackly thing with some tasty food inside. The kits fought over it because there was meat but with stuff on it the color of some of the flowers people kept around them too. They loved it. One of the kits wanted more, so she chased her brother into wide path, and he got run over by a huge, frightening monster. The little one knew that was not right, but these rules are easily forgotten by a hungry kit. She dragged her back to the trees to feed the others. But the meat tasted funny. No, she did not like the big people paths. This new side of the woods was no better than the other. Best to go back to what she knew.

For many moons, the voice remained silent. She hunted and slept, sometimes under the human place, and sometimes in her den in the woods. She smelt the gray creature often now and made sure to keep well away.

One morning, she waited for the humans to leave while crouching behind a brush pile. She wanted to take a nap in her safe place.

"Kill the little one."

That voice had been quiet for a few days.

"Kill, kill, kill!"

Vixen's eyes were afire, her mind no longer her own. She shrieked as she bolted in for the kill.

19

Lin called the security company to find out how to change the security alarm code at both houses. They reset the Salton alarm remotely and instructed her how to change the Bay house code and the Salton code when we got back. And not to use the same code for both. The Maryland detective liaising with Joe had sent away all but a couple of cops. They'd seen no sight of Nick. The woods behind us were thick, and a swamp occupied a good portion of the middle area before the trees opened up to a major highway. Apparently, there were no K-9 officers available in the area.

Dr. Ayre and Auntie watched a children's movie with Rose, seeming to enjoy it as much as the child. After Hunter took Sam out for a quick walk around the house, we locked up tight. I bathed Rose and put her to bed before settling down to a more adult movie.

The next day was Rose's birthday. Lin planned to creep out early to hide little gifts I'd bought, almost like Christmas stocking fillers. It would be like hunting for Easter eggs. Sam would only be allowed out on a leash until Rose had found all of them as some were candy. We wouldn't tell her what day it was until after breakfast; otherwise, she'd get too excited to eat or settle.

We all ate a big breakfast of eggs, sausages, bacon, toast, then pancakes with maple syrup. Dora had the sense to bring the pancakes out a little later after Rose had eaten a boiled egg with toast soldiers and a few strips of bacon. She loved pancakes and managed a couple. I don't know where she put it all, although she was growing fast. She didn't have as many clothes as she used to because she grew out of them in a couple of months. Shoes were a nightmare.

Finally, we broke the glad tidings, and Dora presented Rose with a little quilted bag to put her little things in. Dora almost purred at the hug and kiss she got in return. Lin would wait until after lunch to give Rose her big present. We all trooped out to watch the fun.

My blonde angel skipped around the lawn with Hunter close behind, both whooping every time she found a little packet. They counted each time and reached nine. The last one was near the shed, opposite the back wall of the house, where pots of newly planted herbs provided fragrant summer dishes. Were there herbs in the Salton garden? There must have been, given Dora's flavorful cooking. I hadn't noticed, but then I'd never looked.

Rose peered at a gap under the shed, reaching into it with her hand until Hunter pulled her back. "Sweetheart, you never know what is under there. Do not ever put your hand where you cannot see everything."

She backed up and looked around the herb pots. "I got it!" She pulled the tenth from its spot where it nestled under a group of thriving basil plants. "We go back and put them in Dora's bag now." We all clapped and cheered.

As she turned to round the corner toward the front door, a streak of red fur burst out from under the shed. It growled as it tore toward me, its eyes flashing yellow. I knew I couldn't outrun it, so I froze, hoping Lin or Hunter would save me from a mauling. As it was almost on me, it careened around, clearly making for Rose. Hunter grabbed the creature by the tail and flung it far into the woods.

A bellow reminded me that at least one policeman was still searching the area. He came tearing out into the back yard. "What in hell was that?" he shouted. Another cop appeared on the scene.

"I am sorry, officer," said Hunter, trying valiantly not to look amused. "A fox attacked the little girl here. I caught it and threw it into to woods."

"You couldn't have thrown it that far," the sweaty cop spluttered.

"Perhaps it fell and got up again," Hunter said, nervous now he'd given himself away.

"No, that goddamn thing hit me on the head."

Hunter shrugged. "I simply cannot explain it. I am so sorry you got such a shock."

The cop scowled. "I suppose I'll have to go back and find my cap."

My heart was pounding so hard that I seriously thought it might stop. That fox meant business. Rose began to wail, so Hunter picked her up and sang one of his soulful songs to her as he bore her inside. We all followed, a lovely morning ruined by a near catastrophe.

Lin dried Rose's tears and helped her put her gifts in the special bag while Hunter knelt, holding the child's hand. I sat down, trying to calm myself. Dora went to make coffee. I consoled myself with the thought that the fox was unlikely to have survived being hurled so hard and so far. Dr. Ayre sat down beside me.

"Are you all right, Mary? You look pale."

"I'm fine. That fox shook me up. It would have been terrible if it got Rose," I whispered. "And another thing: its eyes flashed yellow. Maybe that's normal for a fox. But I couldn't help wondering…"

"I saw it too, and so did Lin," she replied. "I went up to my room and fetched a little something I've been working on." She partially withdrew a syringe from her jacket pocket before sliding it back. "I don't believe Loki can survive this."

"I wondered about that eagle disappearing overnight."

"Quite."

Dr. Ayre having that potion made me feel better until I starting working through possible scenarios. Using a syringe would mean having to get really close.

Rose tugged on Hunter's shirt, her cheeks bulging with chocolate. "Beach, Papa. Let's go."

I was astounded that she was ready to go outside again after what she'd seen. She pulled him outside, retrieving her bucket and spade from the patio before they headed down. Rose had to trot to keep up with Hunter's long strides.

Lin played a Chopin CD intended for relaxation. I lay back and closed my eyes. Some of the pieces made me sad because I found their tone nostalgic. I went to the bathroom so I could cry in private. I wept for my parents, for old friends, and for the closeness my sister and I enjoyed when we were small in spite of the four-year difference in our ages. I wept for the tragedy that could have befallen my baby girl. I suppose it was shock because I felt so silly later. I wiped my eyes and washed my face in cold water before returning to the sofa. My eyes stayed puffy for hours, so everyone must have noticed; no one mentioned it.

Dora announced that lunch was ready. Lin went to the beach to tell Hunter. Joe rapped on the door.

"We haven't found him yet. My boss told me to head back," he said.

Dora popped her head out of the kitchen. She soon returned with an extra place setting. "Sit," she told him. She soon returned to set out a light pasta primavera and salad—which I knew Hunter would disdain—before coming back with a bloody steak and some boiled potatoes. Rose sat on a couple of pillows next to Hunter and kept after him for slivers of steak. I couldn't watch her eating that disgusting stuff that left blood on her lips, but she loved it. She ate a couple of his potatoes too. He laughed when he saw my look of disgust.

"It will make her strong," he said.

"Ugh" was my rejoinder.

"Ugh! Ugh! I love steak," Rose chanted. "Ugh!"

We all laughed. I was so relieved she hadn't been traumatized by the morning's events.

We were about to start on our pecan pie when a stream of very British curses reached our ears. Joe rushed outside, his weapon drawn, closely followed by Hunter, Lin, and Dr. Ayre.

It had suddenly gone quiet, so I told Auntie Peggy and Dora to keep Rose inside. Just as well. A grisly scene confronted me. The fox was still tearing at Nick's arm as Joe tried to get a clear shot while trying to avoid shooting the gnome, who lay on his face. The fox stopped briefly and spotted Lin. It roared like a banshee before rushing at her. Joe's shot felled it.

Dr. Ayre darted forward and sank her syringe into the animal. It writhed, growled, screeched something I couldn't make out, and spat. She stepped back as a cloud formed around it. Lin, Hunter, and Dr. Ayre gazed into the mist as if enraptured. Lin told me later that the spirits of their godly kin appeared, floating in a ghostly dance before wafting away. This way they knew Loki had been vanquished before he could enter another form.

Joe's and my eyes were fixed on the fox. It shriveled fast until a fine dust was all that remained of Loki.

"What did you do?" he asked Dr. Ayre, his voice hoarse.

"Oh, just a little something to prevent rabies from spreading," she said.

"Oh, yes?" He went over to Nick and turned him over, gagging when he saw that the gnome's throat had been ripped out. I ran over to the edge of the woods and threw up. I didn't want anyone to see me do that. Hunter patted my back. I tottered back to the group.

"How do you expect me to explain this?" Joe asked.

"A coyote, of course," said Lin. "The neighbor mentioned he'd seen one around."

"Really? I always knew you two were different. And now the good doctor. You're going to have to explain yourselves."

"I suppose we are," said Lin.

"But we trust you to keep our secret," said Hunter. "You know how people are."

"We shall see," said Joe.

The three gods exchanged a long glance. It worried me. They would protect themselves, no matter what.

Joe called for an ambulance and a superior officer, reporting that the suspect was dead due to a coyote attack. He waited for them outside.

We went back in. The anxious faces of Dora and Auntie Peggy turned to face us.

"Loki is finished," said Lin. "Really finished. And so is Nick."

"I'm so glad," said Auntie Peggy. "But who is Loki?"

"A long story for another day," I said.

"Thank the gods," said Dora.

"Good," said Rose. "Loki is bad, and Nick is bad."

I was shocked by Rose's reaction, until I realized that Lin had said "finished," not "dead." Rose wouldn't know what that meant.

"What's that?" Rose asked when the siren wailed and stopped outside.

"Nothing," I said.

"Let's watch a movie," said Auntie Peggy.

"Yes, let's," Rose piped as she rushed to the DVD shelf to pick one out.

That afternoon, Lin and Hunter took Joe upstairs to the study where they stayed for a couple of hours or more. When they returned, Joe looked shell-shocked. We all stared at him apprehensively. Would he feel duty-bound to tell?

"Your secret is safe with me," he said. "I've known for a long time that there was something unusual about your household. But now I understand. And you are my friends."

He drank a cup of coffee before leaving. I noticed he left a pretty package on the table.

"Am I getting any big presents?" Rose asked, her voice plaintive.

We had forgotten. She opened them and spent a few happy hours before dinner playing with new toys. We had the cake after dinner. At bedtime, she had a hard time deciding which new book Hunter should read from.

Next day we returned to Salton and the good doctor to Washington. I was still shaken by the fox incident but also relieved that we could go to the Bay in the future without having to worry about Loki. When Hunter killed and burned the eagle Loki had turned into last year, we'd thought that was it. I'd wondered though, because the eagle had disappeared by the next morning. I guess that fox ate it and became Loki's tool.

We all helped unload the cars. I realized that Rose had not received the gift from Hunter and Lin. I pointed it out to Lin without saying anything aloud.

"She can have it tomorrow," Lin whispered. "She'll be excited to have something extra."

We all went to bed early. I, for one, was exhausted.

Breakfast next morning featured a huge stack of pancakes with strawberries and blueberries. Dora made thinner pancakes thant those I'd had before. Lin told me they were more like French crepes. She sprinkled hers with fresh lemon juice and sugar. Rose tried a bit and pursed her lips when the lemon hit her tongue but got used to it. She ate the fruit later when she'd finished with pancakes. I tried it but wasn't keen. At least pancakes took her mind off steak, which Hunter wolfed down on his own.

Hunter took Rose to his study and Lin disappeared. I went downstairs, not sure if Lin wanted to record or not. I'd been reading down there for about an hour before she came down.

"Shall I turn on the recorder?"

"No, I have something to tell you."

I couldn't quite make out her expression: serious but full of pent-up excitement.

"Yggdrasil has leafed out."

"What does that mean?" I asked. I knew it was momentous and didn't know whether to feel happy or scared.

"It means that our heaven may come back."

"But what does that mean, really?"

"We intend to find a big place, perhaps a farm near the Bay where we can replant the tree. Because it will grow taller than any monument. It's already grown a foot since we left. Things cannot be as they were, of course. But we will always be family. And if the place is big enough, we can stop moving around. And maybe our children can become immortal. And survivors will find safe haven."

"I don't know what to say. If you're happy, I'm happy for you."

"You will always be part of our family, no matter what, Mary. You can move between our world and yours as you wish."

Did I want to live in two worlds, or would one do? I wanted Rose to have a normal life, to have friends and a good education. But she couldn't be separated from her Thoren family. I needed the Thoren family, especially Hunter. And what about Auntie Peggy? She loved her new life. I wanted both the extraordinary and the ordinary. Could I keep them in separate compartments? Could Rose?

"You don't have to make any decisions right now," said Lin. "We haven't made any concrete plans. You can have this house if you like. Or the one at the Bay. We've discussed all that. Rose can go to a local public or private school. Maybe boarding school later. There is a small private school in the Bay area that you might have noticed on our drive. We can play it by ear. We won't keep both houses, but you can choose the house you prefer."

"You're both too kind. The Bay is my special place. I'd rather be there. And I'd be closer to you if you find a place nearby."

Lin looked pleased. "Just one more thing. Too many people know about us. No one can come to the new place who does not already know. We will keep a condo in Salton so that I can keep in touch with Lettie if she needs me, do shopping, and so on. You and Auntie can use it too, and the kids will like having a place there, near their old friends. A condo is easier to deal with than an empty house. That's why you need your own place so that Rose can have her friends over—and you too. You will make friends in the neighborhood."

"Yes, I'd like that. Yes, it's going to be fine. Auntie can live with me, and we will visit you often. Will we keep on with the memoir?"

"Yes, definitely. You haven't heard it all yet, not by a long shot. It might take a few years to complete the next volume though."

Momentous events were unfolding. Perhaps not just for me, I realized with a jolt. What would a renewed Norse heaven mean to the rest of the world? To their religions? How much unrest might this cause? I tossed and turned most of the night, only falling asleep when I told myself it might just bring peace to the world. Some people would have to believe in the new gods for them to exist once more, but it seemed to me that new cults were born every day. This one might be the answer to all that.

20

I t didn't take Lin and Hunter long to find a farm for sale on the Chesapeake Bay. It was only a fifteen minute drive from the house that would become mine. The new spread boasted just under ten acres. Plenty of room to ensure privacy.

The day after closing, they took Auntie Peggy, me, and Rose to see it. It had clearly been unoccupied for quite a while. We could hardly make our way up the path to the old farmhouse because it was so overgrown with brambles. Hunter carried Rose after she got a scratch on her leg.

To say the house loomed sounds melodramatic, but loom it did. It sported gables galore, a small terrace on the upper level facing the bay, and small, cloudy windows. It looked as if it could topple over any minute, it creaked so alarmingly in the stiff breeze.

"Beautiful, isn't it?" Lin asked.

"Well…"

"Well what?"

"It's rather decrepit. And dark."

"Nothing a good architect cannot make nice," Hunter said, buoyant with excitement.

He opened the front door with an enormous iron key. As expected, the hinges groaned like an elderly banshee. The afternoon sun penetrated the grimed windows enough to illuminate the millions of dust motes we'd disturbed. We peered through the doorways that opened from the huge hall into various rooms and made our way through a corridor to the end. Here, the corridor ended in a tee as it opened on one side to the kitchen—which still contained a wood-fired oven—and what was no doubt a dining room on the other side. I thought it odd that the other rooms wouldn't face the Bay. Then we went farther along the corridor outside the dining room to find a very large living room that contained one ragged sofa that had obviously been colonized by mice or rats, judging by the eruptions of its puffy innards, and the reek that streamed our way.

A door led from this room to a wide patio that circled the back and sides of the house. The magnificent view awed me. We could see the bridge that led from Solomon's Island over to St. Mary's County and the marinas beyond. Straight ahead lay the Patuxent River Naval Air Station. I'd read in the local paper that the Blue Angels sometimes performed over there on Independence Day. This would be the ideal place to watch from—for fireworks too.

Plants straggled up the steps and over the edge of the terrace. Ten acres to be cleared. And who knew what lay beneath. Thank goodness he hadn't brought Dora. She would have had one of her conniptions.

"Right," said Hunter. "We will first get a crew to clear the land. I will call the architect who designed our house on Drum Point and get some ideas. I like this house. It is big enough. There is a huge basement too. We will not go down there now. When I first viewed the house, I found some nests and things. I will also call the pest control service."

Oh, god, from bad to worse. Lin hadn't said anything beyond, "Hmm," and "Aha." I could see the wheels turning.

"There is enough space for privacy," she said. "After the house has been renovated, a big wall must be built around the property with a security gate. We can plant Yggdrasil near the water."

"Yggdrasil?" said Auntie, tremulously.

"The world tree," I whispered.

"How high will Yggdrasil get?" I asked.

"Much higher that the Empire State Building!" Hunter exclaimed, his arms spread above his head.

"Well, you're going to have an issue with the planes that fly out of the air station. It's going to pose a significant safety risk, and they will make you cut it down."

Lin wheeled on me. "I will kill anyone who tries to harm Yggdrasil," she grated. Auntie gasped, which brought Lin to her senses.

"I'm sorry," she said. "It has been so long... so very long." Her eyes welled.

"I have thought of that," Hunter said. "There is a way. Yggdrasil has its own properties. Nothing and no one can touch it that threatens its life. And when it is full grown, it will become like a ghost to the human eye above the tallest nearby tree. Its protective barrier will cause the planes to fly around it until it reaches our world."

"They will know there is something diverting the planes," said Auntie. "They will investigate."

"How big will the canopy get?" I asked.

Hunter slumped. "Very. Maybe an acre."

"Then there's a problem," Auntie said.

Rose broke the heavy silence. "Does Yggdrasil know how to curl up, like I curl up when I'm hiding?"

Hunter swept her into his arms. "My brilliant baby girl."

Lin had brightened too. "You know, I think we can warn it to shrink itself when necessary. When Ragnarok began, it curled up like an armadillo. It looked very strange, but it can happen. We can warn it."

"The *Gjallarhorn*," Lin said. "We have to find something that sounds like that."

"Go on the internet and look for an English Horn recording," Auntie said. "It's very different from the French Horn but see how it sounds."

"And there are different horns from all over the world used for calling in the cattle, and so on," I said.

We tramped back through the house. I wanted nothing more than a shower at that point. The stench of rodent nests still hung in my nostrils. I hoped we wouldn't catch anything.

We spent most of the time at the Bay now because Hunter needed to supervise the renovations. Lin went up to town from time to time, sometimes taking Auntie with her. Auntie missed her home and old friends, I realized.

"Auntie, are you all right living with me here?" I asked her one afternoon. "I think you miss your house."

"I do miss it, dear. I've lived there for so long. But now, when I spend the night, I miss being with my new family. Nothing is ever perfect. I'm thinking of selling the house and buying a small condo. I can put my favorite pieces of furniture in it. Then you'll have a place up there when you want it too."

I thought that was a perfect solution. I loved the idea of having a little place up there. I know Lin said they'd get a condo in Salton the family could use, but I wanted a place of our own.

"I think that's a marvelous idea," I said. "Do you have enough to buy the condo and move your stuff in before you put the house on the market?"

"Yes. I would rather do that. Real estate agents are always going on about decluttering, so that will solve that issue. Next time Lin goes up, I'll look around. I'll give my neighbor a call. She's an agent. I know I can trust her."

We got frequent renovation updates at the dinner table. It took a couple of weeks to clear the land. Then another week to clean and fumigate the house's main level. The basement would be a separate issue. Lots of snakes, Hunter told us with relish. A whole nest of them. I didn't know if I could ever be comfortable there if it had slithery things hiding out. How would they know if they'd all gone?

Carol Weiss, the architect who'd designed the other Bay house, came over several times, and we all pored over plans for hours on the dining room table. She suggested that extensions be added to each side of the house because Lin insisted on ten bedrooms and several more bathrooms. That was one bedroom each for the family, which accounted for seven, and three spares. One new wing would have the master bedroom and Hunter's study. The other a suite for Rose, me, and Auntie. There would be a small apartment over the garage for Dora and Stan. I thought it a little strange considering none of us would be living there full-time, but I guessed Lin was thinking of bringing family and friends together for holidays and other special occasions.

Hunter took me over there about six weeks after the first visit. November now, the weather was beginning to feel distinctly wintry, so we needed warm jackets against the breeze blowing off the Bay. I was pleasantly surprised once we got through the electronic gate.

"Does the wall go around the whole farm?" I asked him.

"Oh yes. And our beach is fenced on the sides too."

The land was clear of undergrowth, allowing the old trees to show their glorious forms—some elegant, others gnarled, albeit distinguished. The driveway from the road was still full of potholes, but Hunter said it wasn't worth fixing yet with heavy trucks going back and forth. It would have to be completely redone. The rooms were clean, and open windows ensured the scent of fresh air. The terrace had been power washed and shone under the afternoon sun, apparently needing little repair. The view truly was spectacular out there. The house seemed to stand straighter with its shiny new windows and fresh paint. Building the extensions was still in progress but not far from finished.

"Lin will have great fun furnishing the place," I said.

"Yes, as if I have not paid enough money for it all."

Hunter liked to grumble about money, but he did it in a half-hearted way that showed he didn't mind that much.

"Anyway, you will all choose your own furniture," he added.

"I have a feeling Auntie would like to have some of her own stuff here," I said.

"That can certainly be arranged."

"By the way, have your brought Yggdrasil here yet?"

"No, but we have to next week. It is getting very big. We have to put it far from the house because of the roots—that is partly why we need so much land. I had someone bring a backhoe to dig the hole. See over there?"

An orange plastic net surrounded a hole I couldn't quite see because it was some distance away.

A week later, Hunter went up to town to supervise uprooting and moving Yggdrasil. Lin would meet him at the castle (as we all now called it) to see it planted. They reported that all had gone to plan, and the tree looked happy. I knew how much the tree meant to them so was relieved. Auntie had read about Yggdrasil in various accounts on the internet. Still agog with excitement knowing that these were not, in fact, myths, she demanded to see it. Lin obliged. I joined them.

Yggdrasil's leaves waved gracefully against the blue sky. It was already taller than some of the old trees nearby. I noticed that some roots humped above ground before disappearing back into the soil. I shivered. What was going on down there?

"It's an ash tree," Auntie proclaimed. "Some of the stories said so, but now I can see it for myself. When the leaves fall, they create amazing compost. So beautiful."

"I don't think the leaves will fall," Lin said.

"Well, didn't they fall every year in your garden?"

"It never grew leaves again until Loki died."

"Well, maybe it will act differently in this climate. That will be interesting."

"Very," Lin said, pursing her lips.

"It's time to listen to some horns," I said.

"By the gods, yes," Lin said. "This tree is growing so fast. We have to find the right one and test it."

The next day, we sat in the living room while I scoured the internet for the sound of an English horn and several other ancient horns still available in Europe.

"The English horn will do best," Hunter said. "I will order one."

"You'll have to learn to play it," I said.

"How hard can it be?" he asked.

Frustratingly hard, as it turned out. He managed to achieve a wail or too, but that was about it.

"Papa, you must take some lessons," Rose told him.

Hunter sighed. "Yes, you are right."

Unsurprisingly, Hunter couldn't find any English horn teachers in southern Maryland. He finally ran one down in Takoma Park, Maryland and drove up there every day for two weeks. He complained the teacher wanted to make him do all kinds of silly things when all he wanted to do was make the call of approaching battle. Finally, the teacher gave in, and he managed the call. Then he quit.

By the time he'd finished his ordeal by horn, Yggdrasil had grown another ten feet. He decided to try the call right away, so we all gathered to watch. He took a deep breath and blew. The tree shook and quivered as its massive trunk curved until the top touched its roots. The leaves and branches folded in like an umbrella. The tree became very still. A few leaves fell with a whispery twirl.

"Now what?" Lin said. "How do you tell it it's safe?"

Hunter quivered a little. "I don't know. Do you remember the sound?"

"Hunter, there wasn't a call because the battle ended with nearly everyone dead, including Heimdall, blower of *Gjallarhorn*."

Everyone looked at each other in dread.

Rose marched up to the tree and walked around it, patting its branches, saying, "You're safe now, Yggdrasil. You can get up now." She kissed one of its fallen leaves and threw it into the circle of branches. She came to Hunter and clasped him around his leg.

Slowly, the tree uncurled itself, taking a lot longer to regain its former stance. Everyone followed its progress until it looked as if it almost touched the sky. Its green canopy swayed against a cerulean background with the grace of a gossamer veil.

I looked back at the house. The outside had been painted white and shone against its collar of green shrubbery. It was a welcoming sight, promising safe haven.

21

By the time it got close to Thanksgiving, the farm was still undergoing renovations, so the celebrations would take place in the Bay house—my house. The Thoren's Salton house had been sold, and they'd found a really spacious three-bedroom condo in the center of Salton. Auntie Peggy had found a two-bedroom condo not far away. It had taken a while to find a development that would accept dogs. Her home, sadly, had been bought by a builder, so would be torn down, like so many others in Salton then and now.

Dora's husband knew about the Thorens, as did Joe, although I didn't know if his wife Helen did or Lettie. Lin and Hunter were understandably nervous about too many people knowing who and what they were, but now that they would soon move to the farm, they'd have to let Lettie and Helen know, or they'd hardly see them—which would be especially awkward with Lettie. And Lettie had a boyfriend. The list grew longer.

Lin came into my room one morning the week before Thanksgiving.

"I'm going to make an announcement after Thanksgiving dinner," she said. "The people closest to us will have to know. It has to be done. It worries Hunter, but things could get sticky otherwise."

"I was thinking about that," I said. "Lettie, for one. But she has a boyfriend. How will he take it? And can he be trusted?"

"Poor Lettie, they just broke up. He turned out to be a racist. Apparently, they were eating at their favorite restaurant when he said something outrageous about a white woman having dinner with a black man. She reprimanded him, but he wouldn't see it."

"I'm sorry. She seemed so happy with him."

"Let's hope someone else comes along. Anyway, he would have been most unsuitable to share that kind of conversation with. But Lettie will have to be told. She may have suspected I'm somehow different because she's seen me in action when we worked together on several difficult cases."

"Dora's husband knows. Who else is there? You finally told Sven, I think."

"Yes, we did. There's Reem. She's pretty sure she can get away. I think she suspected I was different. Then there's Helen. I'll ask Joe if he told her. Toni will be with her father this year, very much against her will, poor child."

"Not too many new bombshells then. Reem is a pretty devout Muslim. I wonder if she will start questioning things."

"My guess is she'll put us on the level of djinns, a concept she is familiar with. In Islam, there are good djinns. Don't forget—she hasn't heard the stories you have."

"That's true. And Rose will be there. Do you think she will understand? You know how children talk."

"I hadn't thought of that. Perhaps Hunter and I will just invite them into the upstairs living room, apart from the others."

And that's what happened. Everyone was curious when Helen (Joe hadn't told her), Reem, and Lettie were asked to go upstairs after dinner. After they'd left, I told the others what was going on.

"Lin and Hunter want to share a little something about themselves."

I worded it that way so that Rose wouldn't pick up on it.

"Ah I see," said Dr. Ayre.

"They must have noticed how special Linny and Papa are," said Rose.

Everyone looked at her, their faces etched by surprise and concern.

"Yes, they are certainly special," I said. "That's why we love them so much."

The company mumbled their agreement.

When we heard footsteps descending, we all turned to see their reactions. Helen's eyes sought Joe's. He reached out a hand to her, drawing her close. She was pale and shocked. Reem looked troubled. She slid back into her seat, keeping her eyes on her plate.

Lettie looked bouncy. "Well, isn't this a turn up for the books!" she said. "I knew there was something special but never guessed the truth. Dang!"

The evening progressed uneventfully. Reem didn't say much, Helen chatted normally after a while, and Lettie was her usual ebullient self.

Later, Lin announced that, sadly, the family would be away for Christmas this year. Now it was my turn to look surprised. It was the first I'd heard of it.

The next morning, she came into my room. "We will have Christmas at a nice hotel in Copenhagen. Not too many presents since we are traveling. Just nice food, decorations, and *hygge*."

"What's *hygge*?" I asked.

"It's the Scandinavian word for cozy, although it means more than that. You'll see."

"Oh, I'm invited?"

"Of course you are! Do you think I would leave you for Christmas? And I already checked with Auntie. I told her we'd get a wheelchair so she doesn't have to walk along all those corridors at the airport. She's excited."

After a long trip to Copenhagen, via London, we arrived on December 22 in two taxis at our hotel close to Tivoli Gardens. Rose gasped when she saw the building's domes and crenellations outlined in small yellow lights that created a golden halo against the indigo sky.

"Fairyland!" she squealed.

"Yes, it does look magical," Auntie said. She looked excited but pale, which worried me. I'd get her to bed as soon as I could. We had eaten well on the flight, so there was no need to worry about a meal, even though it was almost dinner time.

When we entered the lobby, Rose immediately ran to the huge tree that proudly claimed the center of its pale marble floor. Hundreds of electric candles were clipped to its branches, and tastefully spaced decorations, all made from wood or other natural substances, finished the picture. Little wooden elves in red and green outfits stood around the base. I found it charming—a nice change from tinsel and bows.

We finally got all the room assignments sorted out. Auntie, Rose, and I would share a suite, which delighted me because I'd be able to keep an eye on Auntie. I mouthed "thanks" to Lin. She was always so thoughtful.

"All right, everyone," said Lin. "Our dinner reservations are at seven-thirty. Let's meet down here a few minutes before."

"Auntie, are you up to dinner? You can just rest, if you prefer. Lin won't mind."

"I am most certainly up to it. Wouldn't miss it for the world."

"Sit next to me, Auntie. I'll take care of you," Sven said, patting her arm.

"And I'll have the other side," said Rose. "We'll both help you."

"You make me sound like an invalid," Auntie protested, "but I'd love to sit with you both."

The traditional Christmas dinner would be on Christmas Eve, our waiter explained, which is when Danes celebrate. After dinner, the hotel would provide transportation to take us around Tivoli Gardens to see the spectacular light display. Tomorrow we'd be taken there again so that we could visit the Christmas market, look at the fabulous decorations, and attend a show in one of the theaters. They had children's rides too.

Hunter ordered wine before we all made the rounds of a sumptuous buffet: roast meats with tangy fruit sauces, fish, both smoked and cooked, mushrooms, potatoes with dill, and a few appetizers and soups, hot and cold.

"Oh, it's been years since I tasted this," Auntie exclaimed, spooning a generous portion of what looked like anchovies, chopped raw onions, and raw egg yolk onto her plate.

"You've been here before?" I asked. "You never said."

"In Denmark, of course, but not to this lovely place," she said airily as if I should have known.

Rose insisted on starting with a cold fruit soup. I wanted something hot. While the dining room was warm, the snow-blanketed terrace set the atmosphere.

We all ate a generous dinner, despite our meals on the plane. We even managed dessert, set out on a side table. We all chose chocolate mousse in individual crystal bowls, each topped with a little sugar mouse. To my alarm, everyone insisted on donating their mouse to Rose. I placed some in a tissue for the next day. I felt a little guilty when I ate my own.

They took us to Tivoli in vehicles like golf carts with bells that jingled as they moved. What a spectacle. Tall trees had been festooned with lights all the way up to their canopies and along their boughs. One massive tree cascaded fairy lights like a golden waterfall. Everything that could be lit had been. Stalls selling snacks and drinks were still open, and colorful wooden elves and Santas stood like sentries throughout. A little island in the lake sparkled like a star-burst, and the boats' outlines glowed with multicolored strands. We were all so awestruck, none of us said a word, even Rose, whose mouth gaped in wonder as she snuggled in her papa's arms.

We all went up to our rooms after the fabulous trip through fairyland. After Auntie got into bed, Rose climbed in with her. The hotel had provided some children's books in English, and one of them described Danish Christmas traditions. Auntie read to her until she fell asleep. After I carried Rose to her own bed, I went back to check on Auntie. She had fallen asleep, her glasses on the end of her nose. I gently removed them and turned off the light. I read for a while before turning off my own light.

Next morning, breakfast consisted of a mind-boggling smorgasbord—myriad dishes offering everything I could think of—as well as an egg station. Rose refused the idea of eggs and asked me to put a little of several foods on her plate. She loved the smoked salmon and paper-thin ham atop hefty crackers with luscious butter but not the red roe so much. She enjoyed the yoghurt with berries and coffee cake after that. Blueberry juice was a big favorite too. I also loved the buttered crackers with all the toppings. Orange juice was fresh squeezed, and the coffee smelled marvelously fragrant. Auntie's plate had so many bits and pieces on it, I couldn't quite sort them out. She seemed to revel in it all. I hadn't seen her quite so animated for a long time. Hunter had predictably gone *al a carte* and ordered steak. Probably off carte at breakfast.

We went back to our suite to freshen up before making our way back to Tivoli. Rose was spellbound as we passed stretches of monumental fir trees that looked almost black in the distance, their branches weighed down with snow. The icy air felt oddly pleasant under a bright sun. We could have walked, but I didn't want to tire Rose out—or Auntie, for that matter.

"Look, Mama, so many Christmas trees!"

We got out at the edge of the market. Hunter hoisted Rose onto his shoulders as it was fairly crowded.

We separated as all of us spied different items that caught our attention. Margareta and Sven flanked Auntie, Hunter stayed with me and Rose, and Lin disappeared. Hunter could not say no to Rose. She pondered over little plush elves, cunning handmade toys, and many other delights. She finally chose a large soft elf, a family of tiny wooden reindeer, and a book about Denmark.

I noticed a colorful carved Santa Claus, or *Julemanden*—Christmas Man, as I learned the Danes called him. I love Christmas ornaments, and even though Lin decorated the Salton house, I had put out a few of my own downstairs.

Now, I would be able to do as I chose. The thought of owning my own home still thrilled me. After buying a *Julemanden* and an elf for the mantle, I picked out some tree ornaments. All depicted fish or birds, some made from wood, and others from pine cones or other natural materials. Next Christmas, I would be ready. I decided to do it all in a natural theme. No going overboard, although Rose would probably disapprove. Hunter wouldn't let me pay for anything.

Finally we came together in a small crowd watching a contortionist on a small stage. I always found that kind of performance fascinating but somewhat grotesque. When the act finished, a juggler pushed his way through the throng, and that was more to Rose's liking.

"What is the thing that man is doing called?"

"He's a juggler," I said.

"I think I'll be a juggler when I grow up."

"Whatever makes you happy," Hunter said, laughing. I knew he meant it too.

Lin still hadn't appeared, so Hunter decided we should all go to lunch without her. We passed several places with long lines but came across one that was less popular.

"Why aren't many people here? Is there something wrong with it, do you think?" I asked Hunter.

"Price, probably," he said.

When I looked at the menu, the prices were listed in kroner. I hadn't yet figured out the exchange rate, so couldn't tell, but the ambience said "pricey."

Hunter ordered steak frites, a repeat of his breakfast fare. No buffet of healthy fresh food could satisfy his carnivorous tastes. I opted for cod with potatoes and cabbage, and Rose had fish and chips, although they called it something more chic. Sven, Margareta, and Auntie, after much discussion back and forth, ordered pork and mushrooms.

Hunter reminded us that the hotel had provided tickets for a matinee, so we all trooped over to the theater, a modern pine building, its entrance flanked by a giant *Julemanden* on one side and a reindeer on the other.

We all enjoyed the entertaining and lively show, in spite of very little of it being performed in English. There was lots of singing and dancing by young men and women in colorful, jingling, costumes, which had most of us bobbing and tapping our feet. Lots of special effects had Rose and all the other children whooping and cheering. Auntie and Rose looked tired by the time we exited the theater. I'd had enough, too, and wanted a rest before dinner. We were still jetlagged, after all.

"What time will the carts come to pick us up?" I asked Hunter.

"I think there are always a few waiting," he said. "Do you want to go back now?"

"I think it's time."

He led the way. Back at the hotel, Rose went to the elves under the tree and patted each one on the head.

"I forgot to say goodbye," she explained. "Now I want to go and cuddle my own elf."

Rose soon slept, her elf clasped to her chest. Auntie slept too. I unwrapped my decorations and fantasized about where I would place them next Christmas. I lay on my bed intent on reading another chapter in my mystery novel but woke up with the realization that it was dark outside. Panicked, I looked at my watch. Six-thirty, so we hadn't missed dinner. But we'd have to hurry because Lin had told us she booked for seven. As it happened, the others were awake. Auntie had turned on her light and was reading a travel guide provided by the hotel while Rose chatted to her elf.

We found Lin already seated in the dining room. "I ran into some friends," she said. Dinner wasn't much different from the previous night, but I tried different things: pork with prunes, crispy roast potatoes, and a salad of greens that were new to me. Hunter, predictably, went straight to the roast beef carving stand, and Rose went with him.

"Rose must have some vegetables," I said.

"Don't want to. Papa isn't having any."

I gave Hunter "the look," and he took her over to the center table to spoon green beans and potatoes onto both of their plates. He looked a little sulky, poor baby.

"I know you're both going to eat up all your vegetables," I said, rubbing it in.

"I will if Papa does."

I couldn't help laughing as I looked at Hunter to see how he took it. He cracked a smile. "Of course I will eat up my vegetables."

No one spoke much for a while until we got dessert. We discussed what we would do next day. Everything in Copenhagen would be closed on Christmas Eve, except Tivoli.

Lin said, "I suggest we go to Tivoli for a couple of hours or so. Maybe go just before lunch. Rose will definitely need her nap in the afternoon because it will be a late night for her."

A little girl sidled up next to Rose. "*Wie heist du?*" she asked.

"She wants to know your name," Lin said.

"Rose," she said, pointing to herself.

"Gerda," said the little girl, pointing to herself.

Her father came up behind her and spoke sternly to the child before turning to Hunter. "I do apologize for my daughter's intrusion," he said in slightly accented English. "She has been complaining she is being bored all afternoon. We arrived this morning."

"Would she like to play with me?" Rose asked. "We could play out by the big Christmas tree. It has elves. We can make stories. I have finished my dinner."

"I can watch them," I said. "It would be my pleasure."

What an ideal situation. A playmate for Rose who didn't speak the language. No embarrassing secrets could be spilled.

I took the two children out to the lobby. Rose clasped Gerda's hand and led her to one of the elves. "This one is called Peter. He is the naughty one and I like him best." She pointed at herself. "Rose." She pointed at the elf. "Peter."

They moved on to the next one. This time Gerda pointed at herself. "Gerda." She pointed at the elf. "Hans."

This lasted until they had exhausted the supply. Then they sat, legs crossed and started telling stories about the elves. Rose made up a story about how the naughty elf, Peter, made his younger brothers do naughty things. When the mother catches them, Peter says it's Hans' fault. But his mother says that he is the oldest and should have… And so it went on. Gerda took over and told her own story, but goodness knows what it was. Finally the other adults showed up.

"We will all go to Tivoli together tomorrow," Hunter said. "The children will have more fun that way."

"That's an excellent idea," I said. "We didn't look at any of the rides yesterday."

We all sat in the lobby, which offered numerous groups of sofas and chairs. Lin ordered coffee, and we all chatted and sipped for a while. The children found picture books on one of the side tables, and those kept them occupied. It seems that Herr Grunewald was an Austrian industrialist. I asked him how he learned such excellent English.

"I went to the London School of Economics in England. I already spoke English quite well as my family visited London very often, but university added some polish."

Frau Grunewald spoke heavily accented English and often had to search for the right word. She was surprisingly dowdy, given her husband's prosperous and suave appearance.

"It is nice for our girls," she said to me.

"Yes. I am very pleased to meet you," I said. "Your daughter is lovely."

She looked pleased. I had the feeling she was often overlooked.

Finally, we parted ways. Rose chatted excitedly about her new friend as the elevator rose to our floor.

23

The next morning the children played outside for a while after breakfast. The terrace had been swept clean, so they threw a big, soft ball to each other before deciding to kick it around instead. Hunter sat watching them with me. I caught a movement in the corner of my eye. A white fox had come up to the edge of the terrace and stood watching the girls.

"Hunter," I whispered. "Do something." My breath came in spurts due to my fear.

"Do not worry. The arctic fox is our friend."

Hunter went outside and crouched down. The fox trotted to him immediately when he held out his arms. He cuddled the creature with the girls clamoring to pet it. The fox seemed to revel in the attention. I'd calmed down enough to join them. The fox looked up at me with beautiful eyes.

"I'm afraid it's time to get ready, girls."

That was met by a storm of protest before Hunter assured them that their friend would be back.

Hunter, Rose, and I rode together again. What a fairytale setting! Gentle hillocks of snow, tall conifers, so dark they looked black, stretching out to the horizon, were interrupted only by the occasional stone cottage. The sun caught Hunter's hair, touching it with gold above his perfect profile—breathtaking. Indeed, my breath had become too heavy. It had been awhile because we had been in such close proximity to family, both here and at the Bay since the Salton house had been sold. Hunter turned and grinned. That damned godly hearing.

I turned my face the other way to take a couple of deep breaths and get ahold of myself. Something streaked along the edge of the dark fencing. Then another. Dazzling white foxes with magnificent brushy tails seemed to be chasing something. A piteous scream confirmed my suspicions and caused Hunter and Rose to look in that direction.

"Two beautiful white foxes," I said. "They ran out of sight before I could tell you. I think one of them caught something."

"Yes, those arctic foxes are truly magnificent," Hunter replied. He put his arm around me, and I rested my head on his shoulder. Bliss. Until we were interrupted.

Rose called out, "Foxy!"

A white fox chased our cart with some urgency.

"Is it the same one?" I asked Hunter.

"Yes, it is. You know how animals like Rose."

We reached the center of Tivoli Gardens soon after.

The fox leapt into the cart and put his paws on Rose's lap. She cuddled and kissed him while he made little noises akin to a human "ooh" and "aah." Hunter finally spoke to it in his old tongue, and the fox leapt down and went on his way.

"Why did you send him away, Papa?" asked Rose, close to tears.

"It is time for us to join our friends. Gerda is looking forward to the rides. Anyway, the fox promised to come back to see you."

Rose cheered up. This time, we focused on rides. Margareta and Sven took charge. I was surprised to hear Margareta speaking German to Gerda. I could tell that her speech was labored, but she managed. She must have visited a German-speaking country during her two-year absence from high school.

The carousel delighted both girls, and they especially loved the richly decked elephant, which they took turns on for four rides, which the older kids alternated so they could keep an eye on the little ones. Then came the train, which they went on twice. By that time, everyone was ready for lunch. We went to the same restaurant, which obliged us by pushing tables together so that all ten of us could eat together. Hunter and Herr Grunewald seemed to hit it off. Lin occasionally tried to converse with his wife. Auntie had made a point of sitting next to her, and another revelation jolted me when Auntie started to chat with her in what sounded like fluent German. Her war work, of course. The table went silent when their conversation started—I wasn't the only one surprised—but everyone soon went back to their conversations. I wondered why Auntie hadn't said anything while we were having coffee in the lobby last night.

"Mama, why is Auntie talking funny?"

"She is talking in German, the language they speak in Germany, Austria, and Switzerland. Gerda is from Austria, so she speaks German. You know how you've heard people here speak in another language? That's Danish. A lot of countries talk different from us."

"Yes, I know. But I didn't know Auntie could talk different." She gazed in wonder at my aunt.

Mrs. Grunewald became quite animated, obviously happy to have someone to talk to. I could see how she would have been quite pretty once. She could have been pretty again if she took care of her appearance.

Rose and Gerda talked at each other from time to time, willing to listen and nod, glad to be together. When it was time to leave the restaurant, they walked ahead, hand-in-hand. We strolled past all kinds of kiosks and booths, some selling snacks and drinks, others local crafts. I picked up a couple more tree ornaments and Rose a book.

A little stage on one side had some stools around it with an audience of about twenty children. A few clowns came on, performing all kinds of silly tricks. I have never been to a circus, but I imagine they must do much the same things. The girls found two stools next to each other and hugged their knees, laughing at the antics. Suddenly, a couple of short clowns wove among the children, handing out candy and throwing confetti.

When one came close to where we were standing off to the side, I heard Lin gasp. The clown heard too and leered at her. "Hello Lin," he said before going back to his performance.

I turned to look at her stricken face. Hunter grasped her shoulders with his hands. "Don't tell me," I said. "Another survivor."

"Must be," she whispered. "Another gnome. I think it's Nisse's brother."

Does it ever end? I hoped there would be no more trouble.

I felt I may as well ask. "So, was he with the dwarves too?"

"No. When Nisse was put in prison, he came to my lady Frigg asking for money to help get his brother freed. She told him Nisse must pay for his misdeeds. Then he came to me to ask me to intercede with Frigg. I said I could never go against my lady. He threatened to harm me. I told my lady and never saw him again. Until now." She shrugged and spread her hands. "I have no idea how he escaped. And Nick never mentioned him."

"He is another bad apple," Hunter said. "We should go."

Suddenly, there was a bang, and we were shrouded in fog. Several people screamed and kids cried. I fumbled my way toward the girls. I could feel Hunter beside me. "Rose," we both called out.

"Over here, Mama. Papa come and get me and Gerda."

My hands outstretched low, I touched first one kid, then another, making them squeal in fright. It was chaos with adults stumbling around and tripping on children. Slowly, the fog began to dissipate. I saw Rose, who was crying hysterically. Frau Grunewald wailed alongside her.

"Don't be scared, darling," I cooed as I hugged Rose.

"I'm not scared. A clown took Gerda."

"Where is Herr Grunewald?" I asked his wife.

"I do not know. He went to find the, er, the toilette." She stifled a sob.

"Rose, did you see which way he took her?" asked Hunter. Rose pointed at a stand of trees.

Lin and Hunter sprinted into the woods. I knew Lin would soon outpace both Hunter and Gerda's kidnapper, if indeed they went that way. Soon security officers arrived and asked the same question. Apparently the woods curved all the way around the back of our hotel. It turned out that the clowns on the stage had no idea who these other clowns were. They were not part of their act.

Herr Grunewald arrived amid the commotion. He flew into a panic when he heard what had happened. "I am very wealthy," he told the officers in English. "They will hold her for ransom."

"You had better go back to the hotel, then. We will send someone with tracking equipment in case they call," the senior officer told him. He turned to another officer. "Take them."

As the officer led the bereft parents away, I told the others, "I think we should go too." Rose was still crying, so Sven carried her. She was getting too heavy for me. We walked back, our festive mood completely dissipated. Poor little Gerda, she must have been terrified.

We sat in the lobby, settling into a group of armchairs in one corner. We ordered coffee for ourselves and juice for Rose, asking the waiter to take a cup to the police officer standing by the entrance. We didn't talk much as no subject seemed fitting in the face of Gerda's dire peril. I remembered only too well Lin's story of the abducted schoolgirl she'd rescued.

I thought at first I was imagining things when Lin marched through the hotel entrance holding Gerda. The policeman gasped and moved toward them, speaking urgently into his phone. We all rose to our feet. Rose tore toward Gerda, her arms outstretched. Lin gently set the child down. The children clasped each other, sobbing.

Soon, the parents emerged from the elevator at full speed, a police officer not far behind. They cried with joy too. But where was Hunter?

It wasn't long before the gawping concierge opened the both doors for Hunter. He strode in with one clown hanging over each shoulder. They weren't even struggling. He dumped them on the floor at the officers' feet.

"They had the child," he said. "Lin caught up with them as they were getting into a van. They put the child in the back. Lin took out the child, and I pulled out these clowns."

The clowns looked up at him in abject terror as he loomed over them. They looked about the same size. Were they both gnomes?

"We should get all that make-up off their faces," I said. "Then we can see who's who." *And what.*

"We will clean them up when we take them to prison," said the senior officer, who had arrived by that time. "We will need to speak more to you and your wife tomorrow," he told Hunter. "Thank you for your help."

Herr Grunewald patted Hunter on the back, trying to hold back his tears.

"All right," Lin said. "Let's go upstairs and rest a little. It's going to be a big evening."

I felt wiped out. The shock of the abduction, the relief that Rose was okay, fear for Gerda's safety, joy at Gerda's safe return—a gamut of emotions enough to exhaust anyone. I could tell Auntie and Rose felt it too.

Auntie and Rose slept a little, me not at all. I couldn't settle. When it came time, I bathed and dressed Rose in a lovely new blue velvet dress and pulled her hair into a high chignon. She looked beautiful. I wore a dark blue velvet top with gray silk pants. Auntie wore black velvet with a large diamond and sapphire pin—which I had never seen before.

"Are those real diamonds?" I asked.

"Oh, yes. I decided this trip was a special occasion, so worth taking it out of the bank. And before you ask, it was a gift from an admirer many years ago."

"Auntie, you are a dark horse. Tell me about your admirer."

Her face clouded. "He died young. So many of them did."

The war again.

The dining room seemed to have sprouted all kinds of extra decorations and lights. The center table, a triumph of artistic flair, had tall crystal vases filled with red and white roses arranged with seasonal greenery. The snowy tablecloths had been set with gold chargers and the array of food made selection a challenge. A piano at the corner played light classical music, accompanied by a harp and oboe—an unusual combination that worked beautifully.

When the Grunewalds appeared, they asked if we could all sit together. The waiters pushed two tables together, and the girls sat next to each other, grinning at each other between mouthfuls. I noticed that Gerda frowned between each grin. Her eyes looked puffy too. How could she not have been traumatized? But she was behaving like a heroine.

We all felt better now that the crisis had been happily resolved and ate with gusto. The dessert was the traditional Danish Christmas rice pudding with hot cherry sauce. We put away a good amount of terrific wine too. German white wine and French red. I preferred German white wine to others I've tasted. Soon, it was time to waddle out to the lobby where the staff danced around the tree singing their Christmas songs. After a while, Gerda and Rose danced with them. We all applauded, and the staff handed out presents to everyone from the selection of boxes amongst the elves. Mine was expensive French perfume—which I think most of the ladies received.

It was eleven by that time, so time for bed. What a strange day.

Hunter and Lin and Herr Grunewald were driven to the police station shortly after breakfast the next day. We had agreed to open our presents on Christmas day, so we'd wait for their return. Rose simmered with impatience. Gerda and her mother wandered around the lobby, seemingly at loose ends. The girls played with the elves while we sat and talked. Auntie had already gone up.

"They wanted to hurt our girl. Because they wanted to steal from my husband."

"I know. It is so frightening. But it ended happily."

"Yes. My husband has too much money. Bad people love that."

"Yes. But she is safe now."

"Is she?"

We didn't say much after that. I was anxious to hear what Lin and Hunter found out about the kidnappers.

After an hour, I decided to go back to our room. Rose didn't like it, but the mother's doubt had disturbed me. Too close to the bone.

Finally, they returned.

"After we have opened presents, I will tell you all about it," Lin said. "Let's go to our suite. I'll record it on my phone."

"All right. I'll just stop in ours to tell Auntie and fetch our gifts. Come along, Rose. Present time."

She didn't need much persuading.

Lin had ordered several pots of coffee and hot chocolate—which was unbelievably superior to any I'd tasted before. Margareta played Christmas music on her phone, and we all had a jolly time opening our secret Santa gifts. Needless to say, Rose got more than one gift. She dutifully planted a kiss on everyone's cheek since only one box had been labelled as coming from Santa, and she didn't know who had given her what. She got a big hug in return from everyone. It brought a lump to my throat. What a lucky little girl to be so beloved by so many.

Lin finally announced she was ready to tell us what had transpired. I had my phone ready in my pocket to record. Lin had only had her phone a little while, and I didn't trust her to get it right.

Tape 9,
Volume 3

We were allowed to see the gnome alone. The other, a teenage girl, occupied a separate cell. Herr Grunewald didn't want to speak to either of them. The gnome was Nick's brother, Iker, for sure. When we entered, Iker spat at me. Fortunately, he missed. Hunter raised his hand, but I stopped him. They're sure to have rules about that kind of thing here in Denmark.

"It's your fault I lost my brother," he said in a whisper more like a hiss.

"Being in that prison saved him," I whispered back. "He found us and tried to steal from us. He robbed houses in our neighborhood. He died just a few months ago. A coyote ripped out his throat while he was hiding from the police in the woods."

Iker's face turned the color of the whitewashed cell walls. "Alive, all these years. And I didn't know?"

"Yes. And I don't think he knew about you. How did you escape?"

"I had climbed the dwarves' mountain to try to find a way down so I could rescue Nisse. It was terrifying. The water rose so fast, soon it carried me away, but I grabbed onto a tree so huge it rose above the surface, and I managed to hold on. I had a rope wound around my body in case of needing to climb into the caves, so I bound myself to the tree. I was there for many miserable years, sleeping, drinking the foul water, eating nothing. Finally, the water began to recede, and I could climb down the tree to Midgard. Everything I knew was gone. The barn I used to live in together with its house. All the houses for that matter. I lay on a sandy beach and slept. I awoke when some wild pigs came snuffling around. Good thing they didn't take a bite out of me. But there was life again, which meant food."

"It was a long journey down the ages. I lived hand-to-mouth most of the time. Had a wife and children a few times, although it's hard to find a girl when most people don't look like me. I always had to leave them when I got old much slower than they did too. I'm tired of it. I just wanted one big score. One where I wouldn't have to worry again. Just one."

"So you decided to terrify a little girl. And what about that girl you got involved?"

"Oh, the child would have been all right." He shrugged. "We wouldn't have hurt her. And the girl? She's just some tart I found on the streets. Addict. She's finished, whatever happens."

"You are as bad as your brother," I said. "Selfish and lazy. Why didn't you learn a trade? Work for money like everyone else?"

"Like you?" Iker sneered.

We left while we could still control ourselves.

The officer in charge assured us that the kidnapping of a child carried heavy penalties. Hunter and I will follow the case and make sure Iker doesn't cause any problems when he gets out.

After one of those pregnant silences, Auntie said,
"Well, well."

Rose said, "I'm glad Gerda is safe from that horrid gnome.
I hate gnomes."

"I do not think there will be any left," Hunter told her.

Let's hope not. Wait. What does he mean by that?

24

We had another few days at the hotel and spent one of them in Copenhagen. It was a lovely old city, a tasteful mix of ancient and modern. I didn't buy anything all morning, although Hunter caved in to Rose's plea for a little furry fox toy. I wouldn't have thought she'd be keen on foxes after our traumatic experience at the Bay. I certainly wasn't keen after what I saw, which is why I'd been so afraid for her when the artic fox had shown up on the hotel terrace. I guess she didn't equate red foxes with white ones. I insisted she keep her toy in the bag so it wouldn't get dirty.

Hunter, Rose, and I separated from the others at the Royal Copenhagen showrooms. We'd had enough of shopping. Lin was making arrangements to have a dinner service shipped home. She chose a delicate blue floral pattern on a white background. Very Scandinavian. I did succumb to the pull of a lovely (and costly) figurine of an arctic vixen with a cub. To me, it epitomized the beauty of the snowy north and brought to mind that ride to Tivoli when the sun anointed Hunter so gloriously, and I spotted the gorgeous white foxes. The clerk wrapped it securely before I nestled it deep in my tote.

We took a taxi down to the harbor. Who can go to Copenhagen and not see the Little Mermaid? Even I'd heard of it before I ever set foot outside the U.S.A. At first, I thought the statue disappointingly small. On further consideration, it was well over life-size, but its panoramic background dwarfed it somewhat. She perched on a large rock, scanning the horizon, promising safe haven for visitors to Denmark's shores. I mentally shook myself out of such sappy musings. She'd made me feel uncharacteristically poetic. Did she have that effect on others?

"Mama, who is she?"

"She is called the Little Mermaid."

"Is she sad?"

"No, she just watches the sea to welcome visitors like us."

"I like her. She's pretty. It's a bit cold to go without her clothes, isn't it? Why doesn't someone put a coat on her? Panties, too. She really needs panties."

I looked at Hunter, who was trying not to laugh. "Ask Papa," I said.

"I don't think Papa has any panties," she said.

Hunter rose to the occasion. "She is made of bronze, Rose. Bronze doesn't feel the cold. Not at all."

That satisfied her. It was time to join the others so we'd get back to the hotel by dinnertime. The fox was waiting against the wall by the front entrance. After a quick kiss and a cuddle, we managed to steer Rose inside. We had one day left to pack and relax before the flights back to Washington. Since the Salton house had been sold and the castle was not yet ready, the Bay house was temporarily home to the entire Thoren ensemble. Much as I loved them all, I looked forward to having the place to myself.

Gerda and Rose wished each other a teary farewell the day we left. The Grunewalds were staying on until after

New Year's. They invited us all to visit them in Austria, and Hunter and Lin invited them to visit us once the renovations were complete on their new home. I hoped that would happen. I was sure they'd have a lovely home. And Rose and Gerda seemed to get along so well. Maybe Auntie should teach her German.

Rose looked around the dining room terrace before we left for the airport, then the front of the hotel. No fox. She burst into tears. Hunter picked her up.

"The fox knew you were leaving. He does not like goodbyes. They make him sad."

She calmed down but stayed sad for quite a while.

I sat next to Auntie on the flight to London. Rose sat with Sven. We chatted about our experiences, and I mentioned how I hoped we would see the Grunewalds again.

"Yes, they seemed to be pleasant people. But we really don't know much about them, do we?" Auntie said.

"What do you mean?"

"Well, some of these industrialists can have rather checkered pasts, you know."

"What makes you say that?" I asked. "Something to do with your experiences in World War II?"

Auntie gaped at me. "World War II! Just how old do you think I am?"

"But your hints about your war work. Your fluency in German. I thought…"

"You do realize that war ended in 1945, don't you? When I was a toddler."

"Oh." I felt myself blushing. What a stupid error. "Well, what were you talking about, then?"

"The Cold War, of course. I was involved in the mid 70's through to the end. And that's all I'm going to say."

"But the German?"

"Berlin was a center point. A hotspot. Now, let's talk about something else."

No wonder it was so hush hush. My cheeks flushed again when I thought of my ignorant supposition. Granted World War II was well before my time, but I should have known better.

We all split up when we arrived at Dulles airport. Auntie was tired and decided to spend a week or so in her new condo in Salton. Lin and her kids wanted to spend some time in their condo as they all had friends they wanted to see. That left Hunter, Rose, and me. How blessed I felt as Hunter drove us down to the Bay house. We stopped for groceries at the nearest supermarket and finally got home. My home, the best home I could ever want.

Rose could barely stay awake. I heated up a can of children's alphabet spaghetti before we put her to bed. Not ideal, I know, but she was at the end of her tether. I grilled two steaks for Hunter and a small one for myself and made a small salad—I knew better than to expect Hunter to partake. We left the dirty dishes, showered, and went to bed.

Next morning, we walked on the beach after breakfast. A frigid wind swept over the waves, and I went back in after a quarter hour or so. Rose wanted to stay longer, so I left her out there with Hunter, who never felt the cold. She was easily persuaded to come back because we needed to get over to the kennel in Leonardtown to retrieve poor little Sam, who'd been left there for nearly three weeks.

When we got there, poor little Sam was having the time of his life chasing another spaniel around the field, his tail wagging furiously, its white tip a blur. Other dogs played with each other or wandered around tracking the scents of whatever wild animals had visited the night before. As soon as Rose called out to him, he raced over to the gate, yipping and dancing with excitement. We couldn't stop anywhere for lunch because we had him with us, but I'd taken the precaution of taking meat out of the freezer.

Hunter and Rose had steaks for lunch. I didn't, preferring a frozen tuna casserole. Enough is enough.

"I need to get over to the compound to check on things," Hunter said. "I have had an idea for training Ygdrassil."

"Oh, what?"

"I will record different kinds of airplane sounds and play them, indicating that it should take evasive action. I hope it will learn to act on its own."

"I think that's a wonderful idea. Shall we come with you?"

"No, there will be no heating in the house, and I will be outside a lot. It is too cold for Rose and for you, I think."

Hunter spent the nights with me until the others came down. It was a glorious time of cozy intimacy. We cooked together and snuggled with Rose while we read her stories. I was more in love with him than ever, and he seemed to be with me.

Lin brought Auntie down after about ten days. While I was happy to see them, it rather burst my bubble.

Auntie was full of news about her new condo. She hadn't had to get rid of anything because half her things had been put into storage and would later be moved to her rooms in the castle. The things she loved best fitted perfectly into the condo, and twin beds and a chest would be installed in the second bedroom for Rose and me.

Lin wouldn't be around for long. She wanted to take measurements and make notes before traveling back up to the Washington area to do some serious furniture shopping. I wished Auntie would go with her. I missed Hunter already. But I told myself I mustn't be greedy. I must accept reality— if I could call it that.

I pondered enrolling Rose in pre-kindergarten but decided it would be better to wait until everyone moved into the castle. Fewer questions and complicated answers. In the event, I'm glad I did because February brought some pretty brutal snowstorms. I was glad to stay home for a few weeks. The roads were a mess, although Hunter always managed to forge his way through. Nothing could dampen his excitement about his castle. He and Lin could stay in a one place for as long as they liked. They could avoid being seen for a generation before getting out and about again. The passing of so much time meant nothing to them. The thought of it depressed me though. I'd get old and ugly. They wouldn't. Hunter would always love Lin. He'd lose interest in me though. He'd still love me but in a different way. Perhaps I wouldn't want more at that age. I must remember to be grateful for the wonderful life he and Lin had given me. *Is gratitude enough?*

26

March came in like the proverbial lion. Exterior work on the castle was just about complete, minus a few minor details, so the crew could finish the interior. I hadn't been back since that glimpse of Yggdrasil's self-preservation stunt. Hunter mentioned that the sound of the planes now caused a slightly different reaction. The tree had grown too massive to fold as before. Now it merely opened out the top branches into a vast canopy. The first time it did that, it flattened the canopies of the trees nearby. After that, it forked a good portion of its branches upward. That way, no harm done. He said it looked rather splendid. I wondered why no one would notice this huge thing towering over everything else. He told me that it had grown so tall that anything above the other tree tops was invisible to humans. When it reached Asgard, or where Asgard used to be, it would not only be invisible that high but noncorporeal to this world too, so planes would no longer be a concern. I concurred with Alice—curiouser and curiouser.

Rose was getting restless. Everyone was, except Hunter. It was high time March settled down and gave us all a break. We walked down to the beach where Rose found plenty to pick up after rough waves had scooped up glass, rocks, and shells from the sea bed and dumped them ashore for her delight. I'd have to do some surreptitious sorting and tossing before long. We had buckets of the stuff. I didn't like to bring it up. We'd already had a meltdown about giving away some of her stuffed animals. Hunter explained that poor children sometimes didn't get anything for Christmas and had no toys to play with.

"Then they don't have good mamas and papas," she retorted.

Then we went into good parents who don't have enough for themselves, not even enough to eat. But she didn't believe us. She couldn't grasp it. When she was old enough, I'd have to show her what poor looked like. We'd missed an opportunity in Egypt. In the event, I took about eight from the back of her closet and gave them away to the local shelter Lin had told me about. Not a week later, I found Rose rooting through her stash searching for Willy the Pig. When I told her he was living with another child now and was very happy, although of course he missed Rose, she threw such a fit, everyone came rushing to her room expecting to see blood. Auntie took charge and led the sobbing child into her room. I could hear them talking but couldn't catch what was said.

At dinner, Rose acted as if nothing had happened. She started talking about school and how much she was looking forward to it. Auntie told me later that she'd told her some stories about the poor people she'd known around the world. How they had to make do without enough food, dreadful housing, and no school for the kids. That had obviously made an impression. I started worrying about Rose going to school for the first time. She hadn't had anything to do with other children besides Gerda. And she was very precocious—or so I thought. I hadn't had much to do with other children either, so had no one to compare her to.

We had a couple of calm, warmer days, so I decided to drive to the castle. I'd brought my car down to the Bay when the Salton house went on the market. It was a nice drive through narrow country lanes. I glimpsed some greening buds among the trees that lined the fields. When I came to the turnoff and entered the code into the gate's security box, I drove through carefully, taking in everything around me. The grounds looked splendid—manicured, despite the fact that most of the trees and shrubs were still bare. I spotted several magnificent holly bushes off toward the bay. They'd be useful at Christmas. I looked around for Yggdrasil and was surprised how odd it looked: a massive trunk with branches that marched up it before coming to an abrupt stop. That's what Hunter was talking about. Above a certain point, it was invisible to humans.

"Wow," Rose exclaimed. "Our tree is so big now. It looks as if it's touching the clouds. It makes all the other trees look teeny."

I stopped the car. "You can see way up, Rose? All the way to the clouds?"

"Oh, yes. It goes up more, but the clouds are hiding the top."

My heart hammered so loud, I held my chest as if that would steady it. What was my child? Part god, I knew. But did she have powers? I would speak to Hunter. No, maybe Lin first. But Rose would talk to Hunter about the tree.

I started the car again and rolled up the drive. The house looked inviting. White with a dark green roof, it was perfectly balanced with a large elegant wing on each side. It appeared rather Georgian, probably because of the columns in front of the original center building. They were new columns, of course, as I remembered the old wooden ones looking half rotten and downright shaky. These were made of white marble with faint gray striations.

Hunter appeared in the doorway and rushed out to greet us. We each got a bear hug after climbing out of the car. Rose was able to extricate herself from her car seat now.

"Come and see," he cried out. "You will be surprised how lovely everything is looking."

"Hunter," I said. "I can't wait to see it. But I have to tell you something. Rose can see Yggdrasil. All of it."

That put the brakes on. His face glowed with happiness. "She is one of us!" he said.

"How much one of you?" I asked, my tone a trifle snippy.

"I expect as much as Margareta. We do not know what powers she has yet. She has not been tested. Sven, I think, not so much. He is strong. And he is brilliant. But the godly powers—I do not think so. Rather sad."

I couldn't speak with my emotions tangling my brain. My daughter would become a splendid creature. But she would be other. And I would be lesser. Hunter put his arm around me.

"Do not worry, Mary. We are all loving each other and happy. What more could we ask? Now come and see."

He was right. No need to worry, at least for now. We walked through to the kitchen. I had never seen such a gorgeous layout of stainless steel and marble. A long counter ran down the center with cupboards underneath, leaving plenty of legroom. It would serve as a worktop and table. A six burner stove, two refrigerators, a huge pantry, lots of pale wood cabinets, and a floor covered with what I thought might be Italian tiles. It took my breath away.

We moved on to the other rooms. There was only one living room, which was massive with a stone fireplace at one end. We emerged onto the terrace. Matching urns stood on each side of the top step, smaller ones at each end of the four steps to the lawn, and ceramic planters had been lined up against the wall, waiting for the weather to get warm enough for planting. The rotting railings had been replaced with wrought iron. The view of a moody, slate-gray sea and scudding clouds chasing away the sun, was awe-inspiring.

"Upstairs still has a lot of work," Hunter said. "But let us look at your wing."

It was like an apartment. Two bedrooms, each with its own small bathroom, upstairs with a small living room for Rose to play in. One bedroom and bathroom downstairs, a larger living room, a kitchenette, and a washroom.

"The downstairs bedroom is for Auntie," he said. "I do not think she will like to do stairs much longer. When we move in here, you can take our bedroom at the other house and let Auntie be downstairs."

"You are spoiling us," I said. "You know we will spend most of our time at the other house, don't you?"

"Oh, yes, and I shall love visiting you there. But you know, Auntie may be here more than you think because she is fond of Dora. And I would like that because you will be all alone and waiting for me over there."

"Ah hah! You've been scheming," I said, laughing. I hoped it would work out that way. "Have you thought about cleaning? Dora can't possibly manage this huge house on her own."

"Yes. We shall get a cleaning company for three hours twice a week, and everyone must behave themselves while they are here. There will be four ladies, so they can easily manage the cleaning and make the beds. We will buy two sets of sheets and towels so they can wash and dry them and swap them out. Dora will do the cooking and the other washing. The ladies will iron also."

"You seem to have it all worked out."

"Of course, Lin has managed everything. She told me what she has arranged. Dora is satisfied."

"The other wing has a side-load four-car garage and an apartment for Dora and Stan."

"I thought you were going to use that for guests."

"We had second thoughts. We will keep the guests upstairs where we can keep an eye on them."

"Good thought."

I wandered to the front window of the living room in my wing. What was Rose doing?

"Hunter! Do something!" Rose sat with her back against Yggdrasil's trunk cuddling a young red fox. "It might be rabid."

"No, no, do not worry. I can see from here that it is healthy. But I will go."

He strode out of the wing's front door with me stumbling behind, my mind whirling with ripped flesh. The fox seemed unconcerned with our arrival.

"Where did the fox come from, Rose?" Hunter asked.

"His mama and sisters disappeared and he's lonely. He's hungry too. Do we have meat for him, Papa?"

"I think we can find something." He turned to me. "The animal is fine. I am going to look for some meat. I put some steaks in the freezer. I do not think the little guy will mind if it is cold." He walked back to the house.

I resigned myself to the situation. There'd be no denying Rose her foxy friend.

"How do you know his family disappeared?" I asked.

"He told me."

"He can't talk, can he?"

"Not with his mouth. But he looked into my eyes and told me with his mind. Why don't you pet him?" I slowly crouched down and stroked the fox's head. He rolled onto his back. "He wants you to tickle his tummy." I obliged and the little animal grunted with pleasure. His pointy face was a thing of beauty. "He will sleep under the tree. He will try to hunt for food. We will feed him sometimes and bring water when it's hot."

"We won't be living here though."

"Papa will take care of him. And when Sven and Margareta are here, they will too. I promised."

"All right. He is a very nice little boy. And he loves you, I can tell."

Hunter arrived with the frozen steak, which he placed on the ground near Rose. The fox jumped up and chowed down, chewing and chewing the hard lump. He finished, looked at us one by one and dashed for the trees.

"Why did he go away?"

"I expect he needed to go to the toilet," said Hunter. "He would not want to do such a thing near you. It would be impolite."

"Sam does."

"But Sam is a family dog. He is trained that way. Maybe he will even be friends with your fox. What is his name, by the way?"

"Hyndla."

Hunter's sharp intake of breath surprised me. "How do you know that is his name?"

"He told me."

"I see. Let us go inside."

"I think I'll sit here and wait for Hyndla."

"All right."

We walked back toward the house. Hunter clasped his hands behind his back and stared at the ground as he strode so fast I could hardly keep up. When we got to the front door, I pulled his arm. "What about that name?"

"It is the name of a supernatural being. A name she could not possibly know unless she was told. That is no ordinary fox." Seeing my frightened look, he added quickly, "Not a harmful creature—far from it. I need to think a little more and will tell you the story later. But do not worry, my darling Mary. Do not worry about your exceptional daughter."

But I did worry.

27

Hunter finally persuaded Rose to leave her new foxy friend and come home with us. The wind carried a sharp edge, and I really wanted to get into a warm house and heat the soup and good bread that Dora had left in the freezer.

"Hyndla likes to sleep in his den in the woods. He is not used to inside. It will make him uncomfortable. And it is too cold for you to be out here all night."

"But won't Hyndla be too cold too?"

"Oh, no, foxes have special thick fur coats that keep them very warm. They curl up and wrap that wonderful bushy tale around their faces. Do you have a bushy tail like that?" Hunter patted Rose's bottom. "No, I thought not. No nice bushy tail. Poor you. You will have to sleep in your bed."

Rose giggled, kissed the fox on the top of his head, and took my hand, turning back to wave as we walked to the cars.

I heated soup and bread while frying Hunter's steak for about a minute. I had to avert my eyes when my baby licked her lips, bloody from the slivers Hunter put on her plate. I made the obligatory salad too.

We ate and took it in turns to read Rose a story, this one from a book by Beatrix Potter that Auntie had given her. The illustrations were charming, painted by the author herself. Some of the words were surprisingly advanced, but Rose seemed to deal with them, although they tripped Hunter's tongue a couple of times. I suppose Rose knew what they meant through the context—a smart way to teach children new words.

Soon enough it was bedtime. Rose dug through her hoard of plush animals until she found the fox she got in Denmark. That was the one she had to cuddle.

"Why is Hyndla red when my fox in Denmark was white?" she asked in a sleepy voice.

"So they can run around in the snow without being seen," said Hunter.

I was glad he didn't mention hunting. A hard truth for a toddler. I was pretty sure she'd become a vegetarian when she discovered the truth about meat.

I went to the kitchen and poured us each a glass of wine before we settled on the sofa. I knew he was going to tell me a story—I could almost see his mind churning—so I had my phone ready to record in my pocket.

He sighed and began.

Tape 10,
Volume 3

You may not know that I am one of three gods who created the first man and woman out of large pieces of buzzing rock we found on the beach in Midgard where we were wandering one day. It was a curious sound, that of bees and birds, of wind and fire. It caught the sun in several places, where there were little insets like mirrors. We knew at once it had fallen from one of the celestial bodies high above. We had no difficulty in breathing life into the rocks. They shimmered and buzzed louder before breaking apart and revealing human forms. It was one of several very important things I did in the earliest days. I gave man the gift of reason, for example.

Well, I liked to walk in Midgard, especially in the summer once the seasons started to establish themselves. Soon— well, soon to me—the land was populated with many people and many creatures. These included foxes with red fur in spring and summer, but they would turn white in the harsh winters. One fox in particular, a lovely little fellow, always seemed to appear whenever I did. Sometimes, I would sit under a tree, and he liked to snuggle up next to me. I got into the habit of bringing him some meat. I would have loved to take him home with me, but we could not take any creature to Asgard that did not belong there. It was unthinkable.

The Jotuns—ice giants, you know—were always trying to make trouble. These ice giants had their own lands but wanted more, so they tried to make sorties into both Asgard and Midgard every now and then. One night, I was in my palace in Asgard asleep when my dreams became troubled by the carnage of war. I dreamt I was on the battlefield surrounded by Jotuns. Suddenly a fox appeared between the legs of one of them, dodging back and forth, obviously wanting me to follow him. I dived between that giant's legs—you see how big I am, so you can imagine how big those fellows were—and followed the fox to the safety of a thick forest too dense for a giant to pass through.

I woke with a start, eyes open and mind racing. I jumped up and ran to the window of my chamber to search for intruders. There was no glass, of course. We didn't need it. When I hung over far enough to see the base of the wall, what did I see but two Jotuns creeping toward the entrance! I rushed out of my room and alerted the guards. They would have killed many of my guards before being vanquished, so I called on my brother Odin to smite them. He was asleep at the time, so I actually had to call on him twice, but he hurled two of the thunderbolts Thor made him. That put a stop to their mission, which I suppose was meant to destroy me. I am not sure why they wanted to kill me because I did not really have that much influence on anything that concerned them. And it would have been very hard to kill me—an immortal. I was puzzled about that, about how they planned to do it.

I went back to bed and finished my sleep, almost dreamless, but not quite. My little fox friend came to me and snuggled up like he did on Midgard. He told me that I was quite safe now, and I should sleep the night through. Which I did.

I could not stop thinking about my dream and how the fox saved me. I went down to Midgard and walked along the beach I favored before settling under a tree on the edge of the forest. Soon enough, my little friend joined me. He settled down by my side, and I put my arm around him. I looked into his eyes, and he spoke to my mind.

"I am happy to see you safe."

"Was it you in my dream?"

"Yes, of course. I am your spirit animal. Your friend and your guide when you need me."

I knew I could take him to Asgard then. He lived in my palace, enjoyed the best meats, and ran around the vast expanses of fields and forests to his heart's content. When Ragnarok began, he jumped into my arms.

"You will be saved," he told me, "although it will be a terrible time, and the worlds will fall into the void for many millennia. This is goodbye. I will not survive." He jumped down and disappeared. I shed tears for my friend and shed many more before that horrific day was over.

So you see, Mary, that fox was my spirit animal, and I still have a rapport with any fox I encounter. I can talk to them, and they can talk to me. When Rose said her fox spoke to her, I believed her. And remember how tame that arctic fox in Denmark was with us? Rose's spirit is the fox. She is my daughter. She has my blood.

"How come you couldn't communicate with the fox that attacked Rose?"

"Because it had been taken over by Loki. I couldn't get into its mind. I knew something was very wrong, but I only knew it was Loki at the last minute when his laughter penetrated my brain."

I didn't know how to feel about all these revelations. Hunter created man? Hunter could talk to foxes? Even more shocking, Rose could talk to a fox. She had Hunter's blood? I didn't think he had blood. I thought they just had white stuff running through their veins. But I suppose he didn't literally mean blood.

"It's all so much to take in. Rose will be so different from me."

Hunter folded me into his arms. "I know this is a lot to digest. You have grown up with another idea of creation. You have a daughter you love a lot, but of whom you do not understand a lot of things. That is very difficult for a mother."

"I feel unworthy to be her mother. Unworthy of you. I am so ... ordinary."

"My darling Mary, you are not ordinary. You are very special to me. To Lin too. How many mortal women would have found themselves in this family and this situation and handled it with so much grace?"

That made me feel a little better. But my daughter terrified me. What would she become? What would become of her? Might she grow to despise me?

Summer was almost upon us. The family had all moved into the castle a couple of months before. Rose and I spent the night there from time to time, and sometimes Rose stayed there with Auntie, who, as Hunter had predicted, spent more time there than at my house. She and Dora had become really close and enjoyed working together in the kitchen.

It was a very satisfactory arrangement as it provided Hunter and me plenty of time together. We had spent so much time in the company of others over the past few years that I felt our relationship had stopped growing. Hunter wouldn't have known what I was talking about as he was supremely content with things as they were. But I needed to know him better—something of his inner life. It's true he was usually easy to read, but I'd found that taking him at face value was a mistake. He was a wise and courageous old thing in a deceptively strapping body.

An old ramshackle shed squatted not far from our wing of the castle. I was surprised Hunter hadn't had it knocked down because it was unsightly.

"I have a plan," he said.

When he made statements in that decisive tone of voice, I knew to drop the matter. One morning, I drove up to the castle and noticed Stan hauling junk out of the shack.

"Hi, Stan, what's up?"

"Hi, there. Hunter wants this cleaned out. He plans to renovate it."

"What for?"

"He didn't say. He wants it empty and the walls cleaned, inside and out."

"Wouldn't it be easier to start from scratch?"

"Wouldn't you think? An electrician's coming tomorrow to run a line from the house. He wants light and plugs for a heater and a fan. I'm to replace that broken window and add another too."

That was more than a little odd. He had so much space inside. Whatever was this going to be for? A hideaway? Too close to the house for that to be realistic. Besides, everyone knew his study was out of bounds unless we were invited in.

I walked up the front steps and let myself in. "Rose, Auntie, I'm here." Silence.

I dropped my bag next to my bed and went in search of the family. It was a moderately warm day, so I guessed they'd be on the terrace. Hunter, Lin, and Auntie sat in the comfortable padded chairs sipping coffee. Rose sat on a cushion on the lawn just beyond with her fox asleep with its head on her lap. She held a forefinger to her lips, miming, "Shh." I still couldn't get my head around the fact that this wild animal behaved like a pet dog around her. Sam sat with Auntie on the terrace. I wondered if he was jealous and sulking about not being top dog any more. I resolved to give him extra attention.

"Morning, everyone." I blew kisses to all and poured myself a cup before sitting in the porch swing.

"How are you, dear?" asked Auntie.

"Very well, thank you, Auntie. I called that private school a few miles up the road to inquire about enrolling Rose for kindergarten. We have an interview next week."

"So soon?" asked Hunter. "She's just a baby."

"She'll be five in August," I said. "It's time for school. You know she must. She's longing to go to school."

"Oh." He scowled.

"It's only half a day," Lin said.

"No, actually, kindergarten is full day now," I said.

"Too much, too soon." Hunter had become agitated.

Auntie stepped in, to my relief. "She is around adults too much. She must learn how to interact with children her own age, you know."

"She did fine with Gerda." Hunter was not persuaded.

"They didn't even speak the same language. It was more as if they were playing side by side. Yes, they had a connection, but they were not truly interacting—negotiating, arguing, learning to see someone else's point of view, and so on."

"I suppose you are right." Hunter puffed out his cheeks.

"Auntie usually is." Lin smiled and patted his hand as she said it.

"What are you doing with that shed? As I came in, Stan was taking all the junk out of it."

Hunter leaned forward and spoke quietly. "It is going to be a playhouse for Rose. I am going to make it a surprise for her birthday. It will have electricity for lights and a radiant heater. Also a fan. There will be a big cupboard for toys and a small table with chairs. I will add a bigger window too."

"She will be so excited," I said. "Thank you. She's such a lucky girl."

I wasn't so sure about her being out there playing all alone. It's not as if she could bring her schoolfriends to the castle. But I couldn't disappoint her daddy. He was so proud of his idea.

"I'll be over tomorrow morning," said Lin. "I want to discuss a book I've been reading."

"What book?" asked Hunter. "I have not seen you with this book."

"It's a book about Greek mythology. You know, gods and all that. I haven't read much of it yet."

"Oh, all that kind of business."

"Quite."

I exchanged an amused glance with Lin. We hadn't told Auntie about the memoir project yet, but she must have known something was going on. She also must have realized that my novel wasn't going anywhere.

"By the way, I read something quite disturbing in the paper this morning." Auntie had subscribed to a local paper that covered southern Maryland.

"Oh dear, what?" I asked.

"There's an arsonist setting fire to buildings. The police think it might be the work of several people, perhaps teens. The first was a garden shed. The next was an abandoned trailer. Unfortunately, a man was in it at the time. Probably a homeless person looking for shelter. I remember reading about that. Nothing happened for a few weeks, but a couple of days ago, a small house in Drum Point, not far from us, went up in flames. The owners were out, I'm glad to say. The police think the perpetrators check to make sure no one is home."

"We are well protected here," said Hunter. "But I must install security cameras at the other house. I will go to buy them now. Stan can help me."

He rushed away. I felt more than a little disturbed. We were mostly alone in that big house. Even if they set fire to it while we were out, I'd be devastated.

I turned to Auntie. "Do you think I should keep Sam with me at the house while we're alone there?"

"I was just thinking that, my dear," she said. "Good idea. No one can come near the house without him raising the alarm."

Two days later, the cameras had been installed, and the installer had instructed me how to monitor activity on my cell phone. That made me feel much better.

Not a week later, Sam's frantic barking woke me. My first groggy thought was of Rose, but she was spending the night at the castle. I looked at my phone and saw two people who looked like teenage boys pouring liquid around the door of my shed. I dialed 911. The police car came barreling down our narrow street, sirens blaring, giving the boys ample notice to scarper into the woods behind. I showed the cops my video.

"As we thought," one of them said. "Kids."

"How do I clean up this stuff around my shed?"

"I'm not sure. Why don't you drop by the fire department tomorrow and ask?"

Well, that was helpful.

"Have you checked with local gas stations? It can't be that usual for kids to buy cans of gas."

"We will continue to pursue every line of inquiry."

Next morning I called Hunter, who sent Stan to deal with it. He arrived with three bags of kitty litter, a huge jar of vinegar, and a waste bin. First he wiped the wood with vinegar mixed with water several times. Next, he poured kitty litter on the grass and left it there for about an hour. We had coffee together while he waited for it to soak up whatever was close enough to the surface to be absorbed.

"All that grass will die, of course," he said. "Watch out for any smell of gas in your water. It's possible it could find its way into the well."

"The police found the can half full, so there wasn't that much. So, are you working for the Thorens full time now?"

"Yes, Hunter made it worth my while. I took early retirement from the Park service, and I have a military pension too, so I have health insurance."

"That's good. I appreciate you taking care of the lawn here too."

"There's some pruning I need to do. Fortunately, there aren't many trees near the creek, but there are a few branches behind the house that need to be taken back."

"There used to be trees at the creek. They died."

Dora hadn't told him about the poor torn up trees, then. Last year, Loki inhabited a snake, slithered up the trees along the creek, and told them that if they pulled themselves up by the roots and smashed the house, they'd become immortal. Dora, a wood nymph, communicated with them when we noticed them moving. She told them it was Loki's cruel trick, and there would be no immortality. Pained and devasted, they withered and collapsed without fulfilling their mission.

"Are you all right, Mary?"

"Yes, sorry, just thinking. What did you do in the military?"

"I was in the army. Stationed abroad several times. Only too glad to get into a quiet humdrum life after some of the shows I've seen." He shook his head. "Let me finish up outside. I need a broom and dustpan."

He swept and swept, pouring the detritus into his bin, and drove away.

A few minutes later, Lin arrived. "I hear you had a bit of excitement last night."

"Yes, it was terrible. If the shed had really caught on fire, it could easily have jumped to the house."

Lin grimaced. "Yes, a second fire here would have been a catastrophe. You remember I told you about the first one."

"How could I forget?"

"Let me tell you about another."

Tape 11,
Volume 3

Hunter and I were living in a small town on the west coast of Sicily sometime in the 1800's—I've forgotten exactly when. In some ways, it was an ideal experience. The local produce, so fresh and abundant, was delectable, and the sea offered a wealth of sustenance. Our rented house overlooked the sea, which was so clear and warm. The culture didn't approve of women swimming, so I had to do it at night, which annoyed me, but it was nevertheless pleasant.

But like most small towns, there were feuds and jealousies, and the people led very small lives. The men's energies focused on their farming or fishing, food, and vengeance. The women waged vicious campaigns regarding who cooked better and whose daughters were the most beautiful. That doesn't mean they were always nasty or ill-tempered. Far from it. When they met with groups of family and friends, they ate, sang, and danced. If any of them needed help, it was gladly offered. They kept us at a distance at first but soon included Hunter in their activities, although clearly expecting him to become an ally in whatever war they happened to be waging at the time.

I wasn't so readily accepted by the women. They distrusted me around their menfolk. It almost tempted me to bed as many of their husbands as I could. When I looked at them closely though, I went off the idea.

One spring lunchtime in April, Hunter and I decided to have lunch in one of the small restaurants in town. Most women did not eat out then, so I was the only woman there, apart from the owner's wife. She stayed behind the scenes cooking for the most part. I didn't have the patience to cook zucchini flowers, which are delectable if prepared properly, so I was looking forward to having some.

The cook came out, proudly bearing our platters, and placed them in front of us. "You are a marvel, Donna Fierra," I said. "No one prepares them better."

The lady clasped her hands over her ample belly and laughed, bobbing her head in pleasure.

"My wife does them better," a voice rasped from the table behind us. "She cooks everything better."

Donna Fierra turned on him and unloosed a stream of invective in Sicilian. We'd been speaking broken Sicilian but were not yet fluent. We'd learned Venetian in an earlier life, but that was completely different. I could only understand a few words. Soon everyone joined the verbal battle, and once the proprietor rushed out from behind the bar and joined in, it became even more heated. The little man danced and gesticulated as he rattled off his grievances. I was too irritated to watch the spectacle. People's faces become so ugly when they turn hateful that it quite takes away one's appetite. I turned back to my food and ate as did Hunter.

"Donna Fierra," I called, loudly enough to get her attention. "That was absolutely delicious. No one could have done it better. Thank you."

The room was suddenly went quiet. Most looked pleased, but a couple looked murderous. We put money on the table and left.

The next night, I was swimming naked, reveling in the feeling of warm water caressing my body when I heard Hunter roar in fury. I ran from the water to find our front door on fire and two men running away. They weren't fast enough for me. I threw them to the ground. They stared up at me slack-jawed. I'd forgotten I was naked. Time to teach them a lesson. I morphed into a dripping monster with long talons and a forked tongue. They scrambled to their feet and ran for their lives. One of them was the man at the restaurant who had belittled Donna Fierra's cooking.

Hunter had put out the fire by the time I got back. The men would, of course, report what they had seen. We could say it was nonsense, and they were drunk. But these people would be all too ready to believe a tale like that.

We decided to go the same restaurant the following evening to get a feel for the townspeople's goodwill. The place fell silent when we walked in.

"Good evening," the proprietor said, without a glimmer of a smile. "I hope you are well."

"We are, no thanks to that man who was rude about your good wife's cooking," Hunter said. "He and another man set fire to our house. I managed to put it out, but our front door is ruined."

"I am very sorry to hear that," the man said. "We heard they were only walking by and saw something very … unusual."

"We ran after them. I knocked them down but let them run away. They were drunk. If they saw something strange, it was in their heads. They are fortunate I did not call the police."

"I see. Guiseppe's son-in-law is the *commissario* here in town, so it would not have been much help."

"What is on the menu tonight?" I asked.

"I am afraid we have run out of food. We had a rush earlier on. I am so sorry."

He didn't look sorry, only frosty. We knew there was an ill wind blowing, and it was our cue to get out. It was a pity because we liked the place. It had been restful after a difficult rebirth in a Balkan country that found itself in the middle of a war a couple of months later. Things calmed down after a few years, so we waited until Hunter grew to manhood before going to Sicily. It wouldn't have been long before we got bored with small town life anyway, but I prefer to leave on my own terms.

"I've heard Sicily is very beautiful," I said. "Have you been back?"

"Yes, although never to that town. It's really lovely, and the food is amazing with touches of Spanish, Arab, and Italian cuisine. We'll go one day."

I hoped so.

We celebrated Rose's birthday at the castle that year because of the new play house. We put all her gifts in there and decorated it with balloons. I couldn't wait to see her reaction. Hunter was almost as excited as Rose as they waited for the big day.

We'd stayed the night at the castle as Rose would wake up early. Sure enough, I heard her open her bedroom door. A few seconds later, she slipped into my bed. I only got a short cuddle.

"Let's go to my birthday."

"I have to get dressed."

"No, just your robe."

"It's too hot for a robe. I won't be long. I'll take my shower later."

While I put on a skirt and top, I watched Rose skip around the living room coffee table, around me, and back to the living room. Round and round she went, working off some of her nervous energy.

We went out to the big kitchen, where Auntie sat at the table sipping her Earl Grey tea. Dora already had two coffee pots going. I'd forgotten that Joe and Helen were also spending the night; Sven and Margareta had also come home for most of the summer. Hence the need for gallons of coffee.

"Where is my birthday?" Rose asked.

"We have to wait for everyone to come downstairs," I said. "Why don't you eat your breakfast while you're waiting? That way you don't have to waste time eating when you have presents to open."

She thought that was a good idea. Motherhood tends provoke manipulative and certainly opportunistic behavior.

Hunter came down first, and the others trickled down soon after.

"What would everyone like for breakfast?" Dora asked.

"Can't we do my birthday before breakfast?" Rose asked plaintively.

"Maybe they're hungry," I said. "You've had your breakfast, remember?"

Hunter said, "Let us pour ourselves some coffee now and have breakfast afterward." He just couldn't help himself. He filled his mug. "Follow me, everyone."

Confused, Rose looked up at me with a small frown and the start of a pout. Hunter scooped her up and strode to the play house, set her down, and opened the door. "This is your own little house for you to play in. Happy birthday!"

She rushed in, turning and marveling, walking round, touching everything, sitting in each chair before curling up in the armchair. Hunter, Lin, and I went in, and the others looked through the windows and door. We gave her our gifts, then Hunter invited people to come in and hand her their gifts while she continued to sit on her throne. She thanked everyone as she had learned to do and seemed almost lost for words. She loved her books, her big schoolroom toy with its miniature students and teacher, her new dress, and her art kit. After she'd opened all the gifts, she stuffed the paper into an empty box and put away the toys in the cupboard. She put the books on a shelf beside the door, and the art kit on the table.

"I like everything nice and tidy, so I know where to find it," she said. "Now I have my own house, I must keep it properly. Thank you for my house, Papa."

"I think it's time for breakfast," I said.

"I will stay here. I want to make a picture."

She stayed there all day. Hunter plugged in the fan and opened the windows as the day began to heat up. I saw her run up to the front door to use the washroom next to it a couple of times. When I went to get her for lunch, she begged me to bring it out to her. I told her I would, but just this once because it was her birthday. But the cake would be with everyone at the castle. When I went to take her a glass of lemonade mid-afternoon, I found her curled up in the armchair, fast asleep with her fox by the chair, also asleep. Poor Sam had stayed in the house.

We had the cake after dinner, for which I insisted she come to the dining room.

She stayed at the castle for a few days, obsessed with her house. I spent a couple of days at my place and joined them for the weekend. I don't know why I still thought of the weekend as different from weekdays. Given our lifestyle, there was no real difference, although that would change once Rose started school.

Labor Day weekend, we were again at the castle. Lin had planned a big barbecue on the terrace. Sven and Hunter had set up umbrellas and chairs on the beach, so we'd all get in our sand, sun and fun before the kids went back to university and Rose to school.

Sven had also set up a net on the beach for volleyball. I didn't participate, as I'd played it once in college and bent my index finger back. It hurt like hell. Sven, Margareta, Hunter, and Joe played a no-holds-barred game while Lin, Auntie, Helen, and I sat under the umbrellas, fanning ourselves and laughing at their outrageous antics. Rose had disappeared back to her house after a quick swim. Lin and I went back into the water as it was getting quite hot.

Suddenly, Lin said, "Look."

A think plume of smoke wafted above the house. We all rushed through the house and out to the front. The play house was on fire.

"Rose, Rose!" I rushed forward before a whoosh of flame drove me back. The house had become an inferno. I bent double and clutched my stomach. A woman I knew must be me screamed and screamed without cease. A mighty roar that could only have come from a god filled my head. I was vaguely aware of a hose wetting the little house, but it was too late. Soon, sirens and lots of men. I cried into the dry earth. Strong arms lifted me and took me to my bed. A sharp sting, then nothing.

30

Weak dawn light glowed in the window. No one had drawn the curtains. I closed my eyes again, drifting into a pleasant dream where Rose slept on one side of me and Hunter on the other.

Then, I remembered. I cried out, "No, no, no!"

A child beside me started to cry in fright. "What's the matter, Mama? You're frightening me."

I sat up, my head swimming. A nightmare? I gathered Rose into my arms, feeling Hunter's arms behind me, holding us both.

"It's all right, Mary. Rose is safe after all. It's all right. Sh, sh, sh."

We rocked together for a while before I said, "I don't understand. The fire. Was it a bad dream?"

"Lin gave you a shot, so you fell asleep quickly. You were crazy with grief. You were out cold when Rose walked out of the woods."

"But how? She was in there. I saw her go in and work on her picture."

"Mama, I heard some boys talking in front of my house. Then Hyndla came in and told me to leave. He kept going to the back door and looking at me. 'Go,' he said. 'Danger.' So I opened the back door, and we ran into the woods, right up to the fence."

She pulled out of my arms and lay down again. "Then two boys came running to the fence, so we hid. They tried to climb it but kept falling down."

"They had used a ladder to get in and forgot about getting out," Hunter added. "Very stupid boys. I thought Rose was in the house when it burned down, so I was not in the mood to be kind. But I knew Auntie had called 911, so I must be careful. I only knocked their heads together hard and picked them up, one under each arm. They were just waking up when I threw them at the feet of the policemen standing around."

"I followed Papa out of the woods, but it took me longer because he's bigger. He acted so funny when he saw me. He fell on his knees and cried. Uncle Joe and Auntie Helen started crying. Sven did too. Margareta just smiled a lot. Linny and Dora were getting in the ambulance, and it went away with all that noise they make. So they didn't see me for hours."

"Ambulance? Why Lin?" I asked.

"It's Auntie," Hunter said. "When she thought Rose was still in the play house, she had a stroke. Not a very bad one. She will be good again, the doctor said. But she must be in the hospital a little while. Do not worry. Margaret and Sven are with her now."

"Please, can we just lie here a little longer? My head feels funny, and I feel as if I've been ill."

"You have, Mary. We all have, but you most of all."

unter wanted to come with us on Rose's first day of school, but I said no. How could I explain him? She would call him Papa. I had listed myself as widowed. Sure, I could invent an explanation—I'd done it before—but it wouldn't hold up for long.

I took her into the building and was pointed to her classroom. I'd check in at the office after getting her settled. I greeted her teacher, Mrs. Grant, and turned to introduce Rose. But she was on the other side of the room by the loaded shelves helping a little boy choose a book.

"I think you'll like this one," she told him. "It has planes and things."

"I like animals more than planes," he said.

She turned back to the shelves. "Oh, this one is my favorite. I don't mind reading it again. We can read it together." They sat on some cushions and opened the book.

"And that is my daughter Rose," I said, laughing. "She seems to feel right at home."

"She's reading the book to Peter," said the teacher. "She is way ahead of the rest of them."

"I hope that's not going to be a problem. She doesn't take easily to being bored."

"I'll see how it goes. We might have to move her up. It depends on her maturity and other skills."

I shook the teacher's hand. "It was nice to meet you, Mrs. Grant."

I waved goodbye to Rose, who didn't notice, and went to the office to complete the necessary paperwork. Hunter was waiting outside in his car, a ball of anxiety.

"Is she all right? How did it go? Was she upset when you left?"

I told him what happened. "She is more than fine."

We went back to the castle, where Lin and Auntie waited to hear about the first day of school. Auntie had been released from hospital the day before. She was still weak and couldn't use her left hand very well. She dozed off frequently. Lin had bought her a fancy electronic wheelchair. Fortunately, our wing at the castle was on the same level as the living areas, so there was no problem getting around.

I regaled them with Rose's behavior with her new friend while I drank my coffee. "They may move her up a grade if she proves too far ahead of the others."

"Be careful about that," Auntie said. "She may be smart, but she's not necessarily emotionally ready to deal with older children, especially when she reaches her teens."

"That's a good point," I said. "But she won't do well if she's bored. And while I don't know much about other children, she seems rather mature to me."

"It's true. She is mature for her age," Lin said. "I think the school will make the right decision."

"I think I'll take a little walk. I need to settle down a bit, myself."

I walked to Yggdrasil and sat with my back against its trunk. The weather, still summery, threw the grounds into a mosaic of dark and light shadow. I closed my eyes, exhausted from the nightmares that startled me awake every night, dread and horror knotting my nerves.

Hunter flopped down and put his arms around me. "You still think about it?"

"All the time. I dream about it too. It's strange Rose has never cried for her little house."

"She did at first, but then I heard nothing more. I thought she would ask for another one."

"I'm not ready for that."

"Perhaps she is not either."

"Everything changes."

"That is natural. I thought our life on Asgard would never change."

"What does it mean, now that this tree reaches so high?"

"I think it has reached our heaven."

"You mean it is still there? Your heaven, I mean."

"We don't know if it will be as it was, whether it is coming back, or whether there is nothing at all. We will find out."

"How?"

"I must climb the tree. It will be a very hard climb, perhaps the hardest thing I have ever done. It is a long, long, way, and it will be more windy and cold than you can imagine."

"You know, I bet Agna could do it easier with her magic."

"We talked about it. Lin is probably stronger than me in some ways. Did Lin tell you anything about Agna's background in Asgard?"

"She did."

"Then you know that Agna was part of Freya's court, and Freya planned to take Frigg's place with magic. Lin does not want anything bad to happen to her lady Frigg. And Lin was handmaiden to Frigg. She does not want to be a handmaiden anymore. She likes our life together better. So it is I who must go. If I find Asgard once more, and all the gods in it, I will pave the way for the others to visit. I am the brother and son of Odin, after all."

"That's been puzzling me. I think Lin told me you were the son of Odin. Then I read somewhere that you are the brother of Odin. Now you say you are both. How can that be?"

"Three of us go so far back, we know only that we are bound together throughout eternity. We are not entirely sure who our parents were. I'm pretty sure Odin is not my father. He may or may not be my real brother. But after so many millennia, what matters is what is in our hearts. He is, to all intents and purposes, my brother. He is our leader, so he is my father too."

Hunter stroked my hair.

"Now I understand. It's rather beautiful, actually, if confusing."

"Do Christians not call their god father?"

"Yes, that's true, they do. That makes sense. The father who takes care of everything."

"Quite so."

"I'm afraid for you making that awful climb. I couldn't bear it if anything bad happened to you. And what happens if a plane comes while you're up there? The tree might knock you off."

"It will not. It is not doing that anymore. Did you not notice? When a plane flies over, nothing changes. That is how I know that the time has come."

"I hadn't noticed. What happens then?"

"Now that it touches the heavens, Yggdrasil no longer exists for humans above the other trees. It has made its own adjustments. It will be interesting to see if it branches out into other realms."

"What realms?"

"The land of the elves, for example. There were others. I hope it will just be Asgard, a heaven free of discord."

"How can the gods come back if no one believes in them?"

"We shall see. It is not difficult to get humans to believe things."

"You know, if we start a movement, the powers that be will start investigating us. They will maybe wonder where your money comes from."

Hunter looked dismayed and sat up. "You are right. We cannot have that. We must find a priest." He looked down at me. "Or a priestess."

"Me? I wouldn't know where to start."

"Look at those people on TV. Learn a few things from them."

"More like what not to do. Most of them make millions from gullible viewers. We would have to make it attractive. No demonizing other beliefs, no asking for money, no moralizing. Except the Golden Rule."

"Yes, we must make the idea attractive. Why should they believe? There must be a good reason."

"Exactly. Anyway, what about your journey. When will you go?"

"After Christmas. We will have a wonderful time, and then I will climb through freezing maelstroms until I find my glimmering Asgard once more. It will take all my strength and endurance. But I will do it because I must find my old heaven. I will climb, and climb, and climb."

Book Club Questions

1. How did the foxes in the story help you learn something important about the main characters they interacted with?

2. Does Rose have powers that will remain limited like Margareta's, or do you think they might both become more powerful? Why?

3. Rose's paternity is bound to be questioned at some point. Who might stir up trouble and why?

4. What was the most intense scene in the book?

5. Auntie Peggy is a dark horse, and it is finally clear that she once worked in Intelligence during the Cold War. Do you think this made it easier or harder for her to accept who and what Lin and Hunter really are?

6. Margareta and Sven have been rather quiet in this book. Do you think they will welcome the gift of immortality if the possibility arises? They are both educated and intelligent. What advantages and disadvantages might they see in gaining immortality?

7. If Odin gains enough believers to become strong again, what might that mean to other religions? Do you think fanatics might rise up and threaten the family?

8. Does it bother you when the author contradicts traditional mythology, for example, female leprechauns, survivors of Ragnarok, and so on?

9. Does Hunter surprise you sometimes? Does Lin?

10. Who is your favorite character and why?

Author Bio

D. A. Spruzen grew up near London, U.K., graduated from the London College of Dance and Drama Education, and earned an MFA in Creative Writing from Queens University of Charlotte; she teaches creative writing in Northern Virginia when not seeking her own muse. Her publications include the first three books in the Sleuthing with Mortals series: *The Turkish Connection*, *The Witch of Tut*, and *The Knight, the Gnome and the Fox*; an historical novel *The Blitz Business*; the first two books of the *Flower Ladies* trilogy; and a poetry collection, *Long in the Tooth*. Her poems and short stories have appeared in many online and print publications. She resides in northern Virginia and southern Maryland.

Discover more at
4HorsemenPublications.com

10% off using HORSEMEN10